CHARACTER LIST

Ron Penrose – Patriarch of the family and retired boat builder.

Amy Penrose – Ron's wife.

Davy Penrose – Ron's brother – owner of the Penrose House Hotel.

Jago Penrose – Ron and Amy's elder son – the harbour master.

Rachel Penrose – Jago's wife – owns and runs the chandlery on the quayside.

Fitzwilliam 'Liam' Penrose – Jago and Rachel's eldest son. Lives and works in London doing something clever with numbers.

Frederick 'Rick' Penrose – Jago and Rachel's second son. Works with his mother in the chandlery and also owns The Hire Hut, a water sports hire company. Sits on the local parish council.

Henry 'Harry' Penrose – Jago and Rachel's third son and the eldest of the twins by a couple of minutes. A chef in a restaurant on the seafront.

Edward 'Ed' Penrose – Jago and Rachel's fourth son and the baby of the family. Training part time for a marine biology PhD and working in a dead-end admin job to support himself. Shares a cottage with his cousin, Matt.

Ryan Penrose – Ron and Amy's younger son – self-employed joiner who works with his son, Matt.

Helen Penrose – Ryan's wife – works from home doing the accounts for Ryan's business and is a support worker at the local primary school during term time.

Matt Penrose – Ryan and Helen's son – works with his dad and shares a cottage with Ed which they are in the process of refurbishing.

Chloe Penrose – Ryan and Helen's daughter – works as a legal secretary at a local solicitor's office.

Issy Kernow – Close friend of Anya, Chloe and Kat – runs The Cosy Coffee Pot, a café, and oversees the Hub, a community space.

Maud Kernow – Issy's grandmother and a long-term resident at the Penrose House Hotel.

Lockie Kernow – Maud's late husband, Issy's grandfather.

Anya Stokes – A widow who is very down on her luck. Helen's niece and cousin to Matt and Chloe.

Drew Stokes – Anya's deceased husband.

Freya Stokes – Anya and Drew's four-year-old daughter.

Kat Bailey – Close friend of Anya, Chloe and Issy – works for her father, who runs a café that is part of an international franchise. Also volunteers part-time at the community library in the Hub.

Gavin Bailey – Kat's father – runs a Java Brava café franchise on the village high street.

Adam Mountjoy – A property developer.

Caroline – Liam Penrose's ex-girlfriend.

Russ Armstrong – Renowned chef and owner of the restaurant where Harry works.

Thomas – Waiter at the restaurant.

Ray Evans – An ex-schoolteacher who retired early to nurse his wife.

Denise Evans – Ray's late wife.

Kathleen – Lives in the village – runs the Beachcombers litter picking group.

Betty – A regular visitor to Issy's café.

Mike Lawton – Village greengrocer.

The Nicholsons – A couple who own the dress shop next to the restaurant.

Steve – Night manager at the Penrose House Hotel.

Jim – The village postman.

Shelly Dean – An old classmate of Issy, Chloe and Kat's. Married with three small children.

Jason Dean – Shelly's husband.

Beryl – Member of the village craft club.

Rosamund Boscowen – Lives at Boscowen Castle.

Felix Boscowen – Rosamund's brother, also lives at the castle.

Gio & Angie – Owners of the village deli.

Sean Hamilton – Friend of Jago and a competitor in the Round the Rock race.

Charles Pritchard – Liam's former school housemaster.

Billy – Works with Chloe at the local solicitor's office.

Tony Reeves – Deputy harbour master.

Alison Reeves – Tony's wife.

Bob – Sean's crewmate.

Morwenna Delaney – Head teacher at the village school.

EVERYTHING CHANGES BUT YOU

HALFMOON QUAY BOOK TWO

SARAH BENNETT

Boldwood

First published in Great Britain in 2025 by Boldwood Books Ltd.

Copyright © Sarah Bennett, 2025

Cover Design by Alice Moore Design

Cover Images: iStock and Shutterstock

Interior Images: Sarah Bennett

The moral right of Sarah Bennett to be identified as the author of this work has been asserted in accordance with the Copyright, Designs and Patents Act 1988.

Every effort has been made to obtain the necessary permissions with reference to copyright material, both illustrative and quoted. We apologise for any omissions in this respect and will be pleased to make the appropriate acknowledgements in any future edition.

A CIP catalogue record for this book is available from the British Library.

Paperback ISBN 978-1-83633-583-2

Large Print ISBN 978-1-83633-582-5

Hardback ISBN 978-1-83633-581-8

Trade Paperback ISBN 978-1-80635-286-9

Ebook ISBN 978-1-83633-584-9

Kindle ISBN 978-1-83633-585-6

Audio CD ISBN 978-1-83633-576-4

MP3 CD ISBN 978-1-83633-577-1

Digital audio download ISBN 978-1-83633-579-5

This book is printed on certified sustainable paper. Boldwood Books is dedicated to putting sustainability at the heart of our business. For more information please visit https://www.boldwoodbooks.com/about-us/sustainability/

Boldwood Books Ltd, 23 Bowerdean Street, London, SW6 3TN

www.boldwoodbooks.com

For the lovely readers in my Facebook author group. x

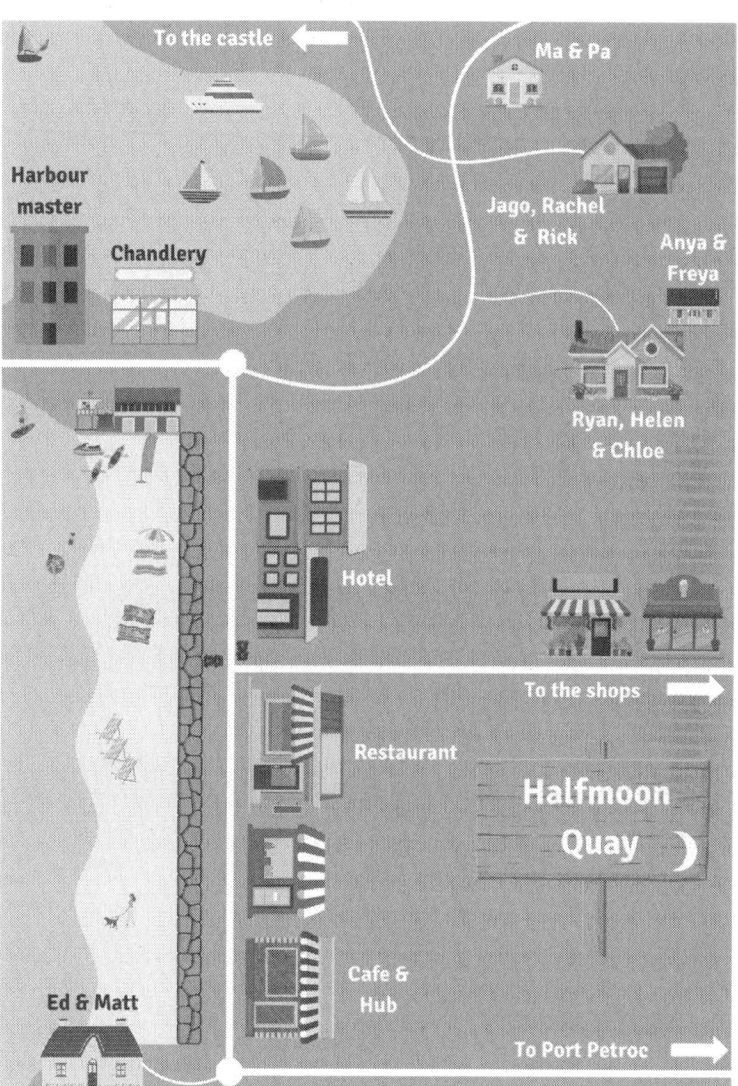

1

Beep. Beep. Beep.

Liam Penrose reached out without looking and cancelled the alarm on his phone. He hadn't needed it since he'd taken time off work to come and visit his family, but he was afraid to switch it off. Afraid if he did, he'd never want to switch it on again. All those late nights and early mornings, all those weekend plans sacrificed to revised deadlines, all those steps he'd taken up the corporate ladder, and now the thought of putting on a suit and setting foot in the shiny glass skyscraper with its views out over Canary Wharf gave him a vertigo attack. Recognising he'd been heading for burnout, Liam had arranged a sabbatical with his boss. He was supposed to be using the time off to rest and reconnect with his family. So much for that. It was like the moment he'd stopped working his body had finally acknowledged how exhausted he was but his brain had yet to get the message.

He stared up at the ceiling with burning eyes and wondered what he was going to do to fill the next sixteen hours before another night spent tossing and turning. He'd thought coming home would make him feel better. And it had for a few hours before his great-uncle had turned his life upside down. It had been a fortnight since his grandmother's birthday. Two weeks since his great-uncle Davy had dropped an envelope in front of Liam containing the deeds to his seafront hotel and told him he could do what he wanted with the place. Liam felt like he'd barely slept a wink since then for worrying about what he was going to do.

Correction. He knew what he wanted to do, but there was simply no way it was going to happen. Liam's future had been mapped out since the summer he'd turned fourteen and his teacher, Ray Evans, had called round to see his parents, promising him the kind of future they'd never had. If his family thought for a minute he was contemplating chucking away a high-flying career in city finance to run a cheap and cheerful hotel, they'd be horrified.

And very disappointed.

A brief knock sounded from the other side of his bedroom door. 'Go away,' he grumbled. 'I'm sleeping.'

The door swung open with surprising force, the thump of it against his chest of drawers barely muffled by the dressing gown hanging on the back.

'Good morning, sunshine!' Liam's brother Rick marched into the room like he owned the place and plonked a mug of coffee on the bedside table, a furrow etched between his brows as he looked down at Liam. 'You look like shit.'

'Gee, thanks.'

Bending at the waist, Rick sniffed at him like a dog before recoiling with an exaggerated gasp of horror. 'Smell like it too. Jeez, Liam, when was the last time you had a shower?'

Liam scowled as he levered himself up into a sitting position with his back against the headboard. 'Yesterday.' No, yesterday he'd spent the day slumped on the sofa watching rubbish on the

TV in his brother's sitting room. 'Definitely over the weekend.' It was hard to be sure as the days blurred into each other.

Rick grabbed the mug he'd just set down and thrust it into Liam's hand. 'Drink that.' Without waiting for a reply, he crossed to the window and yanked open the curtains.

Wincing as the sudden blast of sunshine hurt his bleary eyes, Liam raised his free hand to shield his face. A gust of cold air rudely followed the light as Rick unhooked one of the side windows and swung it wide. Liam had two choices: squint and freeze or drop his hand to yank the quilt up over his bare chest. He chose the second. 'Don't you have something better to do than give me a hard time?' It was hard to glare through eyes he'd narrowed to slits, but he gave it his best shot.

'I do, actually, but I don't want to spend another day with Mum fretting over what's wrong with you, so you need to get a grip. We left you alone for the first few days because we assumed you just needed some time to catch up on your sleep and recharge a bit. I should've spoken to you last week, but between the end of the summer holidays and the madness of the bank holiday weekend I've barely had time to think about anything other than work.' As well as helping their mother run the chandler's shop on the quay, Rick also managed a successful water sports hire company.

Features softening, Rick sank down on the end of the bed. 'What's the matter, bro? Are you having second thoughts about splitting up with Caroline?'

After struggling through several rocky months at the end of their almost ten-year relationship, Liam and his girlfriend had decided it was time to part ways just before he'd arrived back home in Halfmoon Quay. He shook his head. 'No, it was the right decision for both of us.'

Not that he wasn't sad about it, but that wasn't the reason he was hiding away in his room avoiding everyone. He shot his brother a beseeching look. 'Why did Uncle D choose me?'

Some of the tension in his brother's shoulders relaxed. 'My theory, for what it's worth, is that he decided on a clean break from the place. Giving it up can't be easy after so many years; I guess he figured the only way was to walk away from it.'

Liam sipped at his coffee as he thought about that for a minute. 'I suppose that makes sense, but that still doesn't answer why he picked me. It would make more sense if he'd chosen you, or one of the twins, even.'

'What would Harry do with it? You know that working at the restaurant is more than just a job for him, it's been his salvation. We can't let anything derail him again. And as for Ed, he wouldn't recognise a consequence if it jumped up and bit him in the arse. I'd thought losing that part-time job because he was banging his married boss might have been a wake-up call, but apparently not.'

Liam closed his eyes. 'I'd done my best to forget about that.'

Rick sighed. 'You know I adore him but he's still got a lot of growing up to do. The hotel would go broke in six months if he was put in charge of it.'

'Yeah.' Ed wouldn't mean to, but something would happen. And Rick was right about Harry, too. Working at the restaurant wasn't simply a job, it was a vocation for him. 'I don't know the first thing about running a hotel and my life is in London; my work is in London...' Liam was good at his job, but it didn't make him *feel* anything. He'd miss the money, miss a few of the people he worked with, but at the end of the day helping very rich people get even richer wasn't exactly a worthwhile endeavour. Still, it wasn't just about what he wanted. 'I can't give all that up; what would everyone think?'

Rick raised his eyebrows. 'Since when did you care what everyone thinks?'

Since always. Liam shifted uncomfortably against the head-board. 'Come on, you know what Mum and Dad sacrificed for me to get where I have. It'd be a slap in the face if I told them I wanted to chuck it all in.'

And what would the rest of the family think if he didn't? The hotel had been in their family for several generations. Both his grandfather and his great-uncle had spoken more than once with immense pride about how their ancestors had worked their way up from fishermen, risking their lives every day just to make ends meet, to having a building in the village that bore their name. It was a landmark, a physical representation of all the hard work of those who had come before him. His stomach twisted. He was damned if he did and damned if he didn't.

'Is that what's got you so stressed out? Because I don't think Mum and Dad would see it like that. All they've ever wanted was the best for you, for all four of us. If you're not happy in London then talk to them about it.'

'It's not that I'm not happy...'

Rick burst out laughing. 'Have you looked in the mirror lately? If you're having such a great time, why are you homeless, girl-friendless, and seemingly still exhausted after spending the last two weeks sat on your arse?'

'I already told you that Caro and I had simply run our course, and the flat belonged to her folks, so of course I was the one who was going to move out. Finding somewhere else to rent won't be a problem.' The lie of that sat heavy on his shoulders. Unless he was willing to flat share, he'd have to look for a place much further out of the centre of the city, which would mean a longer commute. The thought of spending extra time crammed cheek-by-jowl with strangers on the Tube was enough to make sweat break out on his brow. He took a quick sip of his coffee and did his best to wipe his glistening face without making it too obvious what he was doing.

'And the endless late nights and weekend working? That didn't take its toll on your relationship?' Rick shook his head. 'I wasn't kidding earlier when I said you look like shit, Liam. The dark circles around your eyes wouldn't look out of place on a bloody panda!'

'I'm just a bit knackered because I haven't had any time off since last Christmas.' Truth be told, he'd worked through most of that holiday too, as his company had tried to work out if they were going to buy in on a new IPO launch to the stock market of a tech start-up company. 'That's why I'm on extended leave. I'll be fine once I recharge my batteries a bit.' Assuming he ever managed to get a decent night's sleep. 'This stuff with the hotel, it's just an extra stress I could do without right now.'

Rick folded his arms across his chest. 'If you want the best of both worlds, you could get a manager in to run the hotel on your behalf.'

'You mean Anya?' Liam took another quick sip of his coffee and eyed his brother over the rim of his mug. 'How are things between you two, by the way?'

'Ha!' Rick barked out a laugh. 'Nice try, but we're not talking about me, we're talking about you. And no, I didn't mean Anya. She's happy to hold the fort while you sort things out, but don't be making any long-term plans for her. Not unless you want to deal with Chloe.'

It was Liam's turn to laugh. 'Noooooo, thank you.' Their cousin Chloe was as sweet as sugar until you crossed her and then it was every man for himself. Growing up with an older brother and four male cousins, Chloe had learnt that the only way to win was to fight dirty – and she was very good at it.

Rick grinned. 'Good choice. She's serious about this new

design venture with Anya. Man, you should see the stuff on their website. I knew Anya had an eye for design, but some of the room design sketches Chloe has put up there are breathtaking.' There was no mistaking the pride in his voice.

'Then I'm happy for them.' Setting down his mostly empty mug, Liam sighed. 'Doesn't help me, though. If Anya's heart is set on leaving the hotel, that leaves me in an even bigger mess.'

His brother's expression grew serious. 'You don't have to accept it, you know. Nothing's gone through on paper, so you can hand those deeds back to Uncle D, head back to London and pick up where you left off.'

Liam knew it was true, knew it was the easiest solution to his unexpected dilemma. Hand the deeds back, get a week or two of decent rest under his belt and get back to London. His boss would certainly be happy about it. Although he'd agreed to Liam taking a sabbatical until the end of October, not having him around was an extra burden on the team. They'd all been supportive about Liam's request, and encouraged him to take a break. No doubt his colleagues had envisioned Liam sunning himself on the beach, chilling out with his family and recharging his batteries before returning fresh and ready to plunge headlong into another complicated project.

Moping around was doing them a disservice too. Liam needed to get a grip and stop wasting this precious time he'd been given. Washing his hands of the hotel certainly made the most sense. Once he did that, maybe he'd be able to relax and enjoy himself. And yet... 'Uncle D's got enough on his plate.'

'Is that why you haven't spoken to him yet?' Unfolding his arms, Rick placed a comforting hand on Liam's ankle through the covers. 'Hey, *hey*, don't you dare let Davy's illness guilt you into doing something you don't want to do.'

'It's not that.' Liam quirked a wry smile. 'Well, not only that.' If he upped and walked away, then it would fall to Rick and the rest of the family to pick up the pieces. That or sell it to someone who wouldn't understand the history that ran through every brick. 'The hotel is part of this family. This village is a part of this family and I feel like I need to honour that.' He scrubbed at the ache in his forehead. 'I just wish I knew the first thing about running a hotel.' The financial side of the business wouldn't be an issue, because numbers always made sense to Liam. But the rest of it? Dealing with people all day every day? That was so far out of his comfort zone he wouldn't know where to start. 'I'm not exactly a people person.'

'And Uncle D is? Come on, Liam, I know a piss-weak excuse when I hear one.'

Liam laughed. 'I can always rely on you to be honest, bro.'

Rick patted his leg again. 'Anytime. And here's my last bit of honesty. If you take on the hotel it has to be because you want to, not because you feel some kind of obligation and definitely not because you are trying to second-guess what everyone expects you to do.'

'Yeah. Yeah, you're right.' Still, it was easier said than done. 'I'll give it some serious thought. Thanks, you've helped a lot.'

'That's what I'm here for. So what's on your schedule for today?' He wrinkled his nose. 'Other than a shower?'

Liam yanked a pillow from behind him and tossed it at his brother's head. 'Didn't anyone ever tell you not to cheek your elders?'

Rick caught the pillow and dropped it to the floor. 'Not that I can recall.' He pointed towards the sunshine streaming through the window. 'It's a gorgeous day, at least promise me you'll get out for some fresh air. If you need to borrow some gym kit...'

'My trainers are in there somewhere.' Liam nodded towards the pair of suitcases stacked in the corner of the room.

Rick stood. 'Then I suggest you dig them out and get out for a run. It usually works for me.' He took a few steps towards the door then paused. 'Might help you sleep better too.'

'Yes, Dad.' Though he said it in a sing-song sarcastic voice, it was enough of a prompt to get him moving. Liam tossed back his covers and crossed the room to crouch in front of his cases. He unzipped the first one and began rummaging through the current contents of his life. Sensing Rick still there, he glanced over his shoulder. 'Go and find someone else to annoy already.' He made a shooing motion.

'Okay, I'm going. Hey, do you reckon you'd have time to help me out later?'

Liam raised an eyebrow. 'I'll have to check my busy schedule, but I might be able to squeeze you in.' They exchanged a grin. 'What do you need?'

'It's the monthly community meeting at the Hub this evening and I could do with a hand setting things up. There's a pint in it for you at the Smuggler's afterwards.'

'You don't need to bribe me to help you, so that pint will be on me.' His brother would need a drink after letting everyone bend his ear for a couple of hours. Rick had a deeply seated drive to help whoever and wherever he could. Liam greatly admired his brother's dedication to the community, but was happy to leave the hard work to him. Perhaps if he'd had more of a tie to the village he'd understand it, but Halfmoon Quay hadn't been his home for a long time and Liam didn't know if it was too late to change that.

Maybe this was the perfect time to try and find out.

2

What a beautiful day. Issy Kernow tilted her face upwards, closing her eyes against the sun's bright rays as she let the warmth of it soak into her skin. Days like this, there was nowhere she'd rather be. A familiar sadness threatened to settle over her, but she slowed her breathing and turned her focus inward, counting, pausing, grounding herself in the here and now until the tugging fingers of sorrow eased their grip on her heart. The grief never left her, not completely, but she would not let it spoil her day.

Opening her eyes, Issy tucked a couple of stray bits of hair behind her ears. Though she loved her poker-straight black hair, it's natural silkiness meant it was forever escaping the clips and bands she used to hold it back. It would be more practical to chop it all off, but her mum had always loved styling it and some of Issy's most precious memories were sitting on her bed at night as her mum brushed it smooth before she went to sleep. Issy raised her coffee to her lips and took a long, deep swallow. The bitter-sweetness of it perfectly matched those memories. Working all day in a café might make some people sick of coffee, but not Issy.

She loved everything about it, from the way it heightened her senses to the rich aroma that always smelled like a warm welcome. Not to mention the kick of energy from the caffeine that helped her get through even the busiest of days.

'Skiving off?' a familiar deep voice called from across the road. She glanced up and grinned at Harry Penrose, who was standing watching her, arms folded across his chest. Tall and dark, most women would consider him extremely handsome, but Issy had known Harry all her life and considered him more of an annoying little brother.

'Something like that!' She'd actually been on her feet since before six and this was the first chance she'd had to take a break. Normally she would've stayed inside and puttered about because there was always something that needed her attention, but the sunshine had been too tempting. Besides, she was her own boss, so if she wanted to take five minutes to sit on the sea wall it was nobody's business but her own. 'You want a drink?'

Harry shook his head. 'Nah, I'm good. I need to open up and get morning prep started.' He checked the large metallic watch on his wrist. 'Give me an hour and I'll be ready for an extra-large double-shot though.'

'It'll be waiting whenever you're ready,' Issy promised. 'Oh, and I baked chocolate and walnut brownies this morning.'

'And there was me watching my waistline!' Harry patted his admirably flat stomach. 'Make sure you save me one. See you in a bit, Issy.' With a wave, Harry turned towards the restaurant where he was second in command to Russ Armstrong, one of the county's premier chefs, and unlocked the front door.

Issy finished her coffee and forced herself to move. Much as she'd like to sit there a few more minutes and soak up the sun, she had her own prep to do before the lunchtime rush and the afternoon madness of the summer kids' club she ran in the community hub extension to the café. Thank God school started next week and her days would settle into an easier pattern, an ebb and flow of peaks and troughs that followed the rhythm of the work and school days of the residents of the village. Although the kids' club was primarily intended to support local families, it hadn't taken long for holidaymakers to find out about it, and while she appreciated the extra revenue she earned because everyone wanted drinks and snacks, Issy was definitely counting down the days now.

As she walked back into the café, her eyes moved automatically to the clock and then towards the window. She wasn't the only one in the village with a regular schedule. Ray Evans, her old secondary schoolteacher, walked past carrying a bouquet of yellow roses on his weekly visit to the neat little cemetery in the grounds of St Peter's church. Issy tapped on the window and raised her hand when he glanced her way. Ray raised his hat, returning her greeting, but didn't stop. He'd be in at quarter past three for his afternoon coffee, just like clockwork.

Issy was about to head behind the counter when another figure came into view. Tall, dark and oh-God-why-was-he-so-bloody-handsome, Liam Penrose was a lot to take even when he was fully dressed. Clad only in a pair of black Lycra shorts and a white T-shirt already turning transparent from his sweaty exertions, he was something else entirely. As though sensing someone watching him, Liam glanced around mid-stride. Cheeks flaming, Issy spun on her heel and marched back behind the counter, cursing softly under her breath. She could not get caught ogling that arse, nor the rest of him for that matter. Liam didn't deserve anything from her, not after the way he'd treated her.

A loud knock on the window made her jump and she glanced over to find Liam waving his water bottle back and forth. She narrowed her eyes and pointed towards the water tap she'd had installed outside by the front door. Sure, she'd had it fitted so people could fill bowls for their dogs, but it was fit for human consumption.

Unfortunately.

She amused herself with the thought of Liam on the wrong end of a bout of E. coli poisoning. Nothing too bad, of course, just forty-eight hours of groaning misery. Seventy-two, tops. The bell above the door rang and there he was in all his glistening glory. He really was determined to wreck her good mood. 'There's a tap outside.'

Liam frowned. 'The dog tap?'

'It's not just for dogs, it's connected to the main supply.'

Liam folded his arms across his chest, making the muscles in his upper arms bulge in a very alarming manner. 'There's literally a picture of a dog above the tap. And a sign that says "dog tap".'

When had he got so ripped? He must have a gym membership back home or something because there was no way he'd got biceps like that just from running. No, no, no, no. Thoughts of Liam pumping iron were not happening. 'Fine.' When he took a step forward, she waved him back as she hurried around the counter. 'No, stay there on the mat. I don't want you sweating everywhere.'

'Are you this nice to all your customers, or did I do something to warrant special treatment?' The sarcasm dripped off him, but he did at least move back until he was standing on the large mat in front of the door.

'Oh no, this is just for you.' Issy stopped in front of him and held out her hand. When he didn't do anything other than stare at her, she gestured impatiently. 'Do you want me to fill your water bottle, or not?'

'I'm not so sure. What are you going to put in it, poison?'

Issy rolled her eyes. 'Don't flatter yourself that you're worth the jail time. Now, give it here or go away.'

Liam extended the bottle, but when she took it he didn't release it at first. 'I wish I knew what I'd done to make you hate me.'

This close she could see how dark the circles were under his eyes. Beneath the sheen of sweat his hair looked lank and greasy. He might have muscles to make Captain America do a double-take, but Liam hadn't been looking after himself lately. He looked pale and, she realised indignantly, there was a glitter of hurt in his dark gaze. How dare he give her sad puppy eyes! And as for looking pale, well that was perfect for someone who was an expert in ghosting people. 'If you don't know, I can't help you.' She tugged at the water bottle, annoyed when he didn't release it. 'Stop messing around, I haven't got all day.'

'Forget it. I'll take my chances with the dog tap.' Yanking the bottle out of her grip, he turned on his heel and marched out to shove his bottle under the external tap.

Issy's feet moved without her awareness until she found herself standing on the threshold, watching him. From the set of his shoulders and the muscle twitching in his jaw, his body language radiated anger. Once he'd finished, he straightened up and glared at her. 'I don't know where all this hostility is coming from, Issy. If anyone has the right to be pissed off here it's me after the way you treated me. Do us both a favour and get over yourself, okay?' He jogged away before she had time to pick her jaw up off the floor.

Of all the nerve! She grabbed the edge of the door, intending to slam it, but what would be the point when Liam was already long gone. She closed her eyes and took a deep breath. Why on earth had she let him get under her skin like that?

They'd been inseparable when they were younger. Been

boyfriend and girlfriend since the playground, when neither of them had understood what those words meant beyond playing together and holding hands. They'd told each other everything. Shared secrets, made promises, trusted each other with their hopes and dreams.

And hearts.

Things changed after Liam was awarded a scholarship to private school for the start of Year Nine. The night before he'd left, he'd sobbed on her shoulder and she'd clung to him as they'd both sworn it wouldn't make a difference. His first summer home, they'd done their best to make up for the time they'd lost, spending every waking moment together. But it hadn't been the same, not for Liam at least. Just a few weeks after he'd gone back to school, he'd simply stopped writing to her. The following summer had been dreadful. Liam had barely acknowledged her and she'd certainly been in no hurry to speak to him.

A knock on the outside of the door shook Issy out of her reverie. Blinking away the tears stinging the backs of her eyes, she forced a smile and opened the door. 'Sorry, Betty, I was wool-gathering. Large pot of tea?' Stepping back, she ushered the woman inside. Arthritis had slowed her steps but with the help of her wheeled walker, Betty maintained enough independence to keep active.

'That would be lovely, dear. I am absolutely parched.' She turned her back and let Issy help her out of the beige overcoat she always wore come rain or shine.

Issy hung it on the rack by the door and offered Betty her arm, settling her at a table where she could enjoy a view out over the ocean. While Betty untied the silk scarf from around her neck, Issy took her walker and parked it by the coat rack. 'I'll be right back with your tea. I've got some chocolate and walnut brownies, if I can tempt you with something a little naughty?'

Betty's eyes lit up. 'Oh goodness that sounds heavenly. Just this once, though, and only a very small piece.'

'Of course.' Issy hid her smile until she'd turned away. It was a part of their routine. Betty would order only tea and Issy would tempt her into something delicious. Never more than a mouthful or two, but if one couldn't indulge a bit now and again, especially at Betty's age, then honestly what was the point? Issy was a firm believer in enjoying the good things in life, and she had the curves to prove it, but running the café kept her fit enough, though you'd never catch her out jogging.

As she pottered around in the kitchen of the business that she had worked so hard to build into something special, Issy's irritation faded. It had been foolish to behave as she had towards Liam. He wasn't worth her anger and she should be well past the point of him being able to hurt her. If she had the misfortune to run into him again she'd treat him as she would any other customer. With any luck he'd be on his way back to London before that happened, and she could go back to forgetting he even existed.

* * *

A shrill scream echoed around the café later that afternoon, drilling its way into Issy's skull and giving her an instant headache. She closed her eyes for a moment, wondering if the noise and chaos around her might vanish if she wished hard enough. The noise continued and she sighed. Her fairy godmother was ignoring her, apparently. Issy took a deep breath and reminded herself she'd miss the extra revenue when the kids' club ended. From some of the slightly glazed expressions on the parents sucking in caffeine like their lives depended on it, Issy wasn't the only one who'd be relieved when the school term started again. The Hub would still host the kids' club, but only for a couple of afternoons a week, and the village school was fairly small, so the numbers were more manageable.

She checked her watch – nearly closing time. If she played her cards right she could get everyone out, finish her clean down and be upstairs and soaking in the tub within an hour. 'It's nearly five, folks,' she called out as she started walking around the tables and gathering empty cups and plates. 'Time to make a move.' The customers sitting nearest acknowledged her request and began gathering their things.

Toys and books were scattered everywhere. The large table at the back where she put out jugs of water and the on-their-last-legs bits of fruit Mike Lawton donated from his greengrocer shop was a disaster zone. A couple of the parents were making an attempt to tidy things up, but it would be quicker and easier to tackle the browning apple cores, abandoned bits of orange rind and knocked-over plastic cups once everyone had gone. Issy touched her hand to the nearest mother's arm. 'Don't worry about that, I'll sort it,' she assured the woman with a smile. Unfortunately, some of the other parents seemed more intent on finishing their conversations than rounding up their children. Issy clapped her hands together. 'It's nearly five o'clock,' she announced again, pitching her voice louder this time. 'Come on, everyone, I need to close up now.'

As she'd hoped, the second announcement spurred those lingering into action. Issy weaved between the tables, chivvying people along with a smile and an encouraging word, gathering dirty dishes until she had a stack she could barely see over. The bell over the door rang. 'Sorry, we're close...' She trailed off at the sight of Liam filling the doorway for the second time that day. He'd had a shower and changed out of his gym gear into a pair of black jeans and a red T-shirt that clung to his body. It was so tight she wondered if he'd been shopping in the boys' section. 'What do you want now?' she snapped, forgetting all about her vow to herself to treat him like anyone else.

'Nothing from you.' His tone matched her own sharpness, and honestly she wasn't sure she could blame him. 'Rick asked me to meet him here to help set up for some community meeting?'

Issy felt her insides lurch, and it wasn't that confusing/annoying sensation that being in the near vicinity of this man always seemed to generate. With a heavy heart, she turned to stare at the blackboard of events on the wall then back at Liam. 'It's the last Tuesday of the month.' She couldn't help the disappointment creeping into her tone. Things had been so full-on with the bank holiday weekend, it had completely slipped her mind.

He nodded. 'Yup.'

Issy's dream of a long hot bath and an early night with her Kindle vanished into thin air. 'Well, shit.'

Liam laughed and some of the tension in his shoulders eased. 'Sorry to be the bearer of bad tidings.'

She huffed out a long breath then straightened her shoulders. Nothing she could do other than make the best of it. 'It's not your fault, I just completely lost track of what the date was. Give me a few minutes to tidy up in the Hub and then you can get started with setting up.' By which time hopefully Rick would be here and he could take over.

She hurried back behind the counter to dump the stack of dishes then grabbed the cleaning spray and a cloth, all but bumping into Liam, who had apparently followed her. 'What can I do to help?' he asked.

Go away and leave me alone. She swallowed the words down. Sniping at him wasn't going to make things go any quicker. She couldn't bring herself to smile at him, but she could find it in herself to at least be polite. She held out the spray and cloth to him. 'If I clear off the tables, do you mind wiping them down afterwards?'

'Sure.' He took the items and walked away.

She kept an eye on him at the first table, expecting a quick squirt and a swipe of the cloth, but he was diligent with his efforts and she had to admit that, as much as she'd rather he wasn't there, it was a lot quicker than doing it all herself.

They reached the last occupied table, where Ray Evans was still nursing a half-drunk cappuccino. 'Haven't you got a home to go to?' she said with a teasing smile as she reached out and gently took the mug from him. The moment the words were out she wished them back. Ray didn't have a home as such, he was one of the few permanent boarders at the Penrose House Hotel on the seafront. Her grandmother had moved in there about three years ago, much against Issy's wishes, claiming they both needed their own space. Given how things had recently developed between Maud and Davy, Issy was beginning to suspect her grandmother had been playing the long game. Ray was a more recent addition, having sold his cottage in the village after his wife died last year, and it was now one of many rented out to summer visitors.

Not looking at her, Ray sent a challenging glance towards Liam. 'I don't know, have I?'

Liam frowned. 'Have you what, Ray?'

'Got a home.'

Liam set the cloth and the spray down, looking confused. 'What do you mean?'

Ray scoffed, an impatient, angry sound. 'Word on the street is that you own the hotel now, not that your great-uncle has had the courtesy to speak to me about it. You'd think as I live there he'd at least have had the good grace to mention it to me.'

Liam shuffled his feet, looking so uncomfortable Issy almost felt sorry for him. *Almost.* 'I, uh, I had no idea you were living there. Things with the hotel are still a bit up in the air.'

Issy raised her eyebrows at him. 'What do you mean you had no idea? You know my grandmother lives there as well?' She assumed that Maud was in on Davy's plans at least, given they'd taken up with each other. Issy still couldn't understand what Maud was doing messing around with a man at her age – Issy wasn't yet thirty and she could hardly be bothered with the idea of a boyfriend.

Liam shook his head, looking completely bewildered. 'I swear I had no idea. I, uh, I haven't been around much and I never paid any attention to what my uncle was doing. I still have no idea why he gave me the deeds in the first place.'

'He's making mischief, that's what he's doing,' Ray snapped. 'Best thing you can do is give them back to him and tell him not to be so bloody stupid. You've got better things to do with your life than worry about a rundown old dump. You can't possibly think you can manage the place from London; speaking of which, shouldn't you be getting back there?'

'I'm on a sabbatical until the end of October, actually.' Liam took a step back, clearly surprised by the older man's ire.

End of October? Liam might be around for another two months? The mug slipped from Issy's nerveless fingers to shatter on the floor, sending cold coffee and shards of china in all directions. 'Damn.' She crouched and began to gather the pieces, flinching when she cut her finger on a sharp edge. 'Damn,' she said again as a bright spot of blood welled into the small wound.

'Are you okay? Here, let me look at that.' Liam was far too close for comfort and before Issy knew what was happening, he'd taken her hand and pulled it towards him. He'd produced a snowy white handkerchief from somewhere and was dabbing gently at the cut.

This close, she could smell whatever shower gel he'd used. Something fresh and sharp with a hint of citrus. Her head went all swimmy for a moment, and it wasn't from loss of blood. She yanked her hand back. 'It's fine.' Dark blue eyes met hers, and there was that hurt she'd recognised earlier almost hidden by a clear frustration. She swallowed hard. 'I mean, thanks for checking but it's okay. I'll go and run it under the tap and put on a plaster.' She scrambled up. 'I need to get a dustpan and a mop to clear this up anyway.'

Liam had followed her up and all but loomed over her. 'I can get those if you tell me where they are. You go and sort your finger out.'

The bell over the door rang, automatically drawing her attention. When she saw who it was she could've cried with relief. 'It's fine,' she repeated. 'Look, Rick's here and he'll need your help sorting out the Hub for the meeting.'

The way Liam narrowed his eyes at her she could tell he recognised a dismissal when he heard one, but he moved away without a word, thank goodness. She lifted the handkerchief he'd wrapped around her finger and was pleased to see the cut had all but stopped bleeding and wouldn't be an issue. The same couldn't be said for the mess on the floor, or the state of her trainers and jeans, which were both covered in dark splashes. She glanced to where Ray was sitting. 'Sorry about that, did I get any on you?'

He shook his head as he stood. 'No, but I'll get out of your way so you can clean up.'

'Thanks. Sorry again for the mess.'

'Accidents happen.' Ray took a step away then turned back. 'I think you should have a word with him about this hotel nonsense.'

'Who? Liam?'

Ray nodded. 'We both know the best thing for him is to not

accept those deeds. Don't you go putting any foolish ideas into his head about giving up everything he's worked so hard for.'

'I'm not sure I appreciate your tone, Ray.' Her former teacher might be reserved, but he'd never been anything less than polite before. 'And I can assure you I won't be putting any ideas into Liam's head, foolish or otherwise. What he chooses to do is none of my business.'

3

Liam clenched his fists as he stormed towards the front door. He had no idea why Issy was treating him like something nasty she'd stepped in, but he was sick of it. It had been fifteen years since she'd dumped him without a word of explanation when he'd needed her support the most, and yet he could find it in himself to be civilised, so why couldn't she?

'You all right, bro?' Rick asked as Liam marched up to him. 'You look like you're ready to fight the world.' He glanced over Liam's shoulder then quickly back at him with a more focused gaze. 'What's going on?'

'Issy's doing my head in, that's all.' Liam closed his eyes for a second and drew in a deep breath. He didn't like being angry, didn't like feeling out of control full stop. With an effort he pushed the irritation away. Whatever Issy's problem was, it was exactly that – her problem. He opened his eyes. 'It's nothing, forget about it.'

'Have you two been fighting? That doesn't sound like Issy at all. Do you want me to talk to her?'

'No!' Liam huffed out a breath and moderated his tone. 'Can

you please just stop trying to fix everything all the damn time? Let's sort the Hub out so I can get out of here.'

Rick opened his mouth like he wanted to argue but closed it again when Liam gave him the don't-push-it look. 'Sure. It shouldn't take long.'

As they worked to tidy up the mess from the kids' club and set the chairs out, Liam decided to change the subject. 'Hey, did you know Ray lived at the hotel?'

Rick paused in the act of unstacking chairs and glanced over at him. 'Yeah. There's a couple of permanent residents and he's one of them. Have you been talking to Davy about the hotel, then?'

'No, not yet. Ray was in here just now and he all but bit my head off about it. Told me I should be back in London – not that it's any of his bloody business what I do.' Ray had played a big part in Liam getting to where he was today by arranging a scholarship for him at a private school his parents could never have afforded in a million years. It had done wonders for Liam's education and career prospects, but it had also torn him away from everything that mattered to him – including Issy. His feelings towards his former teacher were ambivalent at best. 'Bloody Davy, I could wring his scrawny old neck for dumping all this on me.'

Rick clapped a sympathetic hand on his shoulder. 'You don't have to accept, remember? As I said this morning, you're not beholden to anyone. If you want to go back to London, then do it and I'll back you all the way.'

For a second he was truly tempted. If he went home he'd be away from all this aggro and stress. Only he didn't have a home there any more, so he'd just be walking away from one mess and straight into another one. Liam sighed. 'Yeah. Look, can we talk about this later? Go through the pros and cons and stuff?'

'Of course we can. And I'll talk to Uncle D with you as well, if you like. I'm used to that old hustler and his ways.' His mouth quirked at the corner. 'Better yet, you should take Anya with you; she doesn't let him get away with anything!'

Liam smiled. It was one thing to tell Rick to stop trying to help, it was another thing to expect him to actually listen. 'How is she?'

Rick raised an eyebrow. 'Are you trying to change the subject again?'

Liam held his hands up. 'No. We've already agreed to talk through the hotel stuff later. I'm not sure what I want to do, but bolting back to London isn't the answer. I wasn't in a good place when I came home, and not just because of breaking up with Caro. Work has been full on and the thought of going back...' He shook his head. 'There's a lot I need to figure out but this isn't the time and place. Plus what you said this morning about worrying Mum really got to me. I've been letting things overwhelm me and ignoring you all in the process. I genuinely want to know how things are with you guys. Your happiness means a lot to me, Rick.'

His brother smiled. 'Anya's good. We're just keeping it friends for now.'

'And you're okay with that?' It couldn't be easy for Rick, who'd been more than half in love with Anya since they were kids. She'd married someone else, a lying bastard who'd left her and their little girl, Freya, up to their eyes in debt when he'd died in a car accident a couple of years ago. Finally admitting she had nowhere else to go, Anya had moved to Halfmoon Quay earlier in the year for a fresh start. For a while that start had seemed like it was going to include Rick, but things appeared to have cooled a little between them.

Rick gave Liam a wry, knowing smile. 'I'm doing my best to be okay with it, but things haven't ended between us, they're just on hold for now. My knight-in-shining-armour dreams have taken a bit of a battering but Anya is determined to get back on her own two feet without my help.'

'Your interference, more like.' Liam adored his brother, but Rick wasn't kidding about having a bit of a hero complex.

Rick grinned. 'My *helpful* interference. It's doing my head in a bit having to take a step back, but I am so proud of the resilience she's showing. Anya knows I'll wait for her to be ready, and most importantly she wants me to wait for her to be ready.'

Liam was pleased for Rick, but he hoped Anya wouldn't keep him waiting too long. His brother had so much love inside him and it was good that he'd found someone to share that with, someone Liam hoped would be able to love him the way he deserved in return. 'I'll be rooting for you guys.'

It didn't take them long to finish setting things up. Liam straightened the final chair he'd set out then turned to Rick. 'If that's everything, I'll head off. Text me when you're done and I'll meet you in the Smuggler's.'

Rick glanced over to the main café. 'We should give Issy a hand putting the chairs up. She doesn't normally bother, but we have to do it when we have an event in the Hub to dissuade people from hanging around afterwards and expecting her to serve them.'

Liam hesitated. The last thing he wanted right now was to be anywhere near Issy. 'This better not be some ploy on your part to get the two of us talking.'

'You already made it very clear that it's none of my business. Just give me a few more minutes of your time and you can get out of here, I promise.'

Rick approached the nearest table, picked up one of the chairs and placed it seat down on the tabletop. Taking his cue from his brother, Liam did the same with the other and they moved to the next table.

'This seems a bit over the top. Do you get a lot of people attending these meetings, then?' Liam couldn't imagine what was so pressing that anyone would give up their evening to sit in on a boring meeting. He always did his best to avoid them.

Rick shrugged. 'It depends what's going on. I do a morning session every Monday, but I had a few requests for an evening one for those who are busy at work during the day. Some people come along simply for a bit of company, others if they have a specific issue they want to raise. And then there are the regulars, of course.' Rick's tone was a mixture of exasperation and amusement.

'The busybodies, he means,' Issy called from behind the counter.

'I think it's good that people take an interest in their community,' Rick protested. 'Who else is turning out on a wet Sunday morning to litter pick, or volunteering for the Round the Rock organising committee?'

'Not me, that's for sure!' Issy replied with a laugh. How could she be all sweetness and light when talking to Rick and not even give Liam the time of day? Feeling himself getting irritated again, he turned his back on her and focused on his brother.

'You already do more than enough, so stop pretending you aren't as community-minded as me!' Rick settled the last chair upside down and folded his arms as he turned to Liam. 'It's a bit of a tightrope to walk sometimes, but I can't do it all myself, so if getting volunteers to help out means I have to get my ear bent now and again, so be it. Besides, I get a lot of useful information from those so-called busybodies about potential problems around the village. I'd rather know about a drain blocked with leaves before a street floods, or a wonky paving slab before someone trips and hurts themselves.'

'Sounds like you've got a regular little spy network,' Liam teased with a grin.

Rick laughed. 'I suppose I have, but they mean well and I've learnt how to differentiate between gossip and information. If I'm first in line for the rumour network then I can try and nip stuff in the bud before it gets out of hand.'

Liam shook his head. 'I don't know how you do it.' He almost said I don't know *why* you do it, but Rick had always had a strong protective instinct and it was clear that channelling it into his community work helped not only his brother but the village as a whole. 'What else needs doing?'

'The urn needs carrying into the Hub so I can get it heating.'

Liam wanted to tell Issy to do it herself but Rick was already hurrying over to help her. Before he knew it, Liam was ferrying cups and saucers back and forth from the counter to the refreshment table in the Hub and people were starting to filter through the front door ready for the meeting. Issy and Rick went immediately into hosting mode, Issy fixing drinks while Rick positioned himself by the door to greet everyone.

Liam couldn't help but be impressed at his brother's easy charm and genuine interest in every person that walked through the door. It wasn't just that he knew their names, he *knew* them. Every greeting was personalised, families asked after or a previous problem enquired about to make sure it had been satisfactorily resolved. A lot of it sounded like the daily niff-naff and trivia that you just had to put up with when you had neighbours. The apartment block he and Caro had lived in had a shared WhatsApp group full of arguments about missing post, bikes blocking corridors and how much they were going to tip the cleaners at Christmas. All stuff Liam couldn't have cared less about and had happily left to Caro.

As he listened to his brother, it started to become clear that what Liam shrugged off as boring nonsense had a meaningful impact on other people's lives. Particularly the older generation. Rick never gave any hint he was bored talking about bins left out too early or taken in too late. Or roadside embankments that hadn't been cut, or potholes springing up overnight. He was either already on the case or reached for his notebook to scribble a reminder. By the time he'd passed people onto Issy to get a tea or coffee they were inevitably smiling, grateful at the chance to be heard and acknowledged as much as anything else. Liam watched his brother with renewed respect and perhaps just the faintest twinge of jealousy. Not that he wanted to get involved with bin disputes – honestly, he couldn't think of anything worse – but Rick was the beating heart of this community and seeing him in action only amplified Liam's feelings of isolation and separation. Life in Halfmoon Quay had moved on without him.

Rick called the meeting to order and Liam slid into a chair on the back row, reasoning that he needed to understand what was going on in the village in order to help him make a decision about the hotel. He soon regretted the decision and his mind began to drift as the topics raised at the door were aired again and other people chipped in their opinions.

He let the conversation wash over him as he watched Issy potter around quietly, clearing up the unused cups and putting away the tea and coffee. He smiled in spite of himself at her silent message that no one would be welcome to hang around for another drink afterwards. He supposed he couldn't blame her. He knew what it was like to work long hours, but he could take his laptop home and at least work in a relaxed environment in the evening if he wanted – though he'd opted to stay late in the office more often than not as things had started to break down between him and Caro.

Issy didn't have that escape – her work was her home as well.

The café had been her family home until her parents had died what must be ten, maybe twelve, years ago? It bothered Liam that he couldn't instantly remember. Whatever was going on with her bad attitude towards him, Issy had been a good friend to him once. And so much more. Surely he should know the date of something so significant in her life even if it had happened after she broke up with him? He tilted his chair onto its back legs and stared at the ceiling as he mentally counted back the years. It was sometime in the autumn because he'd definitely been back in school.

The summer before it happened had been a difficult one all around. Liam had already started to worry about his forthcoming A levels. The step up from GCSEs had been a big one and his first round of mock exam results hadn't been as good as he'd hoped. Desperate to do better, he'd spent much of his time cooped up in his room, going over his notes from the previous year and doing as many practice papers as Ray could get his hands on. His old teacher had given up his time to go over anything Liam had been struggling with and had patiently marked his work and set him extra reading for any areas of weakness he'd identified.

Things had been awkward in their friendship group too. It hadn't only been Issy who had cut Liam dead: his cousin, Chloe, had taken her side and Anya and Kat had followed suit, so their old gang had spent most of the holidays split down gender lines. Then Ed had suffered a terrible fall on the rocks below the castle and Mum and Dad had spent every waking hour at the hospital as his little brother was subjected to a series of difficult operations. They'd saved his leg – thank God – but everything at home had been horrible. Their parents had deemed Rick and Liam old enough to look after themselves, but Harry, Ed's twin and the cause of the accident, had been dispatched to their grandparents' house. And there he had stayed. The past tugged at Liam, horrible memories of his mother crying, his father shouting and Harry refusing to speak to anyone. He and Rick had done their best to keep their heads down and Liam had regarded his return to boarding school as a sanctuary for the first time.

'Liam?'

Startled, he tilted his chair forward to find everyone staring at him. 'Sorry, I was miles away.'

A cross-looking woman he didn't recognise was glaring at him from a few seats away. 'We were asking about the hotel.'

Mind still half in the past, it was difficult to focus. 'The hotel? What about it?'

The woman made a noise of disgust, but before she could say anything else a man near the front of the room spoke. 'Don't play us for fools, young man, we've all heard you're taking over the hotel from Davy.' Unfortunately, Liam recognised him all too well. Kat's father, Gavin Bailey, ran the Java Brava café on the village high street. It was part of an international chain that served the same sandwiches, cakes and drink permutations, whichever one you walked into. It had none of the soul and individuality of Issy's Cosy Coffee Pot.

Feeling like a deer in the headlights under so many gazes, Liam struggled to get his thoughts in order. 'I haven't made any decisions about the hotel yet.'

If he'd thought that would head things off, he couldn't have been more wrong and questions bombarded him from around the room.

'What does that mean?'

'Are you keeping the place open?'

'What if he sells it? Then what? We can't lose all those beds, the pressure on the housing stock is already at breaking point. If we end up with any more Airbnbs the village will die.' That was the woman who'd been glaring at him but she was speaking to the man next to her, who was nodding along to everything she said.

'We have a right to know!' Gavin Bailey demanded, his face turning an unpleasant shade of red.

Feeling trapped, Liam shot to his feet. 'I told you already, I don't know what I'm going to do!'

Thankfully, Rick came to his rescue. 'Everyone needs to calm down, okay? What happens to the hotel is Penrose business. As and when our family decides what to do with it, we will let the community know. Until then, I'd ask you all not to speculate or start spinning rumours. Now then, let's return to the items that are up for discussion this evening. Kathleen, you wanted to say something about the Beachcombers, didn't you?'

There were a few grumbles at that, but most people subsided and turned to face the front of the room as a woman with short grey hair stood and started talking about the upcoming schedule for the volunteer litter-picking group. Grateful that the attention was off him, Liam decided to make an exit while he could, knowing he'd be bombarded again the moment the meeting broke up. He caught his brother's eye and tilted his head towards the door. Rick gave him an imperceptible nod to show he understood and Liam beat a hasty retreat.

He barely made it outside before someone called out, 'Mr Penrose?'

It was the formality as much as anything that caught Liam by surprise and he turned with a smile. 'The only Mr Penrose in this village is my father.'

The tall blond man opposite laughed. 'Yeah, it's a bit like that in my family, too.' He was another stranger and dressed in what Liam immediately thought of as city casual. Smart chinos, a shirt that looked more Savile Row than Marks and Spencer's, silver cufflinks gleaming at the wrists, shiny brown lace-ups with long squared-off toes. He extended a hand to Liam. 'Adam Mountjoy.'

Liam took his hand on instinct and shook it. 'Liam Penrose.' He gave a self-deprecating laugh. 'But then you know that already.'

Adam released his hand and reached into his pocket to withdraw a discreet black leather holder. Flipping it open, he took out a business card and offered it to Liam.

'What's this for?' Liam asked without taking it.

Adam's easy smile never moved as he continued to hold out the card. 'Something that might help you with your deliberations about the hotel.'

Curious, Liam took the card and studied it for a moment. He frowned as he glanced back up at Adam. 'You're a property developer.'

Adam nodded. 'I am. And I'm always on the lookout for a new project. Your hotel is a prime bit of real estate and holds a commanding position on the sea front. I think I could do a lot with it given the chance.' He tucked the card holder away. 'No rush. It's clear you and your family have a big decision on your hands, but I wanted you to know you have options, that's all.'

4

Issy settled her head back against the folded towel and closed her eyes with a sigh as she slid a little deeper under the hot bubble-coated water. She'd applied a deep conditioning treatment to her hair and slathered on a face mask from the basket of treats that one of her best friends, Kat, had given her the previous Christmas. There was a timer set on her phone so she had twenty minutes to do nothing but bliss out and let the warm water soothe the aches of the day away. Her phone started to ring. *Ignore it.* The thought made her laugh because when had Issy ever been able to ignore anything? She'd lie there while her brain catastrophised, so she might as well find out who it was and get rid of them before her bubble of zen completely burst. She sat up too quickly, sending a mini tidal wave of water over the edge of the bath to splash on the tiles below.

'Shit,' she said at the same time as she swiped a wet finger across the screen to accept the call.

'Issy? What's wrong?' Chloe asked, sounding alarmed at the unconventional greeting.

'Oh, nothing. I'm in the bath and I just sloshed water all over the floor.' Issy reached for the towel she'd been using as a pillow to dry her hands but only succeeded in knocking it off the edge into the water. 'Double shit.'

'I take it this is a bad time?' Chloe laughed. 'Let me call you back later.'

'No, no it's fine, but let me put you on speaker before my phone ends up at the bottom of the tub!' Having placed her phone safely on the wide corner of the bath, she fished the sopping towel from the water and rung it out before tossing it into the sink to sort out later. Leaning over, she tugged another towel free from the heated rail and managed to dry her hands this time. 'Right, disaster averted and hopefully you can hear me okay. Although you might have to do most of the talking as my face mask is starting to dry and it's making it hard to move my mouth.'

'I can hear you loud and clear and we both know I'm not going to have a problem talking!' Chloe's bright laughter filled the room once more. She was the most gregarious of their little gang of four, and the most adventurous too. Life was a challenge to be conquered as far as Chloe was concerned, and Issy was sure her friend could succeed at whatever she put her mind to.

Her brand-new venture was building an interior design business with Anya, Chloe's cousin on her mother's side, who had moved to Halfmoon Quay at the beginning of the summer to recover from the devasting mess her late husband had left her in. Issy and Chloe had sworn more than once that it was just as well for Drew that he was dead because otherwise they'd have happily bumped him off and dumped his body out at sea for the fish to feed on. Kat, always the quietest of their quartet, had enthusiastically promised she'd have provided an alibi for them.

'I didn't phone for any particular reason; I just fancied a chat,' Chloe continued.

'That's always a good enough reason to call,' Issy replied as she settled back in the water. 'Do you have any gossip for me?' It was a long-standing joke, because she might always have a lot to say, but Chloe was also the absolute soul of discretion. Working in the local solicitor's office, she knew everything about everybody, but she took her responsibilities seriously and never talked about what came across her desk.

Chloe gave a gusty sigh. 'Not a thing. My life is a barren wasteland of boring and for once everyone in the family seems to be behaving themselves.' Chloe was a part of the big Penrose clan, cousin to Liam and his brothers through their fathers. Between the six members that made up their generation, at least one was up to something – usually one of Liam and Rick's younger twin brothers.

'You haven't heard about Liam making a run for it from the village meeting then?' Issy asked, pleased that for once she was the one with the insider info. Now she'd got over the shock that he was staying longer than she'd expected, Issy wanted to know if he was really serious about taking on the hotel. It seemed a mad thing to do given how long Liam had been working and living up in London, but he hadn't outright denied it at the meeting, so he must at least be considering it. If he was going to become a permanent fixture then Issy wanted as much time as possible to prepare for it. If anyone would know what was going on inside her family, it would be Chloe. Liam legging it from the meeting was the perfect opening to gently coax information from her friend.

'No! What happened?'

Issy opened her mouth to reply, only to be stopped by the hardening clay she'd smeared over her skin. Losing the benefits of her face mask was a small price to pay, so Issy dipped a hand into the bathwater and washed it away from around her mouth. 'Everyone started on at him about what he was going to do with the hotel. He looked so completely poleaxed by the questions I almost felt sorry for him.' Almost.

'Good grief. It's only been a fortnight since Uncle Davy pulled that stunt of his. What do people expect?'

'Word travels fast,' Issy pointed out. 'And two weeks is a long time for a place like this to wait and wonder. Nature abhors a vacuum, so clearly people have been putting two and two together and making forty-three.' Issy rolled her eyes even though the gesture was wasted. 'Half the village is convinced he's going to shut it down, or sell up, or both, and they're either panicking about the impact it'll have on their businesses or the pressure that'd put on the housing stock in the summer with holiday-makers wanting places to stay.'

'You must admit they have a point,' Chloe mused. 'And the hotel is such a landmark in the village it's bound to stir up interest.'

'I suppose so.' Being as close as she was to the beach, Issy was never short of customers during the holiday season, but the hotel was popular all year round, especially with older couples who preferred the peace and quiet of the off season and were less bothered about the weather. She'd feel the impact of not having them pop in to warm up after a bracing walk or take advantage of the packed lunch service she offered if they had plans to venture further afield. If Liam took over she'd have to find out a way to deal with him because their paths would cross regularly. She slid a little deeper into the tub. 'You don't seriously think he's considering moving back, do you?'

Chloe sighed. 'I've no idea. According to Matt, who heard it from Ed, who heard it from Rick—'

'Ah, the famous Penrose whisper network,' Issy interrupted with a laugh.

'Ha! Anyway, according to Rick, Liam didn't come home just

for Ma's party and a visit. He and Caro have called it quits for good, and reading between the lines I'm not sure he's enjoying his job very much either. I get the feeling life in London has lost a lot of its charm.'

The information about his girlfriend intrigued Issy for a moment before she pushed it away. Liam's romantic entanglements were nothing to do with her. She sat up, sloshing the water around, though not enough to send any more over the rim of the tub. 'But I thought he was doing really well at work.' It was certainly the impression she'd got when anyone in the Penrose family had mentioned it, usually in the context of Liam not coming back to visit on the grounds of being too busy on some important project or another.

'Me too, but he doesn't seem to be in any hurry to get back to it. Aunty Rachel told Mum he's spent the last couple of weeks either lying in bed or staring at the TV. Mum thinks he's a bit depressed, but who'd be depressed earning the kind of money he's been pulling in the last few years? Oh to have a London-weighted salary.'

'But then you'd have to live in London,' Issy pointed out, not unreasonably. Poor Liam really had been the number one topic of discussion in the Penrose family by the sounds of it. Issy found herself recalling how tired he'd looked that morning and was immediately annoyed with herself. What difference did it make to her how he was feeling? Liam was big enough and ugly enough to look after himself, and if he was having some kind of crisis then he had his whole family to lean on.

'Oh yeah.' Chloe laughed. 'Well that's the end of that daydream, because I cannot imagine waking up and not being able to see the sea every day.'

Issy didn't reply, because what could she say? There were very few secrets she kept from her friends, but the knowledge that she couldn't abide the one thing that made Halfmoon Quay an idyllic place to live for everyone else would upset them terribly. It didn't take a deep psychological test to figure out why being so close to the ocean troubled her, given her parents had died in a sailing accident when she was seventeen. Thank God for Maud, because Issy didn't know what she would've done without her grandmother. Issy wasn't particularly religious, but she closed her eyes and said a brief silent prayer to implore whatever entity may be listening to keep Maud around for many more years to come.

From the day of the accident it had been just the two of them. They'd clung to each other and Maud had completely changed her life to create a stable future for Issy. She'd given up her home and her job and poured all the money she had into converting Issy's parents' house into the café. Issy had quit school straight after her A levels and started working there full time. Her brief dreams of going off to university had been cast aside by the poor grades she'd achieved. She could've gone back and done resits in the autumn but by then the café had been ready to open and Issy had found a new purpose in life.

She loved the café. Loved getting to spend every day with her grandmother. Loved that they gave the community somewhere they knew there'd always be a warm welcome, and the community had supported the business from day one. Working with Rick and the rest of the council to add the Hub extension had been a moment of great pride to Issy, a chance to give something back to the people who'd stood by her and Maud in their darkest hour.

If she could pick Halfmoon Quay up and move it away from the ocean it would've been perfect, but then again, it wouldn't be the same. The ocean was the lifeblood of the village and always had been. Fishermen and their families had built the Quay, and its bounty had fed and sustained them. As times had changed, the village had learnt to change with them, pivoting from fishing to tourism. The village had grown in popularity, which was a double-edged sword, and everyone in the community recognised it.

Even those whose jobs didn't rely solely on the regular and repeat business of visitors over the summer needed that income to support themselves because without it the village would simply die. They all knew the devastation a bad summer could bring; there were enough boarded-up shops around to prove it. The lack of long-term prospects for younger people was a growing problem and Issy wasn't the only one worried they were reaching a tipping point. Once people moved away it was hard to tempt them back. If Liam did give up his life in London and move back here, he'd be one of the few that did.

There was a beautiful clothing shop on Harbour Road next door to Russ Armstrong's restaurant, but the owners were already talking about closing down at the end of the year. Once upon a time, it was the sort of business that would've been handed down through the family, but the Nicholsons' children had both left the village years ago and built lives for themselves elsewhere. The village rumour mill had already started speculating about who might take on the property and what they might do with it. Issy didn't care what happened as long as it sold quickly, because a boarded-up premises in such a prominent position would drag the whole look of the area down.

'Hey, you know about the Nicholsons' plan to retire at Christmas? Maybe you and Anya could think about taking it over.'

Chloe sighed. 'Yeah, we talked about it for a wild minute, but it's simply too much risk for us. We don't have enough stock to fill a whole shop and honestly, while the online selling is a great side-line, I don't want us to end up diverting our efforts solely into retail. It's the design side of things where I really think we have a long-term future. I just need a few clients first.' She gave a rueful laugh. 'Well, one at least.'

'The hotel would be a good place to start,' Issy mused. Whoever ended up running it was going to have to do something with the place because it was starting to look very tired.

'Now why didn't I think of that?' Chloe said in a knowing voice.

'Ha! I should've known you were already on the case. How far have you got with it?'

'I might have persuaded Anya to make a copy of the floor plans and take photos of all the rooms and communal spaces,' Chloe said, in a not-so-innocent voice.

Issy grinned to herself. Of course she had. 'Next you'll be telling me you have a mood board and half a dozen designs already worked up on your computer,' Issy teased, knowing there was more than a 50 per cent probability.

'Might have.' They both laughed.

'Have you shown anyone else in the family? Even if Liam decides not to take it on, you're going to have to work out what else to do with the place. If Davy ends up selling it, having some suggestions for improvement would make it a more attractive prospect – and with any luck they'd give you the contract to do it. I'm sure Rick mentioned he was going with Liam to the Smuggler's for a drink. You could just happen to drop in on them. If you get them on board, the rest of the family would be too.'

'I could...' Chloe was silent for a moment. 'But I'd want Anya to be there too, and she'll be busy with Freya's bedtime.'

'Oh, I should've thought of that.' Issy wracked her brain for a moment. 'Maybe you could persuade your folks to have a barbeque at the weekend to celebrate the end of the summer holidays. I'm sure you'd find an opportunity to speak to Liam in a nice, relaxed environment.'

'You, my friend, are a bloody genius!' Chloe cried. 'I'd better go and chat up Mum while there's still time to organise something. Love you, bye!'

'Bye.' The phone was already dead before she could pick it up to end the call. Scrolling through her apps, Issy found a relaxing playlist, then set her phone back down. Her face mask was a write-off, so she pulled away what was left now it had dried across her cheeks and forehead, wincing slightly at the tug on her skin. The water had cooled a little, but that was soon rectified with a quick blast from the hot tap. Settling back, Issy closed her eyes once more and wondered if she'd done Liam a favour or simply added another problem to his plate. She pushed the thought aside.

Liam was big enough to take care of himself. Besides, she reminded herself once more, he wasn't her problem.

5

'Sorry, bro. It took me forever to get away!' Rick jogged along the path towards where Liam was sitting on the sea wall.

'Hey, no worries.' Liam stood and gestured towards the beach where he'd been watching the waves lap over the sand. 'This view isn't one I'm ever going to get bored of.'

Rick nodded, but he still looked harassed as he set his hands on his hips. 'I'm really sorry I put you in that situation, Liam. I should've realised word had already got around about the hotel and that people would be curious.'

Liam reached out and placed a hand on Rick's shoulder. 'You really don't need to keep apologising. We both know what this place is like for gossip. Buy me that beer you promised after all and we can call it quits.'

Rick glanced across the road towards the brightly lit brick building opposite. The roof tiles sagged in places and the once-red bricks were dulled with decades of dirt. Extended several times over the years, the Smuggler's Den rambled over the space it filled rather than occupying it. The gold and black name banner across the front was in need of a fresh coat of paint and it was hard to make out the image on the hanging sign of men unloading barrels from a small boat into a shadowy cave. For all it showed its age, the pub was still the heart of the village for many. 'Are you sure you want to go in? What if you get another round of questions?'

Liam shrugged. 'I'll tell them what I told the others: that I'm thinking about it.' At least he would be expecting it this time.

His fingers strayed to his front pocket where he'd shoved the business card Adam Mountjoy had given him. Enough thinking about things, he needed to start talking his options over and there was no one whose advice he valued more than Rick's – except their dad's, but that conversation would be way too loaded. If he chose the hotel, he'd be turning his back on the opportunities they'd worked so hard to give him. If he sold it, he'd be giving away a part of their family's history. For as long as the Quay had existed there'd been Penroses living there. Generations of toil had put them in a relatively stable and healthy position, at least compared to many others in the village. If Liam pulled a brick from the foundations, would it all come crashing down? 'Come on, I really need that drink.'

Thankfully, the pub was relatively quiet. Their entrance drew a few glances, a couple of nods of greeting, but no one came over after Liam claimed a booth in the corner. Rick joined him a few moments later, carrying two pints. Liam barely waited for his brother to sit before he lifted his drink and drained a quarter of it in a few long gulps. The bitter-cold liquid went down a little too easily and he forced himself to set down the glass, and pushed it away a few inches for good measure. 'So, you got any bright ideas how I get myself out of this mess?'

Rick, who had taken a far more measured sip of his own pint, peered over the top of the rim at him. 'Is it a mess, or is it a golden opportunity?'

Liam raised an eyebrow at that. 'What do you mean?'

His brother placed his glass on a mat but didn't release it. 'A casual observer might think that you've not been happy for a long time.'

'You're talking about Caro?'

'Amongst other things. It was clear this morning that you aren't exactly enjoying your job.'

Liam hid his defensive feelings behind a laugh. 'Does anyone?'

Rick didn't join in. 'Yes. I love my job because I get to spend the summer outside helping people make the most of their holidays. When I'm not on the beach I'm helping Mum in the chandlery or sorting out council business.'

'And that's an absolute barrel of laughs,' Liam scoffed, trying to hide his discomfort at the direction of the conversation. The trouble with Rick was he was too damn sharp for his own good.

'It might not be your idea of a good time, but it means a lot to me.' Rick's shoulders were as stiff as his tone.

Liam understood at once that he'd overstepped and hurt his brother in his clumsy attempt to deflect. 'I'm sorry. I know it's important to you and thank God you were willing to step up and take it on.'

Rick's face was stony for a few moments before he visibly relaxed and took another sip of his beer. 'Forget it. We're not here to talk about me. Be honest, Liam, with yourself first and foremost. Do you enjoy your job?'

It was Liam's turn to bristle. Not everyone got to follow their dream career – not everyone *had* a dream career. Liam had a gift for numbers and he'd found something that paid him very well.

Wasn't that the important thing? Not having to stress about bills and being able to afford a few of life's little luxuries. 'I'm very good at what I do.'

'You're very good at avoiding the question too.'

Liam made a grab for his pint then clenched his fist to stop himself. Getting drunk was not what they were there for, even if it sounded like a bloody good idea right now. The thought stopped him short. He'd never been much of a drinker, so why was he contemplating it now rather than just being honest? Enough thinking about things, he needed to start talking his options over and there was no one whose advice he valued more than Rick's. 'I've never been so bored in my life. I scamper like a hamster on the corporate wheel, crunching numbers, producing endless reports and forecasts so that the company I work for can turn huge amounts of money into even more ludicrous amounts of money, and they pay me handsomely for it. I leave home when it's dark and I come home when it's dark. I eat crap, I get forced to socialise with people I have nothing in common with because we happen to work in the same department and it's expected of me. When I do finally get home I'm then forced to spend my weekends with a different set of people that I have even less in common with because they happen to be friends with my girlfriend.'

Rick's expression barely changed, as though nothing in Liam's admission had surprised him in the least. 'Technically, you don't have to do that bit any more,' he pointed out in a bone-dry voice.

Liam shook his head. 'Stop trying to make me laugh. I'm pathetic. My life is pathetic. Almost thirty years old and what have I got to show for it? No home, no partner, terrible posture and even worse eyesight from sitting in front of a screen all day.'

'And the start of a pot belly.'

Shocked, Liam dropped his hand to press against his stomach

and was relieved to find it still flat, though he couldn't deny he'd lost a bit of definition after too many skipped gym sessions. 'Cheeky bastard.'

Rick grinned. 'You had to check, didn't you?' Expression growing serious, he reached across the table and gripped Liam's forearm. 'No thinking. No weighing up the pros and cons, just come out with it. Do you want to go back to London or do you want to stay here in the Quay?'

Liam shook his head. 'It's not that simple though, is it?' He remembered his brief meeting with Adam Mountjoy. Fishing out the business card, he placed it on the table between them. 'Maybe I should just give this guy a ring in the morning and tell him he can have the hotel.' Removing the current uncertainty he was feeling might give him the impetus to stop hiding away and get back on with life in London.

'What are you talking about?' Rick picked up the card, looked at it for a moment then frowned at Liam. 'A property developer? When did you arrange to speak to him?'

Liam shrugged. 'I didn't. He was at the meeting in the café and followed me out. Gave me his card and said I had options.' Reaching out, he took the card back. 'It makes sense when you think about it. What the hell do I know about running a hotel?'

'If it's what you want to do, then you are smart enough to turn your mind to anything. If it's not, then I think you should at least give someone else in the family the opportunity to take over the hotel rather than selling it to the first person who approaches you.'

'Like who?' Not liking the chastisement he could hear in his brother's tone, Liam folded his arms and sat back. 'You've got more than enough on your plate. Harry is settled at the restaurant and Ed's not going to give up his studies – nor would I want him to!'

'I'm just saying you shouldn't rush into anything. If you don't want the hotel, then what happens to it should be a decision for the whole family.'

Liam shook his head, not willing to be put off the point he was making. 'Matt and Uncle Ryan have their joinery business. Anya would be the perfect candidate but you've already told me she's not interested and, besides, didn't you say her and Chloe are setting up some design company, so that knocks them both off the list.' Liam reached for his beer. 'Unless we've got some secret relatives I don't know about, it's me or it's nobody.'

Rick held his hands up. 'Okay, okay, you're right, it just seems a shame to let a stranger take over something that's been part of the family for so long. If you're sure you don't want to do it, then maybe you should give this guy a call just to at least see what he's proposing.'

He didn't sound happy about the idea, and to be honest, Liam wasn't either. 'It would be the smart thing to do.'

'But is it the right thing?' Rick reached out and placed his hand on Liam's arm. 'And I'm not talking about the family, I'm talking about you. Forget all the noise in your head about what's smart or sensible, or easy. Tell me what you want to do.'

Liam had to close his eyes against a sudden burning. 'I want to stay. I want to stand on my own two feet. Do a job where it's all on me. I'm sick of being a drone in the hive. More than that, I miss you all so damn much, the thought of leaving again hurts me physically. Everyone is already moving on without me and I hate that I don't fit in here any more. I want to feel like a Penrose again.' It would be up to him to put the work in to reclaim his place within the family, but he was ready to do whatever it took. And those weren't the only bonds he'd have to repair. He doubted he and Issy could get to a point where they could be friends again, and honestly, he wasn't sure he wanted to. But given the proximity of the hotel to the café, they were bound to run into each other, so they'd at least need to get to a point of civility.

When he opened his eyes, there was nothing but compassion and understanding in his brother's gaze. 'Right. Finally, we're getting somewhere. Now all we have to do is figure out how we're going to make it happen.'

6

The Thursday after the monthly meeting, Issy found herself once more wishing for closing time. The weather had turned the view outside into a misty veil of grey rain and she was stuck in that liminal space between the lunch rush and the kids' club influx, although given the terrible weather she wasn't sure how many people would bother venturing out. The beach had been empty all morning apart from the odd hardy dog walker, and the café hadn't seen a customer for over half an hour. Tempting as it was, she couldn't risk putting the closed sign up to take a break in case someone came seeking shelter from the bad weather. Well, she could in theory put the sign up, but the last thing she wanted was a reputation for unreliable hours. She needed to maximise her revenue before things quietened down. She glared out the window at the rain. If the bad weather continued for long, all the businesses in the village that relied on the tourist trade would begin to suffer.

It was already a struggle during the off season to compete with the Java Brava coffee shop franchise in the centre of the village, as most of her lunchtime regulars had to walk past it in order to come to her. Gavin Bailey, the manager there, ran an endless stream of giveaways and special promotions that was growing increasingly difficult to compete with. It was one of the reasons she'd started offering the packed lunch deals, including an online ordering service. Her days were longer as a result, but being her own boss at least meant she could open when she liked (within reason) rather than at the hours stipulated by corporate headquarters.

So here she was, mopping up the wet, dirty footprints left by her lunchtime customers and would likely be finished just in time for the families coming to use the Hub to turn her nice clean floor into a disaster zone. What was it about kids and their desire to jump in every muddy puddle they encountered? Issy laughed at the thought, wondering when she'd turned into such a curmudgeonly old woman. She'd been a puddle jumper at that age too. She'd loved everything about the water, even the rain. From the moment she'd been able to toddle, her parents had barely been able to keep her off the beach. She'd practically lived in the pond – the safe swimming area demarked by a string of coloured buoys in full view of the lifeguard stand on the beach. She'd progressed from bobbing around with water wings to surfing and paddle boarding. The thing she'd loved more than anything, though, was sailing with her father.

She hadn't been in a boat since the accident, and the comfort she might have gained from her memories was tainted because so many of them revolved around the ocean. She'd avoided them at first and now, when she might bring herself to think about them, they were hazy at best. The images in her mind of her parents from those times were the ghosts who haunted her nan's photo albums. The stories she held close all second-hand recounting of days she couldn't always recall for herself. Maud had reassured her that once she got to her age all she'd have in her head were memories of long bygone times, but Issy wasn't sure she believed her. She cast a glance towards the window, seeing only the dim outline of her reflection against a wall of grey. At least the endless rain meant she couldn't see the beach today. A small mercy she'd tolerate every dirty footprint for.

She spun at the first jangle of the bell above the door, her thoughts still mostly stuck in the past. Instead of a customer, it was Maud, her short lilac bob and clothes protected from the rain by a sunshine-yellow sou'wester hat and matching raincoat. 'Goodness me, with a face like that you'll turn the milk sour!'

Issy smiled automatically at the familiar words her nan always uttered if she caught Issy sulking. 'Hello, Nan. What are you doing out and about on such a filthy day?' Hurrying over, she hung up Maud's hat and coat while her nan brushed imaginary bits of fluff off a black T-shirt covered in sparkly rhinestones tucked into her trademark drainpipe jeans. She might be pushing eighty, but Maud hadn't let age slow her down one bit.

Turning with a smile, Maud hugged her. 'Oh, I was going stir crazy sitting at home, so I thought I'd come and annoy you.'

'You never annoy me, Nan, you know that,' Issy replied, giving Maud an extra squeeze of reassurance. 'It's always a pleasure to see you, but what's wrong at home?'

Maud sighed. 'Davy's gone to the hospital for a couple of final tests before the consultant signs off on his treatment. Of course he refused to let me go with him, the stubborn old fool, so I was left staring at the walls and checking my watch every five minutes.'

'Come and sit down and I'll make us a cuppa.' Taking her nan's hand, Issy led her to a table near the counter where she left her to fetch a pot of tea.

It was too much to expect that Maud would actually sit and watch her work, so it was no surprise to Issy that, when she turned to open the back of the cold counter to retrieve a little treat for them both, Maud had made herself useful and was finishing up the last bits of mopping. 'You didn't have to do that,' Issy told her, with a fond smile and a shake of her head.

'As if I'm going to sit around like Lady Muck while you wait on me,' Maud countered. 'It's done now in any case, so you've got time to sit and keep me company.'

Picking up a tray with their tea and cakes, Issy carried it to the table and set it down with a sigh. 'If this rain doesn't let up, it might just be the two of us for the rest of the afternoon.'

'Which wouldn't be such a bad thing, would it?' Maud asked as she passed by carrying the bucket and mop. 'I'll just put these away and be with you in two ticks.'

It was pointless to try and intervene and offer to do it, as Maud hated any hint from anyone that she couldn't manage. Still, it was an effort to keep her eyes on the tea and not track her nan's every movement. Issy was just pouring out when Maud sat down opposite, her hands still a touch damp from where she must've washed them. 'Oh, this looks yummy,' she said, eyes widening as she took one of the plates with a generous slice of Swiss roll sitting on it. 'What flavour?'

'It's lemon sponge with a lemon and lime cream and lemon curd.' Issy handed her a fork and Maud immediately dug in.

'Worth every calorie I'm sure,' she said with a happy sigh. 'I'll have to do an extra Jane Fonda session, but it'll be worth it.'

Issy smiled to herself as she added a dash of milk to her nan's mug. Maud had been over the moon when Issy had found her favourite 80s workouts on YouTube, the original video cassettes having been worn out and the replacement DVDs somewhere in the stacks of boxes in the attic above the upstairs flat. Maud hadn't had space for much when she'd moved into a room at the hotel on what was supposed to have been a temporary basis several years previously.

Issy wasn't sure if all that pulsing and bouncing Jane and her leotard-clad gang went in for met the latest scientific recommendations, but there was no denying that Maud looked damn good on it, so she kept quiet as she tugged her own top down over the slight roll perching on the waistband of her jeans. She might be on her feet all day, but it was too easy to graze while at work and take upstairs whatever leftovers needed eating, because the last thing she wanted to do after cooking and baking all day was set about making a proper meal for herself. She looked down at her own slice of cake and wondered if she'd better put it back, then decided what the hell. There were many things in life to feel guilty about, but cake should never be one of them. She'd just have to take a page out of Maud's book and find her own YouTube workout to do. 'So it's just a scan today for Davy?'

Maud nodded. 'He's had all his bloods and everything done; this is just a final check and then hopefully he can start his treatment.'

Issy reached over and took her nan's hand. 'I know you must be worried but at least he's finally facing things head on and not avoiding it.'

Maud nodded. 'You're right. It's a miracle he's gone this far with it given his propensity for avoiding things.'

Issy raised an eyebrow at that. 'You're a fine one to talk. How long did it take you to admit you had feelings for him?'

'I knew how I felt about him all along; he's the one too daft to recognise a good thing when it's right under his nose.' Maud set her fork down with a sigh. 'I honestly thought he'd get the message when I moved into the hotel, but he told me he never dared to hope I'd give him a second chance after he made such a mess of things when we were young.'

It had been a surprise to Issy to know that Maud and Davy had been childhood sweethearts. When Davy had messed her around and refused to commit, Maud had made the decision to move on and had started dating Issy's grandfather a few months later. 'Do you ever look back and regret the choice you made?'

Maud frowned for a moment as though not sure what Issy was getting at, then her face brightened into a wide smile. 'You mean marrying my Lockie instead of waiting for Davy to get his life together?' Issy nodded and her nan threw her head back and laughed. 'Good lord, darling, not for one single second. I loved your grandfather with all my heart and soul and I think about him every day, but it gets lonely on your own.'

'So you don't love Davy, then?' Issy tried to puzzle her way through a tactful way to word what was bothering her. Davy wasn't well, there was no getting around that, and it was a serious burden for Maud to take on a relationship with someone who might be running out of time. Issy felt sorry for Davy but Maud was her number one priority and she would be lying to herself if she didn't wonder if her nan was setting herself up for more heartache.

'Of course I do, but it's not the passion we had for each other when we were twenty.'

'Nan!' Laughing, Issy raised a hand to her cheek, which she was sure must be flaming red. 'I don't need the details, thanks.'

Maud's grin was entirely unrepentant. 'And it's not the same deep and abiding love I felt for your grandfather either. It's about companionship, mostly. Someone to talk to, to hold and have hold you. Someone to share the best, and yes, the worst that life has to offer.'

Issy bit her lip, wondering if she should move the conversation on to something else, but she wanted to be sure Maud was okay. 'What if he's not got much time left, though?'

Maud clasped her hand and gripped it hard. 'Oh, darling, is that what you're worried about?'

Issy nodded. 'I can't bear to think of you hurting again like you did when we lost Gramps.' *Or when we lost Mum and Dad.* She couldn't say that, though, not without crying.

'When you get to my age, death is a fact of life. Davy could die tomorrow or he could die in ten years' time. I hope to God it's the latter, but whatever happens I'll face it when it comes. In the meantime, I'm going to make the most of having him by my side. What's the alternative? That I spend what time I have left on my own?'

Issy shook her head. 'No, I don't want you to be lonely, I just don't want you to get hurt, that's all.'

Maud squeezed her hand once before releasing it. 'Might as well want the sun and the moon to switch places, because trying to live your life without getting hurt is just as impossible.' She picked her fork back up. 'Enough of all that, let's enjoy this cake and spending a few quiet minutes together.'

'You're right and I'm sorry if you thought I was questioning your decisions, Nan. It comes from a place of love.'

'I know that, because everything you do comes from that same place.'

They spent a happy half an hour together until Maud's mobile beeped. She checked the message and set her phone back down with a sigh. 'The wanderer has returned, so I'd better get back and see how things went.'

Issy rose and began stacking their tea things on the tray. 'Well, thank you for coming to see me; you saved me from a very boring afternoon.' Leaving the tray, she stepped around the table and gave Maud a big hug. 'I hope you didn't think I was prying earlier.'

'Not at all.' Maud stretched up and pecked a kiss on her cheek. 'Besides, family is allowed to pry and I'd always rather you said something than worried on your own.'

Pulling back, Issy smiled down at her. 'But I'm not going to worry about this any more, because you're happy and that matters more than anything.'

Her nan cupped her cheek. 'That's right, I am. Now promise me you'll stop worrying about me and focus on your own happiness.'

Issy laughed. 'I'm happy, Nan. I've got everything I need already.'

Maud patted her cheek. 'Now say that like you mean it.'

'What are you talking about? I *am* happy.'

'If you say so.' Her nan made a beeline for the hooks on the wall and lifted down her raincoat, handing it to Issy so she could hold it out and help her put it on.

Starting to feel a bit miffed, Issy frowned. 'I do say so.' She moved to open the door, only then realising that the rain had stopped. The sky was still a threatening purple-grey that promised more bad weather to come, but the faintest rainbow shone against the dark clouds.

'Make a wish before it fades,' her nan urged.

'I thought it was a shooting star that you were supposed to wish upon.'

'Well if you won't, I'll do it for you.' Turning to face the cloud bank, Maud stretched her arms wide and raised her voice as she said, 'Rainbow, bring my granddaughter a love to last a lifetime.'

'Behave yourself!' Issy said with a laugh as she leaned down to hug Maud. 'Between you and my friends, I have all the love I need.'

Maud hugged her hard before stepping back and regarding Issy with bright eyes that missed nothing. 'Don't let old fears rule your whole life, Isabel.'

'I'm not, Nan. I'm fine just the way I am.'

Her nan stared at her for a long moment before nodding once, not so much acknowledging Issy's point as correct, more indicating that she'd said her piece – for now, anyway.

'Message me later and let me know how Davy is, okay?'

'I will. Bye for now.' With her sou'wester dangling from one wrist, Maud trotted off down the pavement.

Issy watched her go for a moment before turning to look back at the sky. The rainbow was barely visible now. Beneath its watery arch a lone figure ran along the sand. Even from this distance, something deep inside told her who it was. She turned away with a snort. If Liam Penrose was the rainbow's idea of a love to last a lifetime she'd stick to wishing on stars.

7

'Explain to me again what this evening is all about?' Liam asked his mother as she handed him another stack of containers from the fridge.

'Helen just thought it would be a nice idea to get everyone together before we get more dismal weather like we did yesterday.' Rachel paused to shoot him a pointed look over her shoulder. 'Why does it matter? It's not like you have anything else planned, is it?'

Oof. Liam felt the blow of those words in his solar plexus. 'I was only asking,' he muttered as he stacked the boxes in the large bag at his feet.

Handing over the last couple of boxes, his mum closed the fridge door with a sigh. 'I'm sorry, love, but you have been rather hiding away since Ma's party. It'll be nice to do something all of us together, won't it?'

Liam bent over to place the final boxes in the bag, hiding a wince as guilt lanced through him. 'I didn't mean to make you worry about me, I've just had a lot on my mind.'

She nodded. 'I know, I just don't like it when you go quiet on us.' Reaching up, she caressed his cheek with her thumb. 'You might be all grown up, Liam, but you'll always be my baby and I'm always going to worry about you. It's a mother's prerogative.'

Movement caught his eye and he couldn't help grinning. 'I thought Ed was the baby, not me.'

'What did I do now?' his youngest brother protested, holding his arms out in a why-me gesture.

Rachel tapped Liam on the nose in gentle admonishment. 'Don't tease your brother.' She turned to welcome Ed with a hug and a kiss on his cheek. 'Ignore him. How was your day?'

Ed gave Liam a quick side-eye then puffed out his cheeks. 'My brain hurts. Whose idea was it to do a bloody PhD?'

'That would've been yours!' Laughing, Liam slung an arm around his brother's shoulders that quickly turned into a wrestling match.

'Oh good God, what did I ever do to deserve nothing but boys?' Rachel exclaimed, turning away from them with a shake of her head. 'It's all your father's fault.'

'What's my fault?' Tall and broad-shouldered like his sons, Jago filled the kitchen doorway. 'I've packed everything you wanted in the car, though I don't understand why we need to take so much stuff when Ryan and Helen are supposed to be the ones hosting.'

'It's just a few bits of salad and a couple of things for dessert,' Rachel said. 'You can't expect them to do everything.' She picked up the bag and held it out. 'There's just this to go in and then we're done.'

'You know we'll only end up bringing half of this back again,' Jago said with a shake of his head, but he still took the bag. 'Okay, I'll run this all down quick and bring the car back. Are you going to wait for me or shall I just see you there?'

Rachel raised her eyes to the ceiling through which came the hum of the shower. 'Rick's still getting ready, so we might as well wait.'

'He'll be ages,' Ed said with a wicked grin as he gave Liam a playful slap on the arm then dodged away before he could retaliate. 'Shall we go upstairs and help him choose a shirt that matches his pretty eyes?'

The chance to tease another one of his brothers was too good to turn down. 'Sounds like a plan.'

'Play nicely!' Their mother's exasperated call followed them out into the hall.

'Has she met us?' Ed asked Liam.

'It's an age thing,' he replied, shaking his head and pretending to frown as he followed his brother up the stairs.

'I heard that, you cheeky little broom handle!' Jago growled from behind them.

Turning, Liam raised an amused eyebrow. 'Broom handle?'

Their father curled his lip. 'Your mum's been on at me for swearing too much, so I'm having to be creative, though I'm not sure what she expects from me, because you lot would try the patience of a floundering saint!' Still grumbling, he turned and walked out the open front door.

'Hurry up, broom handle!' Ed called from the top of the stairs.

'No.' Liam pointed a finger at his brother. 'Absolutely not.'

'Oh, Broomy, don't be such a spoilsport.' Ed's face contorted as he tried to hold back a laugh before he darted along the landing towards Rick's room.

'I swear to God, you must have a death wish.' Liam followed him more slowly, knowing it was pointless to argue any further. The more he pushed back, the more Ed would latch onto the stupid nickname. Once he shared it with his twin, Liam would never shake it off. Hopefully torturing Rick would be enough of a distraction to make him forget about it.

They walked in on the rather unedifying sight of their brother's naked backside. 'Put some pants on, bro,' Liam protested, raising a hand to cover his eyes as Ed flopped down across Rick's bed, uncaring of the neatly laid-out clothes on top of the covers.

'Get off, you idiot!' Rick shoved Ed out of the way and retrieved his jeans and red and white checked shirt which he held in front of his body to shield his dignity. 'What are you doing in here anyway?'

'We came to help you get ready,' Ed said, rolling off the bed and heading to the dressing table, which was littered with bottles of aftershave. He picked one up and gave it an experimental sniff. 'Ugh, smells like cat's piss.' He set the bottle back down with a shudder.

'That's the one you gave me for Christmas,' Rick pointed out in a voice as dry as the desert.

'Must smell better on me,' Ed replied with an unrepentant shrug. He caught sight of the shirt Rick was clutching and pulled a face. 'You're not wearing that, are you?'

'Why wouldn't he?' Liam asked, glancing down at his own choice of shirt, which was a navy, burgundy and white variation of the same design.

'Apart from the fact you look like you've been taking fashion tips from Dad?' With a shake of his head, Ed crossed to the wardrobe and pulled open the doors to cast a critical eye over the contents. While he rummaged, Liam and Rick exchanged a look and a shrug before Rick tossed the clothes he was holding back on the bed and turned to his dresser and pulled out some underwear. By the time he was – finally! – decently covered, Ed had selected a black moleskin shirt. He tossed it to Rick. 'This and a white T-shirt. Anya won't be able to keep her hands off you,' Ed added, that impish grin of his firmly in place.

'You know she and I are taking things easy, so try for once in your life not to be a complete muppet, okay?'

Rick turned back to the dresser while Liam leaned down to touch the material of the shirt. It was so soft he found himself stroking his fingers over it. 'This is nice. I don't think I've seen it before.'

Having tugged a T-shirt on, Rick picked up the shirt and shrugged into it. 'I think it was a birthday present from Chloe.' He reached for his jeans and stepped into them and Liam had to admit that the outfit looked good.

He glanced back down at himself. 'Maybe I should go and get changed.'

Ed flopped onto the bed once more. 'What for? It's not like there's going to be anyone there you're trying to impress, it's only family – and Anya and Freya, of course.'

Liam snorted. 'It wouldn't matter who was there, I'm not looking to impress anyone.'

'Not even Issy?'

Liam whipped his head around and stared agog at Rick. 'What are you talking about?'

Rick finished buttoning up his shirt and met his gaze. 'You can't deny you were inseparable once upon a time. I just wondered if there was anything still there, especially with you considering coming home, and all.'

Liam couldn't help but laugh. Rick might love to fix things but he was barking so far up the wrong tree if he was thinking of trying to matchmake him and Issy. 'If you're looking for someone to double-date with you and Anya, I'm going to have to disappoint you. The only thing that's between me and Issy is dislike, at least on her part.' He sighed. 'I wish I knew whatever it was she thought I'd done to cause her to break up with me, because what-ever it is, she's clearly still holding a grudge. Not that I'm in any hurry to retread that path,' he added, quickly. 'But if I do decide to stay I'll need to try and resolve this tension between us. The café and the hotel are too close for us to be arguing all the time.'

Rick frowned. 'I'm confused, bro. I thought *you* were the one who ended things.'

'What are you talking about?'

His brother shrugged. 'Well you did stop writing to her. I remember her asking me about it at the time.'

Liam shook his head. 'You never mentioned it.'

Rick scoffed. 'I assumed it was because you wanted to concentrate on your school work. You never talked about it either, so I assumed you'd rather forget about it.'

Liam supposed he had a point, but he was still confused as to how Rick could've got it all so back to front. 'Well, I don't know what she said, but somehow you got the wrong end of the stick. Issy was the one who stopped writing to me. I was gutted at the time because being away from everyone was hard enough.' Broken-hearted more like, but they didn't need to know that.

Rick stared at him for a long moment before shaking his head. 'I could've sworn you were the one who ended things.' He looked over at Ed, who was still flipping through Rick's wardrobe and muttering disparaging comments about most of its contents. 'Isn't that what everyone thought?'

Ed abandoned the wardrobe and raised his hands. 'Don't ask me. I don't keep track of your love lives, I've got enough of my own drama to deal with.'

'Now what?' Rick folded his arms and glared at Ed.

Their younger brother gave a faintly embarrassed shrug. 'Nothing you need to worry about. Come on, I'm starving.' He beat what could only be described as a hasty retreat out the door.

Liam exchanged a look with Rick. 'What was that all about?'

'I have no idea.' Rick picked up his wallet and keys from the bedside cabinet and tucked them in his pocket. 'But whatever it is, I'm pretty sure I don't want to know.'

On that they could both agree. Liam was going to pursue the confusion over his break-up with Issy, when their mother yelled their names from the bottom of the stairs. He shrugged the thought off as he followed Rick. It was ancient history when all was said and done, so who'd done what and when really didn't matter any more.

8

The moment they arrived at their aunt's house, their mum disappeared into the kitchen with Aunty Helen while their dad made a beeline for Uncle Ryan, who was fiddling around with the enormous gas barbeque that took up one corner of the patio. A large bucket sat in the middle of the wooden outdoor dining table, stuffed full of ice and beer; their cousin Matt, stationed nearby, already clutched a condensation-soaked bottle. 'Good timing,' he said by way of greeting, setting his bottle down to fish three more out of the bucket, which he deftly popped the lids off and handed around. 'I hate to drink alone.'

'Cheers.' Ed clinked bottles with Matt and they took seats next to each other. 'Hey, you still want to sand down those kitchen cupboards tomorrow?' The pair of them shared a cottage by the beach that belonged to an elderly resident who'd moved into the Blue Horizons retirement complex when she'd begun to need extra support. They were living there for a knockdown rent and doing the place up as part payment. Their long-term hope was that she would eventually sell to them, but they knew it was hard for her to let go of somewhere she'd lived all her life, so they weren't pushing the point.

Matt nodded. 'Yeah, if that's all right with you? It'd be good to get them sanded and varnished over the next couple of weekends while the weather's still mostly on our side and we can have the door open to keep the fumes down.'

Liam took a spare seat next to them. He'd promised himself to make more of an effort to reconnect with everyone and this seemed like a perfect opportunity. 'If you need an extra pair of hands, let me know.'

His cousin tipped his bottle towards him. 'Cheers. We might just take you up on that.'

Liam tapped the bottle with his. 'I'm serious. I'd love to help if you think I can be of use.'

'Nine o'clock suit you? There'll be a bacon butty waiting with your name on it.'

'I'll be there.' He'd better get his arse in gear in the morning and go for a run if that was the case. Even on the longest days at work he'd tried to make time for regular exercise, packing gym kit and taking a circuitous route home from the tube station so he could squeeze in a couple of miles. Getting back into the habit was something he was enjoying and he didn't want to let it slip again.

It didn't take long before they were summoned to the kitchen to ferry various plates and bowls and platters outside. 'Dad wasn't kidding when he said we'd be taking half of this home,' Liam observed to Rick as he squeezed a basket of rolls into one of the final gaps along the centre of the table.

Rick paused in his task of laying out cutlery and plates to shoot him a grin. 'We'll all be sorted for lunches next week, that's for sure.' Something must've caught his attention over Liam's shoulder as he immediately straightened up. From the increased wattage of Rick's smile, Liam didn't need to turn around to know Anya must've appeared from the summer house at the end of the garden where she lived with her daughter, Freya.

'I'll finish this,' he told his brother, holding out his hand for the remaining cutlery.

'Cheers.' Rick barely glanced at him as he thrust the knives and forks into his waiting palm and walked away. With a smile and a shake of his head, Liam finished up laying the table.

'Hey, Liam.' He looked up from setting down the final knife to find Chloe standing beside him.

'Hey, yourself. I was wondering where you'd got to.'

'Anya wanted to give Freya a bath now so she can put her straight to bed later, so I gave her a hand. Though perhaps I should've waited until afterwards to get changed.' She pointed out a wet mark on the front of her pretty blue floral top.

Liam shot her a sympathetic smile. 'It's not very noticeable,' he assured her.

Frowning, she brushed at her front. 'Are you sure? I was wondering whether I should nip upstairs and get changed.'

'I'd much rather you sat down and told me what you've been up to. I hardly got the chance to talk to you at Ma's party.' He reached for a pair of chairs and pulled them out, gesturing for her to sit while he took the other one.

Chloe's face lit up as she plopped down. 'It was a bit manic that night, wasn't it?'

Liam nodded. 'Rick tells me you and Anya are setting up a design business. How are you getting on with that?'

If she'd looked happy before, she was positively beaming now. 'It's great! I mean it's still in the really early stages, so we're not much more than a glorified Etsy shop, but I've got so many ideas!' She laughed. 'Can you tell I'm excited?'

'I wouldn't have known if you hadn't mentioned it,' Liam

deadpanned. 'Honestly, Chlo, I'm really chuffed for you and I'm sure you'll make a big success of anything you turn your mind to.' She'd always been driven and while her enthusiasms didn't always have staying power, Liam hoped this would be different because it was great to see such a light in her eyes.

'Thanks.' Chloe gave him a considering look. 'What about you? I know it must've been a shock when Uncle Davy gave you the hotel deeds with no warning, but have you had a chance to think what you'll do with the place?'

Liam took a sip of his beer. 'Let's just say I'm giving it some very serious thought.'

'Does that mean you'd be in the market for, oh, I don't know, a design proposal from someone who is setting up a new business and looking for their first big client?' She said it in an oh-so-casual way, but Liam didn't miss the hint of excitement in her eyes. It hadn't occurred to him to think about doing up the hotel, not when he'd barely got beyond even daring to consider taking it on. Now she'd placed the idea in his head it was obvious. He hadn't had a chance to check things out properly but given how tired the exterior was looking, it was reasonable to assume it wouldn't be much better inside.

Chloe was watching him intently, practically vibrating with excitement. He took another sip from his beer and tried to hide a smile. 'And if I was in the market for such a thing, do you know someone who'd fit the bill?'

'Let me show you what we've been working on!' Chloe grabbed his hand and all but hauled him down off the patio and began towing him towards one of the garden sheds.

'Where are we going?' he protested with a laugh.

'To our workshop.' She paused for a second, eyes scanning around the garden until she spotted Anya. She was standing next to Rick, shielding her eyes from the evening sun as she smiled at

Freya, who was perched on Rick's shoulders. 'Anya!' she yelled across. 'Urgent business meeting!'

Liam was amused and not a little bemused as Anya abandoned Freya and Rick and hurried over. 'What, now?'

'It's as good a time as any,' Chloe said as she pulled Liam the last few feet to the shed. She released his hand and pulled the door open with a flourish. 'Welcome to Penrose Duncan Design!'

Liam's amused laughter faltered as he entered the shed. He didn't know what he'd expected to see, but it wasn't a wall of well-organised shelves full of neatly labelled boxes. On the opposite side was a wide bench that ran the length of the shed, a couple of stools tucked neatly under it. At one end of the bench sat a sewing machine beneath a bright wall light, while boxes of craft tools sat in a neat row at the other end. The majority of the bench was taken up with a stack of what looked like blueprints and a large cork board above it was covered in printouts from websites, paint colour charts and swatches of material.

Brushing past him, Chloe reached for a large ring binder and opened it on top of the blueprints then pulled out one of the stools and patted it. Curious, Liam sat down and the two women immediately came to stand on either side of him. 'Before we start,' Anya said in her soft voice, 'we need to be clear that this is about business, not family, so you are under no obligation.' She glanced past him. 'Right, Chloe?'

Chloe screwed up her nose. 'Listen to you, Miss Integrity.' Her expression brightened as she patted Liam's arm. 'Of course it's business.' She grinned. 'Family business.'

'Of course.' He managed to keep his face straight and his tone serious, though he knew if Anya wasn't there Chloe would likely have him in a headlock by now. She might be smaller than the rest of them, but she'd learnt to fight dirty in order to hold her own against five boys. 'These are the blueprints for the hotel, so we've got all the correct dimensions and those are reflected in the proposed costings at the back of the file.'

'Costings?' Liam couldn't hide his surprise. He'd expected some sketches and a few samples maybe, but he was beginning to realise he'd underestimated both of them.

Chloe rolled her eyes. 'We're not messing around here, you know.' She tugged the folder closer so it was angled between them. 'There are a few different options,' she said, using the side tabs to flip back and forth through each section. 'The top one is the cheap-and-cheerful, mostly status quo one and includes a full redecoration inside and out and options for replacing furniture as close to like for like as we could find.'

Which would be the quickest and easiest, especially if he decided he wanted to sell the place. 'What about the others?'

'The middle one,' Anya said, reaching in front of him to tap the top cover of that section, 'is a bit more ambitious and includes options to completely refurbish and modernise all the existing rooms.' She straightened up. 'When was the last time you were in the hotel?'

Liam shook his head. 'I honestly couldn't tell you. Probably one summer back when we were still kids and used to dash in and pinch lollies from the jar on reception.' He smiled at the old memory of their great-uncle waving his fist in mock anger as one or other of the boys did a dash and grab. The jar was always full, though, and always in easy reach of small hands.

She laughed. 'The jar's still there. In fact, I doubt anything has changed since your last visit, and that's part of the problem. The hotel has a fairly loyal clientele but it's starting to look very tired. I tried to update the website with a few pictures but, honestly, it's hard to find many appealing shots.'

So things likely were as rundown as he suspected. He'd better find out for himself before he got too carried away. 'If I come in

Monday will you have time to show me around?' He needed to talk to Davy too, find out from him what the financials were looking like. Part of him wanted to do it tomorrow, but he'd already promised to help Matt and Ed and he didn't want to let them down. He also wanted some time on his own to sit and go through the proposals because it was hard to concentrate on anything when Chloe was watching him with such hope and interest in her eyes.

Anya nodded. 'Of course.' Her face fell. 'Oh, but maybe we should make it another day because Davy's having a couple of days off. It's part of his deal with Maud to try and take things a little easier.' She gave a wry smile. 'I wouldn't be surprised if he shows his face, though, as he's not very good at sticking to it.'

Liam considered it for a moment. 'It might be best if I take a look when he's not there.' If things were bad, he'd rather know before he talked to Davy.

'Of course.' She reached out and patted his arm. 'I know we've given you a lot of options, but if the thought of making big changes is too daunting, I promise a lick of paint and maybe a few updated furnishings will make a huge difference.'

He grinned. 'You must be a mind-reader.'

Anya laughed. 'Let's just say you have a very expressive face.'

'That explains why I've never been very good at poker, I guess.' They all laughed. He turned to Chloe. 'What about you? Will you be around on Monday?'

She shook her head. 'I'll be at work and it's too short notice to take the day off. I can do it any evening or even next weekend, though.'

'No, it's fine, don't worry about it. Let's see how things go first.'

Liam didn't miss the disappointment in her eyes, but before he could say anything Anya spoke again.

'I'll be at the hotel from eight-thirty on Monday, so any time after that will be fine.'

Liam felt energised for the first time since he'd come home. There would be a hell of a lot to do and he still wasn't sure he knew the first thing about running a hotel, but if he could run a project with hundreds of thousands of pounds on the line, surely he could figure this out? Still, he'd have to have all his ducks in a row before he decided anything. If the hotel was failing, Liam didn't have anywhere near enough savings under his belt to rescue it. He was comfortable, had made sensible investments for his future, but bankrupting himself for the sake of family loyalty was not on the cards.

Conscious of what Anya had said about him having an expressive face, he made sure to school his features as he nodded. 'Would ten o'clock suit you? I'll call in at the café and grab us a coffee if you like.' And maybe have a quick word with Issy while he was at it, try and get to the bottom of this break-up nonsense.

'Sounds good to me.'

He picked up the folder. 'Can I take this with me?'

'Oh, wait, there's another proposal in there we haven't shown you yet.' Chloe reached for the folder but Liam pulled it gently out of her reach. 'It's okay, I can take a look at it for myself.' Tucking the folder under his arm, he reached for Chloe's hand. 'I want you to know how much I appreciate all the hard work you've done.' He made a point of looking at Anya and including her. 'And I promise I am going to give this some really serious thought, but please don't get your hopes up, okay?'

Chloe opened her mouth as though she wanted to say something, but eventually she just nodded and said, 'Okay.'

He squeezed her fingers, hating to see her enthusiasm wane, especially when he knew he was the cause. It wasn't just his own future he needed to consider. 'Come on, let's get back to the party before your mum sends out a search party.'

'Good idea,' Anya replied, moving towards the door. She turned to her friend. 'You coming, Chloe?'

His cousin smiled, but Liam couldn't help noticing it didn't quite meet her eyes. 'I'll just tidy up and then I'll be out.'

The shed looked pretty spotless to him, but Liam let it go with a nod. He wanted to offer Chloe assurance, but now wasn't the time. He couldn't afford to let his heart rule his head when it came to the hotel, and he really couldn't afford to get anyone's hopes up until he had a clearer picture.

Including his own.

9

Issy was in the middle of switching out her chilled display cabinet from breakfast staples to the cakes and treats more popular with the morning coffee crowd when the bell over the door rang and she looked up to find Liam standing there. He seemed a little hesitant which was understandable given her awful behaviour to him the previous week. She'd promised herself she'd make the best of things, so now was as good a time as any to start. 'You are allowed in, you know,' she said with her best happy-to-help-you smile.

'I wasn't sure I'd be welcome.'

A tiny flare of irritation sparked inside. She was doing her best to be gracious; he didn't need to make things any more awkward than they had to be. 'Everyone's allowed an off day now and again, I hope.'

Liam adjusted the leather satchel hanging from one shoulder as he approached the counter. 'Of course, as long as that's all it was.'

What did he want from her, an apology? Well if that was the

case he was going to be sorely disappointed. She tried again. 'What can I get for you this morning?'

'I'd like an extra-large cappuccino, please, to take away.'

She couldn't help raising her eyebrows. 'Rough night, was it?'

Liam laughed. 'Not especially. I'm going to look around the hotel shortly, so I thought I might need the extra caffeine to fortify me. Oh, can you make whatever Anya's usual is? She's going to need some caffeine to deal with all the questions I'll no doubt bombard her with.'

That doused her improving mood as effectively as a bucket of cold water. 'You're taking it over?' She couldn't keep the shock out of her voice.

His expression shuttered. 'I'm considering it. Is that a problem?'

'Why would it be a problem?'

He held her gaze. 'You just didn't seem very happy to see me the other day.'

All her good intentions flew straight out the window. 'What did you expect? That I'd welcome you back with open arms? You've barely said a word to me in the past fifteen years, Liam.'

He tried to fold his arms across his chest, dislodging the bag from his shoulder. Clearly annoyed, he dropped it on the floor and shoved his hands in his pockets. 'And whose fault is that?'

'Not mine!' She braced her hands on the edge of the counter, it was that or risk grabbing the milk jug and clonking him in his stupidly handsome, stupidly annoying face. '"I hate it here, Issy. I can't stand not seeing you every day, Issy. Promise you won't forget about me while I'm away, Issy. You're the only girl for me, Issy."' She threw the words that she hated were still imprinted on her mind at him. 'Well, you sure got over that, didn't you?'

Liam took a step back as though she had tried to brain him with the jug.

'I realise you weren't the person I thought you were back then, but I never realised you could be so cruel.' She covered her face with her hands, furious at the tears she could feel welling up behind her eyes. Why was she putting herself through all this again? Liam didn't deserve her tears, or the hurt he was still apparently capable of inflicting upon her. 'Forget it,' she said, dropping her hands. 'You didn't have the decency to explain yourself back then, so it's pointless to expect you to do it now. I'll get you that coffee and you can be on your way.'

She turned to lift a couple of her reusable takeaway mugs down off the shelf then stopped and bent instead to rifle in the cupboard under the coffee machine where she kept a small supply of one-use cups. She didn't want to give Liam any excuse to return. She went through the process of making the drinks on autopilot.

Part of her had hoped he would have walked out while she had her back to him, but when she turned around he was watching her, his jaw clamped so tight she could see a muscle ticking in his cheek. She placed the two coffees on top of the counter. 'Eight-fifty, please.'

Liam ignored the drinks. 'What is it that you think I've done to you that's so awful? You can't speak to me without biting my head off, and now you're accusing me of being deliberately cruel.' He shook his head. 'I've wracked my brain over the years trying to figure it out, but I swear to God I cannot think of a single reason why you treated me the way you did.'

Issy swallowed around a huge lump in her throat. 'You lied to me.'

He bristled. 'I never lied. *Never*.'

'You played me for a fool then, using me as a prop to lean on during that first year you were away at school. Even worse, you strung me along when you came home for the summer, acting like everything was fine between us. You could at least have had the courage to dump me to my face instead of cutting me off without a word after you went back.'

'What the hell are you talking about? You stopped writing to me!'

She wasn't listening, too caught up in a head of steam, the words she'd held in all these years forcing their way past her lips. 'What was it? Too ashamed to admit to your new posh mates that you had a girl back at home? A girl with the same funny accent you told me they took the piss out of you for? Did you decide you could do better and get yourself an upgrade, someone you could take to the kind of fancy dinners that would help your career?' It hadn't passed her notice the way Caroline had spoken like she had a plum in her mouth – and a stick up her arse. She'd hated the way it had made her feel less, when she'd always been proud of who she was and where she came from.

Liam was staring at her, his mouth no longer clamped shut but hanging open in a proper 'O' of surprise. 'Is that what this is about? You thought I'd be ashamed of you because I ended up at a private school through no choice of my own? I admit I softened my accent, but only because I was trying to fit in there. I've never been embarrassed of you. I could never be embarrassed of you. You meant everything to me!'

She clenched her fists as frustration surged through her. 'So why did you stop writing to me?' she shouted.

'I didn't!' he shouted back. 'Jesus fucking Christ, how many times do I have to say it? I wrote to you every day. Even after you stopped replying, I carried on writing for months.'

His words finally registered, but they didn't make any sense. She shook her head. 'No, that's not right. You were the one who stopped replying. I was going to speak to you about it when you came home for half-term, but then you stayed at school and I assumed it was because you didn't want to see me.'

'I was falling behind in a couple of subjects, so my house-master suggested I use that week to try and get back on track.' Liam's tone had softened. 'Truth be told, I was glad of an excuse not to come back because I couldn't face talking to you after you broke things off without a word.'

'Only I didn't.' Still struggling to comprehend what was happening, Issy wandered half in a daze from behind the counter and sank into one of the empty chairs. 'What the hell is going on?' she murmured half to herself.

Liam pulled out the chair opposite hers and rested his folded arms on the table. His expression was urgent. 'You're being serious about this, yeah? This isn't some kind of sick joke?'

Issy sighed. How little he understood about her if he believed she was capable of such a thing. 'I wouldn't do that.'

'Tell me again what you think happened.'

'What difference does it make? It was fifteen years ago, Liam.'

'Tell me anyway.'

She looked away as she tried to get everything straight in her mind. Not because she thought there was any chance she'd made a mistake, but it had been a long time ago and she'd done her best not to think about it over the intervening years. 'You came home for the summer after your first full year at school. You were your-self, and yet also somehow not.' She turned back to look at him. 'Your accent had already started to change a bit.'

'It was the best way to try and blend in.' Liam slumped back in his chair. 'I never meant to give anyone the impression I was ashamed of where I was from.' He held her gaze. 'Nor to make anyone else feel ashamed either.'

She nodded. 'Okay. Anyway, we had a good summer overall, though it got harder as September came closer. You got really quiet, and kind of went into yourself. I thought it was because you were trying to come to terms with going back to school. It never occurred to me at the time that perhaps you were trying to find a way to break up with me.'

He shot forward in his seat again, his too-long hair tumbling over his forehead. He brushed it back with an impatient hand. 'I wasn't trying to break up with you. It never entered my head for a moment. You were everything that was sweet and good in the world, Issy. You were the lifeline I clung to in order to get through the lonely days.'

That lump was back in her throat, but she swallowed it away. 'The last letter I received was about three weeks after you went back to start Year Ten. They came every day, or pretty much every day, and then nothing.'

'It was the same for me.'

She knew he was telling the truth and yet she couldn't make herself accept it. 'I don't understand.'

He shook his head. 'I don't either.'

His phone rang, startling them both. Liam pulled it out of his pocket with a soft curse, then gave a small resigned sigh as he answered it. 'Hi, Anya. No, sorry, I lost track of the time.' At his words, Issy glanced over her shoulder towards the clock and saw it was nearly ten past ten. 'No, no. I still want to do it. Give me a couple of minutes. Yeah, yeah, see you.' He set the phone back down. 'Sorry about that.'

Issy stood and moved to the counter to retrieve the two coffees while Liam stood and retrieved his bag. She handed him the drinks, relieved he was going because she was still struggling to get her head around everything. 'On the house.'

He took them. 'I can call Anya back and push things back until tomorrow so we can talk about this properly.'

The bell over the door rang announcing another customer.

Issy shook her head. 'It's fine. We're both busy. Besides, I'm not sure what else there is to say.'

His eyes widened. 'What are you talking about? If neither of us stopped writing, then that means someone else interfered and we need to figure out who it was.'

She had to admit the same thing had occurred to her. The list of candidates couldn't be very long, and she didn't like any of the names that had popped into her head. She couldn't imagine her parents doing such a thing, but who else would've had access to her post? If it had been them, she wasn't sure she wanted to find out, not now they weren't around to explain. 'It was a long time ago, Liam; maybe we should just let it go.'

He shook his head. 'No, we need to talk about it,' he insisted, keeping his voice low so they wouldn't be overheard. 'We need to find out who would do such a thing.'

He obviously hadn't jumped to the same immediate conclusion she had. If it wasn't her parents, then it had to have been his, somehow. 'Have a long hard think about who it could've been, and then ask yourself if that's a can of worms you really want to open. Let the past be, Liam.' She stepped past him, the best approximation of a smile she could muster on her face as she addressed the couple who'd just walked in. 'Good morning! Is this your first time at The Cosy Coffee Pot?'

The woman smiled and nodded. 'We're staying over in Port Petroc for a few days and decided to venture a bit further afield.' She looked around. 'It's lovely, really charming and so much nicer to find a family-run business. We try to choose local whenever we can, but it's so hard sometimes when it's all chain coffee shops and Wetherspoons pubs everywhere.'

The bell over the door sounded again and it was all Issy could do to focus on the woman and her husband and not run after Liam and call him back. She smiled at the customer again. 'Well

I'm very glad you chose to pay us a visit. Take a seat anywhere and I'll grab you a menu.'

The revelation might have changed what she thought she knew about what had happened between her and Liam all those years ago, but nothing had really changed. The questions that had haunted her had been replaced with different ones she wasn't sure she wanted to know the answers to.

She couldn't think about that now. Didn't want to think about it.

10

Liam couldn't remember getting from the café to the hotel, his head was too full of questions following his argument with Issy. The idea that someone had somehow intercepted the letters they'd been sending to each other was almost impossible to accept. He simply couldn't imagine who it might have been or why they would do such a horrible thing. It would have to wait until later, though, because he was already late and couldn't keep Anya waiting any longer.

With his hands occupied by the coffee cups, he set his shoulder against the revolving door and gave it a push. The first thing that struck him was how dark and dingy it was inside; the large overhang above the door blocked out a lot of light. The enormous reception desk was as he remembered it, though the worn areas along the edge where the wood stain had been rubbed away by countless hands and bodies brushing up against the front of it were not part of those memories. Chloe hadn't been kidding about how tired the place was looking. Shifting his attention away from the desk to the slight woman perched behind it, Liam smiled. 'Morning, Anya. Sorry again for being late.' He placed her coffee on the counter. 'As promised.'

She accepted the cup and immediately popped the lid off and took a sniff. Her smile widened as she looked back up at him. 'Hazelnut latte, thank you!'

He shrugged, not willing to take the credit. 'I just asked Issy to make whatever your favourite was.'

'I should've guessed.' Anya popped the lid back on and took a sip through the opening. 'Oh, that's good. Right, do you want the grand tour, or do you want to take a look at the books first?'

Liam glanced down at the worn edge of the desk. If this was the first impression guests were getting, how bad was the rest of it? 'I'd better look around so it's clear what I'm up against.'

He put his bag in the office behind the reception desk while Anya put up a 'back in five minutes' sign on the desk with a mobile number and locked up the cabinets and drawers. 'No one can get past this without knowing the code,' she assured him as she led him through a door to the right and closed it firmly behind them. 'And we change it manually every week, and the one on the back door from the car park.'

Liam looked at the old-fashioned number lock. 'That must be a pain.'

Anya shrugged. 'It's part of the routine, so I'm used to it, but one of the optional extras we put in the basic proposal was to upgrade everything to a key card system which we could programme from the front desk computer.' She met his eyes with a sheepish grin. 'The second optional extra is to upgrade that too.'

Liam didn't know whether to be pleased that she'd already thought of everything or start panicking about how much there was to be done. 'This is going to cost me, isn't it?'

She shrugged. 'It depends how deep your pockets are. I meant what I said on Friday night. We can make a lot of improvements on a pretty limited budget.'

'But you'd like to do more than that?' Truth be told, he'd like to do more than that too. A lick of paint would tide things over but it would only be a short-term fix. If he was going to commit to taking on the hotel, giving it a full overhaul now would give him the best chance of success.

'It would be nice to do more, but not if it's going to put you in financial difficulty.'

'I appreciate that, but let me worry about the money, okay?' He gestured down the corridor. 'Lead on and don't hold back. I want this to be the full warts-and-all experience.'

By the time they'd circled back to the reception area about an hour later, Liam was regretting his request and silently cursing his great-uncle. Even if he decided to sell the place and walk away, they'd lose thousands on the potential asking price. Whatever he decided, doing nothing was no longer an option. It made him wonder why Davy hadn't spent what was necessary for at least a decent paint job. Was he in dire straits and the hotel nothing more than a money pit? If that was the case, Liam would need to steel himself against any tug of family loyalty when he made his final decision.

'I know it looks a bit rundown,' Anya said for what must have been the tenth time as she returned to her seat behind the desk. 'But it won't take a lot to make this old girl shine again.' Reaching for the jar of lollies that sat on the top of the reception desk, she offered it to him. 'A bit of sugar will help to sweeten everything up.'

'I wish I had your enthusiasm,' Liam muttered, as he put his hand in the jar and pulled out a lolly. The colourful rainbow stripes should've been a warning but he unwrapped it and popped it in his mouth. 'God, that's sweet.' He didn't take it out though, but rather gave it another experimental suck. 'Not bad, actually.'

'It's hard to be grumpy with a mouthful of sugar,' Anya said with a grin as she unwrapped her own lolly.

'That's true.' Liam gave himself a mental shake as he let the treat melt against his tongue. None of the neglect he'd seen was Anya's fault. He'd asked her to show him everything, so it was unfair of him to take out his low mood on her. She'd only been working at the hotel a couple of months and the level of decline he'd witnessed had to have been years in the making. Davy hadn't been coping for a long time, that much was clear, and as he began to recover from his initial shock Liam wondered why it had taken the old boy this long to admit it. Well, whatever his reasons, the future of the hotel was in Liam's hands now, so he'd better make sure he had the full picture. He gave Anya what he hoped was an encouraging smile. 'Right, let's take a look at those books, then.' He nodded towards the screen on Anya's desk.

Standing, Anya held out a key to him. 'Let yourself into the office and I'll go and make some more coffee.'

'Sugar *and* more caffeine? Just how bad are things around here?'

Anya laughed. 'Honestly, I think you'll be surprised how many guests we get, all things considered.'

When she returned a few minutes later carrying two mugs, Liam's attempt at a good mood was starting to wear off. 'Where the hell is the computer? I've got my laptop with me, but I need to be able to transfer the files across to it.'

'Computer?' Anya frowned as she offered him one of the mugs. 'Oh, Davy doesn't have a computer. The booking records and suchlike are on the one in reception, but he does pretty much everything by hand.'

'You can't be serious?' Liam watched in disbelief as she

rounded the desk and pulled open one of the bottom drawers to reveal a neat stack of red-leather-bound ledgers. 'Oh, please tell me you are pulling my fucking leg!'

Still balancing her mug in one hand, Anya started taking the ledgers out one by one and stacked them in the middle of the desk. 'I only wish I was, but it's not only the décor that's stuck in the past, I'm afraid.'

'Jesus Christ.' Liam rubbed at the stress headache that had bloomed into full life. 'How the hell does he file his accounts?'

'There's some software on the computer, but I don't know the ins and outs of it as Steve does most of the data entry overnight.' Anya flushed, looking faintly embarrassed.

'Steve?'

'He's the night manager. Numbers aren't my forte I'm afraid, and Steve was happy to carry on doing it as there's not all that much else to keep him busy. He did tell me that Davy records everything in here first, though, so hopefully you'll get some idea...' She trailed off. 'I should've thought about it earlier, I'm sorry. I can speak to him when he comes in tonight, ask him to make a copy for you, or at least give me the login details so you can pop back tomorrow and have a look for yourself.' She glanced at the clock. 'I could try and give him a call now, if you like, but he might still be asleep.'

Liam swallowed a sigh. 'No, no, don't disturb him. It's not your fault.' He placed his hand on the stack of ledgers and gave her a smile he hoped was a lot more reassuring than he was feeling. 'This will give me a good starting point and I can always return this evening if I need to.' He looked around the room again. Apart from the desk and the chair, the only other furnishings were a lumpy couch that had seen better days and a wall of grey filing cabinets. 'Invoices?' he asked, nodding towards them.

Anya nodded. 'They're filed in alphabetical order. The keys to the cabinets are on the ring.' She took a step backwards. 'I'd better get back to the desk. I'm expecting a couple of guests and I need to make sure everything's ready for them.'

'Go on, I'll be fine.' Liam waited until she'd closed the door before he allowed himself to sink into the chair with a soft groan. So much for being worried about getting his hopes up about taking over. If he had any sense at all he'd walk out the door and keep on going until he was safely back in London. Suddenly that corner desk with its top-of-the-range computer system all linked up to a company mainframe was looking pretty attractive.

11

When Chloe called Issy later that afternoon and invited her for pizza and Prosecco at Anya's, she hadn't known how to refuse. Though part of her wanted to shut up for the evening and hide away in her flat, there was a real prospect that Liam might show up and try and continue their conversation, and she wasn't ready for that. She wasn't sure she was ready to talk to her friends about what she'd found out either, but they would be there if she changed her mind. Besides, she wanted to know how things had gone at the hotel and she wasn't about to call Liam and ask him.

'So how did it go earlier?' Issy asked as she and Chloe settled on the small sofa in Anya's open-plan main room. The summer house had originally been Chloe's home, but she'd agreed to move back into her old room in the main house to give Anya and Freya the privacy they needed when they'd moved to the Quay just before the summer.

'Hard to tell,' Anya said from the tiny kitchen island where she was pouring Prosecco into four plastic glasses. 'He seemed quite positive about the changes I suggested, but you should've seen the look on his face when I showed him Davy's idea of record keeping.' She picked up two of the glasses and carried them over.

Issy accepted one with a smile. 'Thanks. Do you think that could be a stumbling block, then?'

'Well he wasn't exactly thrilled,' Anya replied with a laugh as she returned to fetch the remaining two glasses, one of which she handed to Kat, who had taken a seat in the armchair opposite the sofa. 'He was locked in Davy's office all afternoon, didn't even stop for a sandwich when I offered to get him one. When I left this evening, he and Steve were going over the accounting system on the reception computer.'

'At least he didn't walk straight out,' Kat pointed out. 'If it was that bad then surely he'd have done a runner?'

'Ever the optimist,' Chloe said with a grin before her amusement faded into a huge sigh. 'I don't know what to think about it all. I know Liam warned us not to get our hopes up after we showed him our proposals on Friday, but it's hard not to. There's so much we could do with the hotel given half a chance.'

'It's a hell of a big ask expecting him to take it on,' Anya cautioned as she set a tray of nibbles down on the small coffee table. She sat on the floor in front of Kat's chair, resting her back against it. 'Not to mention how much money it would take.'

'You sure you're all right down there?' Kat asked as she tugged a cushion out from behind her back and offered it to Anya.

'Fine, honestly, thanks.' Anya propped the cushion behind her and leaned back once more. 'Who knows if Liam can even afford it.'

'That's true,' Chloe said as she helped herself to a handful of crisps from the selection on the table. 'I always got the impression he was doing well for himself in London, but he'd surely have to take out some kind of loan unless he's a millionaire and it somehow slipped his mind to tell any of us.'

Issy surprised herself when she managed a laugh. 'As if anyone could keep a secret like that in your family!'

'Good point.' Chloe laughed. 'Well there's not much more to say until Liam gives us an update.' She turned to Issy. 'How was your day?'

She shook her head. 'Don't ask.' All three of her friends stared at her, and Issy wished she'd kept her mouth shut. She took a swig of her Prosecco and tried not to choke as the bubbles fizzed up her nose. After a couple of splutters, she gasped a laugh. 'I always knew I had a drink problem.' When none of them joined in, she sighed. 'I shouldn't have said anything.'

'But you did.' Chloe nudged her gently with her foot. 'Come on, you know you can talk to us about anything.'

'Yeah, I know. I had a very odd conversation with Liam this morning when he came in to pick up coffees for him and Anya and I'm not sure what to make of it.'

'I thought there was something bothering him when he arrived. I assumed he was worrying about the hotel.' Anya leaned forward. 'What happened?'

That bloody lump was suddenly back in her throat. 'You know all this time I thought Liam was too much of a coward to break up with me properly so he just stopped writing?' Her voice almost wobbled, so she paused a second to pull herself together. 'Well it turns out that he thought I'd done the same thing to him.'

'What?' Kat exclaimed.

'But how can that be?' Anya said almost on top of her.

Issy shrugged. 'I have no idea. I've been a bit pissy with him since he came back. I know I shouldn't have let it get to me, but when I realised there was a chance he might be thinking of sticking around, it all kind of got on top of me. We had a bit of a row in the café today and, well, he swears he wasn't the one that broke off contact. He says my letters stopped at the same time as I stopped getting any from him.'

'But how is that even possible?' Kat asked, her nose wrinkled in confusion. 'Did they somehow get lost in the post?'

'One or two might have gone astray,' Issy said. 'But I sent dozens before I finally gave up, and Liam said he did the same.'

'Someone must've intervened,' Chloe said, cutting straight to the point, the way she so often did.

Issy nodded. 'They must've done.'

'But who would do that to you? And why?' Always the most sensitive of the four of them, Kat's eyes were shiny with tears.

Issy leaned over and placed her hand on Kat's leg. 'Hey now, don't go getting yourself upset. It was a long time ago.' Truth be told, Issy couldn't afford for Kat to cry or she might end up joining in. Sitting back, she rubbed her hands over her suddenly tired eyes. 'The only people I can think of who were in a position to do it were my parents.'

'Surely not!' Anya protested. 'Why would they do such a thing?'

Issy slumped back against the sofa. 'I have no idea. They always seemed to adore Liam. They knew I was missing him a lot while he was away and I'd talked to them about how unhappy he was at school, but they were never anything other than support-ive. Mum even offered to talk to his folks about it, but I knew Liam didn't want them to know he was struggling, so she promised she wouldn't say anything.'

'Do you think they could've had something to do with it, then?' Kat speculated. 'Liam's parents, I mean.'

'No.' Chloe shook her head vehemently. 'They're not like that. They wouldn't sneak about behind your back, and besides, how would they be able to intercept post that was being delivered to your house?'

'That's what I keep stumbling over,' Issy admitted. 'I hate to think it of them, but who else could it have been if it wasn't Mum and Dad?'

'But how did they stop *your* letters getting to Liam at school? It doesn't make any sense unless they were in on it with Aunty Rachel and Uncle Jago.' Chloe shook her head. 'Even saying it out loud sounds mad, like some sort of conspiracy theory.'

'It really does sound weird,' Anya said. 'What does Liam think?'

'We didn't really get a chance to talk about it because he was already late coming to meet you. I told him I thought we should just let it go, and I wish I'd followed my own advice because I hate the fact I'm even considering the possibility that Mum and Dad could've had anything to do with it, especially when I can't ask them about it.' Her voice hitched on the last word and she covered her eyes with her hands once more.

'Oh, darling, don't cry.' Chloe's arms came around her and Issy rested her head against her friend's shoulder as she tried to hold back the tears. Kat and Anya were there in a second, their hands and voices gentle as they tried to soothe and reassure her.

Issy sniffled a couple of times before managing to get herself back under control. 'I'm okay,' she murmured, then repeated it in a stronger voice as she pulled her hand away from her face. 'I'm okay. It's just times like this that bring it all back.'

'It's bound to. Here, wipe your face.' Kat handed her a clean tissue. 'I'm sure they wouldn't have had anything to do with it.'

Issy managed a nod and a smile as she took the tissue and quickly tidied up her face. 'Yeah, deep down I know that must be true, but it doesn't make it any easier.'

'Poor Liam.' Anya sighed. 'He must be going through the same doubts as you are.'

Issy nodded. 'I wish I'd kept my mouth shut this morning and just taken his order.'

'But then you wouldn't know the truth!' Kat exclaimed.

'I'll admit it makes it easier knowing Liam didn't deliberately set out to hurt me, so I can finally make peace with him about that. If he is going to move back to the village, at least we won't be at loggerheads any more.'

As for who was behind it? She feared finding out the truth would only lead to further heartache for one or both of them. At least she wouldn't have to face it alone when they did find out, because she had the best friends anyone could ever ask for. They'd see her through this, just like they'd seen each other through everything else. Issy sucked in a deep breath and managed a smile. 'I didn't mean it just now when I said I wish I hadn't said anything. I'm so grateful to have you all on my side.'

'Friends forever,' Chloe said with a grin as she held her hand out to Issy.

Issy grinned at the reminder of the pledge they used to share when they were kids. She placed her hand in Chloe's and replied, 'Friends forever,' before offering her free hand to Kat. Kat took it and repeated the pledge, then shared it with Anya who shared it with Chloe until the four of them had formed a circle with their joined hands. They looked at each other and laughed before releasing their grips. 'Right, now I've trauma-dumped on you all, let's order that pizza and move onto something more cheerful.'

Forty minutes later they were making inroads into a large veggie special and a medium margherita and Issy was feeling much more relaxed. Not wanting to dig back into the situation with Liam, she cast around for a less personal topic. 'So, what's the gossip on the Nicholson shop? Anyone heard anything yet about a potential buyer?' Talking to Chloe about it the other day had brought the future of her near-neighbour's property to the forefront of her mind.

Chloe sat forward, her eyes bright. 'Oh, I'm glad you reminded me! I've done a few discreet enquiries and word is it won't just be the shop that's up for sale, it'll be their cottage too!' Her boss at the solicitors did all the local conveyancing work for the estate agent, so she'd know if anything was happening behind the scenes.

'They're leaving the village altogether?'

Chloe nodded. 'They want to move closer to their daughter and her husband. See more of the grandchildren. I can't remember what the husband does but he's away a lot, so I think Gabby struggles a bit with childcare and what-have-you.'

'It'll be an end of an era.' Issy sighed. She knew people had always come and gone from the village, but still she would be sad to see the Nicholsons leave. They'd been so supportive when Issy and her grandmother had first opened the café, and she'd miss one or other of them popping over to grab a coffee and pass the time of day.

'I could ask Rick if he's heard anything about the shop,' Anya offered before blushing a delicate shade of rosy pink. If she wasn't one of Issy's closest friends, it would be annoying how Anya managed to look pretty even when she was embarrassed.

'Planning on seeing him, are you?' Chloe teased, nudging Anya's leg with her foot in a playful gesture.

'He, uh, we were chatting at the barbeque and there's a new series of a TV show we both like starting, so he's coming over on Friday to watch the first episode with me.'

Kat rested a hand on her shoulder, causing Anya to glance back up at her. 'Hey, it's a good thing if you're spending a bit of time together, isn't it?'

Anya nodded. 'I think so. I know I'm the one that wants to take things slow, but I miss him when he's not around.'

'Watching TV together doesn't sound like anything too heavy to me,' Issy said, gently. 'And I'm sure Rick's happy to spend time with you.'

'Yeah, and it was my idea. I mean, he mentioned the show was coming back, but I was the one who suggested we watch it together. I don't want him to think I'm messing him around, that's all.'

'I don't think he'll think that for a minute. He seems to be trying really hard to give you the space you asked for.'

Anya nodded again. 'He really is. I'm the one that's having a problem staying away.' Laughing, she buried her face in her hands. 'The moment I set eyes on him all my self-resolve melts away and I want to tell him I love him, but it's far too soon for that.' She took a deep breath and added, 'I've been on the Cruse Bereavement Support website and downloaded a few of their booklets.' She glanced down at her hands clutched around her wine glass. 'I haven't let myself grieve for Drew, not properly. I got as far as anger and just got kind of stuck there. I need to deal with it, or I'm never going to be able to move forward and have the life I want with Rick.'

'I think it's a really good idea,' Issy reassured her. 'And if you ever want to talk, we're here for you.'

'Absolutely!' Chloe agreed. She set down her plate and slid off the sofa to hug her cousin. 'I am so proud of you for being so brave.'

'Me too,' Kat added. 'I also think a snuggle on the sofa with Rick won't do any harm either. I know I wouldn't mind one, that's for sure.' Her cheeks flamed and she stuttered, 'N-not with Rick, of course!' Her inadvertent faux pas was perfectly timed to ease the mood once more.

'You can snuggle with me anytime,' Chloe offered, releasing her hold on Anya and opening her arms wide towards Kat.

'That's very kind of you,' Kat replied with a giggle. 'But not quite what I had in mind.'

'I hear you,' Chloe said with a sigh. 'But let's not talk about the sorry state of our love lives or we'll all end up sobbing into our wine.'

Issy turned to Kat. 'What about your dad? Has he heard anything about the Nicholson place through his connections?' Gavin was a member of the local business forum, so if there was any gossip in that group, he'd be in the loop. Issy had been a member for a while but had ended up leaving, mostly because it was full of men like Gavin who enjoyed the sound of their own voice a bit too much.

Kat started so hard she spilled wine all down her front. Anya jumped up and fetched a cloth, ignoring Kat when she protested that she was fine. Issy watched her closely, noting the dark circles under Kat's eyes, the lank dullness of her hair. She looked like she hadn't had a decent night's sleep in days. 'Is everything okay?' she asked when Anya had finished fussing and refilled Kat's glass and they were all settled down once more. 'You look tired.'

Kat pressed a hand to her forehead. 'I'm okay, just had a couple of nights of broken sleep. I think it's the weather. I changed my quilt over after we had those few cool days and now it's too hot to sleep.'

Issy paused. All of those things were true and she'd been opening and closing her own bedroom window the past couple of nights as she was either too hot or too cold. But she hadn't missed the way Kat had jumped at the mention of her dad. 'We haven't seen you for a while at the Hub; things still busy at Java Brava?'

Kat swallowed. 'There's a lot of pressure when you run a franchise. It's not just working for yourself. They seem to want more and more reports, so Dad's busy in the office and needs me out the front. I'm sorry I haven't been able to cover my shifts at the lending library.' It sounded like she was reading from a script, or more likely repeating one of Gavin's many diatribes. Issy didn't think she knew anyone who was as disgruntled with his lot in life as Kat's father.

The family had relocated to Halfmoon Quay when Kat had been around ten. Issy could still remember the day her friend had first walked into the playground, gripping tightly to her mum's hand. She'd been a tiny waif of a thing and Issy's heart had immediately gone out to her. Their teacher had asked Issy and Chloe to make her feel welcome and they'd been firm friends ever since.

Issy waved off the apology. 'Hey, don't worry about that. I love it when you have time to volunteer at the Hub because it means we get to spend time together, but I know how much your dad relies on you.' Gavin's general bad mood extended to his employees, and even with job opportunities being in short supply, he struggled to hold on to staff for long. One of his baristas had quit at the start of the summer and Kat had been pulling extra shifts ever since.

Kat bit her lip but didn't say anything. Issy looked at Chloe, who widened her eyes, and then Anya, who gave a micro shrug. Well, if they weren't going to say something... 'Maybe you should try and find another job, Kat. Something that gets you out from under his thumb.'

'Oh, yeah, sure. Where am I going to magic that up from?' Her friend's laugh was bitter and ugly and full of years of pain from living with her father's oppressive attitude.

Anya rose up on her knees and put her arms around Kat. 'It's awful that you are stuck like this. I wish there was something I could do to help.'

Kat hugged her back, hiding her face for a moment in Anya's

shoulder, so her next words were muffled. 'There's nothing anyone can do, you know what he's like at the best of times, but the pressure from above is making everything worse.'

Hating to hear Kat sound so desperate, Issy knew something had to change. She couldn't give Kat a job, though God knows she wished she were in a position to do so, but she could at least try and help Kat win a bit more autonomy. Leaning forward, she touched Kat's knee to get her attention. 'Hey, why don't you move into my spare room for a bit? Living at home and working with your mum and dad all day is clearly too much.'

Kat shook her head at once. 'I couldn't do that, you don't have enough room.'

'Nan and I managed quite well for years in the flat, so I'm sure we'd rub along with each other just fine. And it doesn't have to be forever. Stay for a couple of weeks and then see how you feel.'

Tears welled in Kat's eyes. 'Are you sure?'

'Absolutely! It'll be fun to have some company in the evenings. We can pamper ourselves and binge watch the new series of *Reacher*.'

'Oh my God, I want to come round for pamper and *Reacher* night!' Chloe exclaimed. 'Promise you won't do it without me.'

Kat wrinkled her nose in confusion. 'I didn't think action-adventure stuff was your bag.'

'Oh, please, have you seen the lead actor?' Chloe scoffed as she rolled her eyes. 'No one is watching that show for the *plot*.'

'I promise you are invited,' Issy assured her friend with a grin, then turned her attention back to Kat. 'So, what do you say?'

Kat took a deep breath then nodded. 'Your spare room sounds perfect, thank you.'

12

It was just before six-thirty the next morning and Liam was filling his water bottle at the sink in preparation for his daily run. He'd been making good on his pledge to himself to sort out his fitness and was pleased at how quickly he'd got back into a routine. Apart from one morning last week when he'd woken up to torrential rain and had to delay his run, he'd been out of the door within fifteen minutes of waking up.

The first couple of mornings when his alarm had gone off had been a struggle, but he'd stuck to his plan and forced himself to get up. It had only taken a week but today his eyes had been open before his phone even had a chance to beep and he'd rolled right out of bed. True, he hadn't had a great night's sleep, what with his brain insisting on chewing over both his conversation with Issy and the state of the hotel, but he hadn't wanted to slide back into that funk he'd come home in. He was a man on a mission. Well two missions really. He was going to get his head around the hotel's finances by the end of this week, and he was going to try and find out who had stopped Issy's letters getting to him.

A sound behind him startled him and he turned to see his dad walking into the kitchen also dressed in running kit. 'Morning, Dad. I hope I didn't wake you?'

Jago shook his head. 'No, I'm awake by six most mornings, but listening to you creep down the stairs every day made me feel guilty about lazing about, so I decided I would join you – that's if you don't mind?'

'I don't mind at all.' While his father filled his own bottle, Liam opened the back door and stepped outside. Setting his water bottle on the windowsill, he braced his hands against the wall and began his stretch routine.

'How far have you been going?' Jago asked as he joined him.

'I start with a brisk walk to the quay to warm up, then down to the beach where I follow the water's edge to the base of the sand dunes. From there I take the Port Petroc road as far as the top of the hill. Sit there on the bench for a bit as I try not to expire from the effort and then a leisurely jog back.'

'I might have to power walk up the hill rather than run it, but other than that, I'm game.'

'I'm not sure you could actually call what I do at that point running,' Liam confessed with a grin as he began to stride down the path, swinging his arms at his sides to get the blood flowing a bit quicker. 'Sometimes I think I'm going backwards.'

They both laughed, their voices muted so as not to disturb the neighbours. As they wound along the residential streets that would take them to the front, they gradually built up speed, and by the time they emerged onto the main road they were jogging side by side. The crescent-shaped harbour that gave the village its name opened out before them and they both paused at the edge of the sea wall to stare out over the moored boats as they gently bobbed on the rising tide. Gold sparkled all across the expanse of blue water beyond the harbour where the early morning rays of the sun caught the tops of the waves. Liam closed his eyes and tipped his head back as he sucked in a great lungful of clean air, the tang of salt on his tongue a familiar comfort. 'This is what I miss the most when I'm in London,' he said. 'The taste of the sea on the air. Half the time it feels like I can't take a proper breath, especially during the summer when the heat feels so oppressive.'

'I can't imagine not being by the water,' his father admitted. 'It's like the sea is in my very bones and any day I'm not in sight of it feels wrong. I'll admit your mum and I were worried about you moving, but we know how important your work is to you, so it made sense for you to be where you could make the most of your opportunities.' Jago sighed. 'I love having your brothers so close, but I worry about them missing out too. I thought Harry might follow you up to London once he finished his training under Russ at the restaurant, but he seems to have tamed that wild side of his.'

'It's good to see him doing so well.'

Jago nodded. 'I'm glad that someone was able to help him find his way.' The regret that it hadn't been him was clearly etched across his face.

Harry had always been the most restless of the four of them. A miniature dynamo from the moment he'd taken his first steps, which more often than not had led him into trouble thanks to an ever-curious mind and no sense of danger whatsoever. Ed had been his little shadow, always one step behind but never hesitating. Where Harry went, Ed went, it was as simple as that.

Liam had lost count of the number of times either he or Rick had rescued the intrepid twins from near disaster, and all that pair of little numbskulls had ever done was giggle. They'd been so bloody adorable it was hard to stay mad at them for more than about five seconds, though, which is probably why they'd kept getting away with stuff that would've seen Liam's backside parked on the naughty step at the same age.

Things had begun to change at secondary school. Harry had begun to struggle while Ed had made great strides. They'd done their best to hide it, and Liam could still remember how angry their father had been when he found out Ed had been doing Harry's homework for him. It was one of only a handful of times Liam could remember him truly raising his voice. When the school had found out, the twins had been put into separate classes.

Without Ed to help him out, Harry had started getting into trouble. Getting kicked out of class had been easier on his pride than admitting he hadn't been able to cope. And it wasn't only at school. He'd pushed the boundaries at home too. Staying out past curfew, refusing to do his chores, generally sulking around the place when he'd always been such a sunny little soul. And all the time Ed had stuck by him.

Things had come to a head a week before the twins turned fourteen. They'd gone exploring the rocks and caves beneath the castle promontory and Ed had broken his leg in a terrible fall. With the blame falling squarely on Harry's shoulders the decision had been made to separate the twins, and he'd been sent to stay with their grandparents while Ed recovered in hospital. He'd never come home. Liam didn't know how Harry had crossed paths with Russ Armstrong, but the chef had taken Harry under his wing and set him back on the straight and narrow.

Liam placed a hand on his father's arm. 'You mustn't blame yourself, Dad. No one could get through to Harry back then, and you had enough on your plate with Ed's rehab.'

'Wait until you have kids, son, and then you'll understand.' Jago gave himself a little shake. 'Come on, let's get moving shall we?'

Liam didn't think there was a distance far enough they could run that would help his dad escape the demons of past decisions, but he simply nodded then led the way down the steps onto the beach. Once they reached the solid wet sand just below the high tide line, they broke into a slow trot. The chat about Harry felt like an opening, so Liam took a deep breath and admitted, 'It's not all it's cracked up to be, you know, living in London.'

'You're not happy there.' It wasn't a question.

'No, not any more. Not ever, really, if I'm being totally honest about it.'

Their eyes met briefly and once again Jago's expression was one of deep regret. 'We thought we were doing the right thing by you, sending you off to school and that. When Mr Evans told us he thought he could sort out a scholarship for you, well it was like all our prayers had been answered because it was an opportunity we could never have afforded for you ourselves.'

'I know, Dad, and I'm grateful for everything that my education has brought me.'

They ran in silence for a few moments before Jago huffed out a slightly breathless laugh. 'That might be the biggest unspoken "but" in history, lad. You know you can tell me anything.'

Liam swallowed. It was true that he'd always been able to confide in his dad when he was younger, but going away to school had strained that relationship. Liam knew how important it was for his parents to think he was doing well and he hadn't wanted to let them down, so he'd begun keeping his feelings to himself. Over time that guardedness around them had become second nature, but perhaps it was time to change that. 'I hated school every single day. Not the lessons, but being stuck in that alien environment with a bunch of strangers who mocked me for being a yokel because of the way I talked. I stopped putting my hand up in class, even when no one else knew the answer, because I'd hear them whispering behind me.'

Jago halted so abruptly Liam was a few paces ahead of him

before he realised. When he turned back, his father's face was ashen. 'Christ, that's awful. Why didn't you say anything?'

Liam shrugged. 'I didn't want you to worry. Come on, let's keep moving.' Without waiting for a reply he started running again, mostly because he couldn't bear to see that look on his father's face. There was a reason he'd kept things to himself all these years.

Jago soon caught up with him. 'I want you to tell me everything,' he demanded, eyes fixed on the road ahead. 'Every single thing.'

Well, the genie was out of the bottle now and it seemed like his dad wasn't going to let him stuff it back inside, so he did as he was told. Step by step along the path he laid out all the secrets he'd withheld. The loneliness, the worry about not being able to get the grades they expected of him, the teasing that had occasionally veered into bullying, the loss of connection to everyone at home. The guilty relief that September after Ed's awful accident when he'd been glad to escape. The mixed feelings he'd had when he'd aced all his exams and he knew university couldn't be avoided. Meeting Caro, falling in love with her, the slow sad realisation as those feelings faltered when they should've strengthened. His boredom at work. Jago never uttered a sound, only the slap-slap of his trainers on the path any indication that Liam wasn't talking to himself. The only thing he didn't bring up was breaking up with Issy because he was still trying to get his head around what they'd worked out the day before.

By the time they reached the base of the hill leading towards Port Petroc, Liam was glad of the breath-stealing steepness and he grimly focused on putting one foot in front of the other. When they finally crested the top of the rise and the vista opened out before them, Liam felt as empty and cold as the sea below them. He collapsed on a nearby bench, head hanging between his parted knees as he laboured to suck in enough oxygen. A few minutes later, Jago slumped down beside him and the air was loud with the rasping efforts of them both.

Eventually, he recovered enough to sip at his water bottle until the parched feeling in his throat dissipated, but still he didn't speak. He wasn't sure what there was left to say, other than he was sorry for dumping everything out like that.

The silence stretched between them until Jago heaved a sigh. 'Well, shit.'

A shocked burst of laughter escaped as Liam turned on the bench and met his father's eyes. 'Pretty much.'

Jago gave a rueful chuckle. 'I guess that parent of the year award is cancelled again.'

Liam leaned closer until they were resting shoulder-to-shoulder. 'I'm sorry, Dad, I should've told you earlier how I was feeling.'

His father turned and pressed a quick kiss to his temple. 'And I should've paid closer attention to you. The problem is that both you and Rick were such good lads it was easy to fool myself into believing you didn't need me as much as the twins did.'

'Rick took on a lot more than I did. I wasn't kidding when I said I was grateful to be back at school in the end. And I could've tried harder over the years to reconnect with everyone.'

'Your mum will be devastated when I tell her.'

Liam nodded. It was on the tip of his tongue to say they didn't have to say anything to her, but there'd already been too many things left unspoken. Wasn't that how he and Issy had gone all these years suspecting the worst about each other? If they'd been a little older they might have found a way to communicate rather than retreating into hurt silence. If he'd come home that half-term instead of staying at school and leaving that silence to grow until it felt insurmountable. If his worry about disappointing everyone hadn't led him to keeping things to himself.

If. If. If.

Issy was right about one thing: it had been a long time ago. But unlike her he didn't think they should let it go. She was right that there could only be a limited number of people who'd had anything to do with it...

Liam stared at his father. He couldn't have been responsible for it, surely? It felt like too much of a betrayal of trust. Still, the need to know itched at his brain until he had to say something. 'I spoke to Issy yesterday.'

Jago's expression brightened into an affectionate smile. 'How is she? I keep meaning to pop into the café and check up on her, but it's been manic at work with all the summer visitors around so I haven't had chance.'

'You check up on her?'

His father nodded. 'Of course. Me and your mum both. She always felt like one of the family when you were kids, and after she lost her parents like that, well it broke our hearts.' He looked away and then back at Liam. 'I'm not sure if it's my place to say anything, but as we're being honest with each other, we were always sorry that things didn't work out between the two of you.'

He sounded so genuine, Liam immediately knew there was no way Jago had had anything to do with it. 'Breaking up with her wasn't my choice.' A bitter laugh escaped him as the crazy truth hit him once more. 'And I found out yesterday that it hadn't been her choice either.' All those years when they'd hated and hurt... and for nothing.

'What do you mean?'

'Someone interfered somehow and blocked the letters we were sending each other.' Liam was shaking his head even as he said it. It still sounded almost unbelievable.

Jago frowned. 'But who would do such a thing?' His eyes

widened. 'God, you don't think your mother and I had anything to do with it?'

A guilty flush heated Liam's cheeks at the fact he'd even entertained such a thought. 'Perhaps for a moment or two, but only because I couldn't figure who would have the means to do it.'

'Well, I swear it was nothing to do with us. We loved Issy. We still love her and it was clear as day the two of you were meant for each other.'

'Once upon a time, perhaps, but too much has happened since then.' Liam had only recently broken up with Caro, and even if he was ready to entertain the idea of dating again, he had no idea if Issy was even single. There was no reason to suspect she would be. A smart, beautiful woman like her would have them queuing around the block for a chance, even in a small place like Halfmoon Quay. His stomach twisted.

Jago regarded him thoughtfully for a moment. 'I'm sure the last thing you want from your old dad is dating advice, but the pair of you are still young enough to make a go of things.'

Liam shook his head. It was too much to think about right now, even if the idea of Issy with someone else had stirred a possessiveness inside him he'd assumed was long dead. 'You're right, I don't want advice about dating.' He softened the rejection with a laugh. 'Although I am going to need plenty of it when it comes to deciding what to do about the hotel.'

Jago settled back against the bench. 'What does your gut tell you?'

'That I don't know the first thing about running a hotel. That I'm not sure that I can afford it, not without bankrupting myself in the process. That I should stick to what I do know, what I'm comfortable with, what I'm good at...' He laughed again as he leaned back so his shoulder was touching his father's. 'That I should ignore all of that and seize the chance to come home where I belong.'

'Sounds like you've made up your mind and what we need to do now is figure out a way to make that happen.'

Liam grinned. 'You don't have a spare hundred grand tucked under the mattress, I suppose?'

Jago shook his head. 'If I did, it'd be yours, son.' He hesitated for a moment. 'I could speak to your mum about remortgaging the house...'

'No way!' Liam shifted to face his dad properly. 'God, Dad, it was a joke!' Though perhaps an ill-judged one. 'If I'm not prepared to risk my own financial stability for this, then I'll be damned if I'm going to let you do it!'

Jago nodded, and Liam could tell he was a little relieved. It touched him deep inside that his father would even consider putting everything on the line for the chance to make him happy. It was also entirely unsurprising. 'Okay. Well, I'm not sure I know anything about running a hotel either, but Davy sure does, so make sure you pick his brain.'

Liam nodded. 'He's next on my list to talk to. He probably should've been my first port of call but I didn't want to get his hopes up until I'd had a chance to think things through a bit.' He sighed. 'I might still be getting his hopes up if I can't figure out a way to make it feasible.'

Jago patted his leg. 'It's not just him, either. Rick should be able to help you with planning and regulations.'

'He's already offered that.'

His father grinned. 'There you are, then. And you've got Chloe and Anya's design plans, plus Chloe's got connections through her job at the solicitors for legal advice.' Jago started counting things off on his fingers. 'Ryan and Matt should be able to help you with the building work, and if it's too big a job for them they're bound to know someone else you can talk to.'

Liam found the laugh that escaped his throat was more than a little wobbly. 'Team Penrose to the rescue.'

'Damn bloody straight.' Jago rose and held out a hand to pull Liam to his feet. 'And with you at the head of it, that team is in great shape because you've got brains enough for all of us combined.'

'You sound very sure I'll figure it out.' Liam wished he had that much confidence in himself.

'I've never been more sure of anything, because I have faith in you, son.' Jago clapped a hand on Liam's shoulder. 'As it sounds like you're sticking around, how would you feel about entering the Round the Rock race with me?'

Round the Rock was the final event in the village's sailing calendar and usually happened in the middle weekend of October. It was for experienced sailors only as the weather could be unpredictable, and most competitors were local, although a few boats came from other towns and villages up and down the coast. Liam and his father had entered a couple of times when he was younger and though they'd never come close to winning, they'd had a great time trying.

'Seriously? I haven't crewed a boat for years.'

'But you practically grew up on the deck of one.' Jago shrugged. 'I just thought it would be fun to get the old team back together.'

Casual as his tone was, it was clear to Liam how much it would mean to his father. And as he'd said, Liam had all but grown up in a boat; how hard could it be? He glanced out at the open water, all but able to feel the sting of salty air on his cheeks as they skimmed over the waves. 'Let's do it.'

13

How was it still only Tuesday? Issy had woken that morning with a thick head and a mouth that tasted like she'd been licking a dirty carpet. Having messaged the group WhatsApp to blame the others for letting her drink a third glass of Prosecco, she'd dragged herself into the bathroom. A hot shower, a couple of paracetamols and an endless supply of coffee had kept her on her feet so far. She might have been in a better mood, but the morning's sunshine had been washed away by a storm that had rolled in just before lunchtime and was still lashing against the windows.

It was the first day of school and the café had been quiet since breakfast. A few regulars had braved the weather to grab some lunch but the endless rain had kept the afternoon walkers away. In order to keep busy, Issy had already taken apart the coffee machine and cleaned every nozzle and filter, and the tables were still damp from a recent wipe over. She plied a mop over the tiled floor, more for something to do. It was that or put her head down on one of the tables and treat herself to a little nap.

The bright jangle of the bell above the door was a welcome

relief from the boredom and Issy spun to greet her customer with a cheery smile that faltered as she took in Liam's broad-shouldered frame filling the doorway. His dark hair was slick against his head from the rain, apart from a few curls that had sprung up around his nape. He really needed a haircut. She'd been half expecting him all day, but now he was here she wasn't sure what she was supposed to say to him. She decided to keep it simple. 'Hi.'

'No wonder this place is empty if that's how you greet people!' He said it with a laugh in his voice, but she didn't miss the flash of hurt in his eyes. 'I thought after we'd talked yesterday we might be on better terms.'

Oh God. She gripped the handle of the mop tight between her hands as the implications of everything began to wash through her. Liam was still standing in the doorway, not moving. Waiting for her to say something. She gave herself a mental shake. 'Sorry! I just wasn't expecting you. Anya said you still had your head buried in the hotel accounts when she left last night, so I assumed it'd take you a few days to go through everything. Have you sorted it all out already?'

'I wish!' Liam unzipped his waterproof jacket to reveal a leather shoulder bag, which he patted briefly. 'It's impossible to work in Davy's office with him looking over my shoulder. Your grandmother's efforts to get him to take things easy aren't going too well, and he's in and out every five minutes. I'm already starting to worry about whether he'll actually be able to hand over the reins when the time comes. I hoped a change of scenery would give me chance to concentrate.' He pointed at the mop in her hands. 'But I can work at home if I'm going to be in the way.'

'Oh no, please stay, I'm going stir crazy here on my own.' She shoved the mop into the holder in the bucket and hurried over to him. 'Here, let me help you with that.' Reaching up to take the

collar of his jacket so she could help him out of it, she acciden-
tally brushed the skin of his neck with her knuckles. It was cold
and clammy from where the rain must have dripped off the ends
of his curls and trickled inside. He flinched as though her touch
had scalded him, and she immediately backed off. 'Sorry.'

His cheeks were red from more than just the cold, wet wind
now. 'No, I'm sorry. You just took me by surprise.' He turned his
back, ostensibly to make it easier for her to take his jacket as he
shrugged it down his arms, but she wondered if he was hiding his
face. She took the opportunity to rub her thumb over her
knuckles to chase away the lingering awareness of his skin against
hers then set about stripping the soaking wet jacket free. 'Here, let
me hang this up so it can dry, and you go and grab a seat.' She
paused then added with a wry laugh, 'Take your pick.'

Liam glanced around as though confused by so much choice.
'Anywhere with access to a plug?'

She pointed him to a table near the window. 'There's a socket
there you can use.' It was one of the few she'd had installed when
she and Maud first designed the layout so they'd have somewhere
to plug in the hoover without draping a long extension cable
across the room. Improving the power supply for customers was
at the top of the dauntingly long list of improvements she wanted
to make to the café. She wished she'd been able to manage it
when they'd extended the café to build the Hub a few years previously. She wouldn't have been able to use the funding from the
council, but the workmen would've been in situ. Unfortunately,
her budget hadn't quite stretched that far at the time.

Still, it was one of the most asked for things from people
hoping to charge up their phones while they were there, and
she'd noticed the increase in people choosing to look elsewhere,
particularly young people. She glanced over at Liam, who was
unpacking a laptop and several folders from his bag. He wasn't

the only one who needed to do some number-crunching. She did her best to keep on top of her accounts, but it wasn't always easy during the busy summer months. Now things had slowed down she'd have to catch up on everything so she had a proper picture of where exactly things stood. If she could afford the upgrade, then the coming winter months would be the ideal time to do it. It would be a gamble, but one she was beginning to think she didn't have any choice about.

Giving Liam time to get settled, and herself a chance to calm her whirling thoughts, Issy put the mop and bucket away out the back and washed her hands. When she returned to his table, he had his laptop open, the screen filled with numbers and a leather-bound book open in front of him. She frowned at the neatly labelled columns filled with spidery writing and numbers. 'Is that an accounting ledger?' She couldn't keep the disbelief from her voice. 'Anya told me about the post book, but I didn't think even Davy was still such a dinosaur as to be doing his accounts by hand.'

Liam gave an exasperated chuckle. 'Thankfully, there's a digital record as well.' He waved a hand towards the screen. 'But a lot of the descriptions are so brief they're practically written in a secret code. I'm using the ledger to help me work out what everything means.'

Issy winced. 'That sounds like a bit of a nightmare, even for a numbers whizz like you.'

'It's certainly keeping me on my toes.' He glanced up, his expression curious. 'What system do you use?'

She laughed. 'If that's your idea of a chat-up line, Liam, you need to work on your material.' The moment the words were out of her mouth, she regretted them. Whatever the circumstances of their break-up, it was too late to retread old ground.

The widening of his pupils was enough to telegraph his

surprise that she'd opened that doorway into the past, but it was too late to slam it closed. 'You always used to love maths, though. Have things really changed that much?'

'It helps with running this place, sure, but not all of us got the same opportunities to pursue the things we were interested in as children.' She needed to stop throwing that in his face, especially when the choices made had been outside of his control. 'I'm sorry, Liam, that wasn't fair of me. I know how hard it was for you. At least you got a decent education and a career out of it.'

He reached out and took her hand, surprising her once again with how right that contact felt between the two of them. 'I didn't ask for it. I didn't want it, but there was no way to say no. Not then at least.' His final words were said in a thoughtful tone that made her think the unthinkable.

'Are you serious about taking over the hotel, then?' Though she'd hoped for her friends' sakes they might get an opportunity to help refurbish the place, in her heart of hearts she hadn't truly expected that Liam would choose to give up his life in London.

As though suddenly aware they were holding hands, Liam released her fingers and folded his hands in his lap. 'I want to do it. I'm just not sure if I'll be able to do it.'

Which made sense, she supposed. 'Sounds like you've got a tough decision on your hands. Well, I'd better stop bothering you and let you get on. What can I get you? Coffee? Tea? Something to eat?'

He glanced past her to where the display in the front counter was mostly cakes and snacks to tempt any afternoon grazers. 'I haven't eaten anything since breakfast, unless you count those ridiculously addictive lollies they keep on the reception at the hotel. Am I too late for a sandwich?'

She shook her head. 'Not at all. I'll happily make you anything that's up on the board. I've got some homemade chicken or vegetable soup left over if you fancy something warmer on such a miserable day.'

Liam's face brightened like she'd offered him a gourmet meal. 'Chicken soup and a cheese sandwich would be heaven.'

'Do you want that sandwich toasted?'

He laughed, the rich deep timbre going right through her to the tips of her toes. 'Now who's flirting?'

Was she? Surely not. 'Perhaps I'm just bumping up your order to get my hands on more of your money.' She gave him her most winning smile. 'Would you like a drink and a slice of cake to go with that?'

Reaching into his pocket, Liam pulled out an overstuffed wallet and placed it on the table in front of her. 'When you look at me like that, Isabel Kernow, I'd give you the world.' His words were said with a teasing smile that matched hers, but oh there was something in those dark blue eyes of his that made her want to run away. Or even worse, clamber into his lap.

Trying to still the fluttering of her heart, Issy flipped opened his wallet and slid out the debit card in the top slot. 'This'll do for now. You'll be wanting a receipt, I take it?'

'Please. And I'll take a coffee and a slice of cake. Just to help your profit margin, of course.'

She couldn't help but laugh at that. 'I tried a new Battenberg recipe with lemon and ginger sponges this morning. You can be my taste-tester if you like.'

'You must've made that with me in mind.'

'You wish.' Even as she dismissed his comment with a laugh, she wondered if it was true. He'd been in her thoughts so much since he'd been back, and lemon and ginger had always been his favourite flavours growing up... She had to stop letting him get under her skin like this. Especially if he was seriously thinking about coming back. Getting mixed up with Liam again would be a ridiculously bad idea. Even if his dark eyes sparkled when he smiled at her and the curls at his nape made her fingers itch to touch them.

'Maybe I do.'

She closed her eyes briefly. She should've gone to the kitchen when she had the chance. But she hadn't and now he was smiling up at her, that dimple in his left cheek as tempting as it had ever been. 'This isn't a good idea.'

The dimple vanished, his expression shifting from amused to wary. 'I thought things were better between us now.'

Issy sighed. 'They are, Liam, but we can't turn back the clock.' Even if a part of her wanted to do just that. Things had made so much more sense when she'd had Liam by her side. Coping with the loss of her parents without him there to support her had been the worst moment of her life. Her nan had been amazing, but the loss had taken its toll on her as well. Even in the depths of the worst of her grief, Issy had done her best not to put everything on Maud. 'We've both been through so much, Liam, we're not the same people any more.'

'You can't just expect me to forget about it! I talked to my dad earlier. You should've seen the look on his face when he realised I thought he might've had something to do with it.' He scrubbed a hand through his hair. 'Whoever it is who manipulated us back then is still messing with us now.'

'Not if we don't let them.' She placed a hand on his shoulder. 'I'm serious, Liam. I'm tired of being angry about all this.' And she'd been angry for such a long time. 'You've got the luxury of being able to ask your parents, which is something I'll never be able to do.' He opened his mouth to speak, but she shook her head. 'No, listen a minute. I choose to believe they didn't have anything to do with it because the people I remember wouldn't be so underhand. I can't afford to let anything taint those memories, Liam, not when they're all I have left.'

'I let you down when you needed me most. I should've swallowed my pride and sought you out, but I honestly thought having me around would only make you feel worse.' His sorrowful expression shifted to something harder. 'I would've been there if whoever it was hadn't ruined it for us. When I find out who it was...'

Issy shook her head. 'Don't, Liam, please.' She shifted her hand from his shoulder to cup his cheek. 'You didn't let me down and that's all that really matters.' She stepped back. 'I'll go and sort out your lunch.'

Liam reached for her, his hand encircling her arm in a grip that was gentle but insistent. 'I don't think I can be as calm as you about this, but if you truly don't want me to dig into this, then I won't. I don't want anything else to stand between us.'

'There isn't any us. I meant what I said about not turning back the clock.'

'I'm not looking to turn back the clock.' She wasn't sure whether to be relieved or disappointed, but before she could make up her mind he'd released his hold on her arm and slid his hand down to tangle their fingers together. 'I know we'll never get back the time we've lost, but that doesn't mean we can't think about the future, does it?'

Her heart did a dangerous leap in her chest and Issy raised her free hand to press against it. 'It's too soon to think about that. You still don't even know if you're going to move back here full time.'

He squeezed her fingers. 'I'm going to do my damnedest to make things work with the hotel, and even if I can't, I'm not going back to London.'

If she'd thought her heart had been beating fast before, it was racing now. 'Are you serious?'

Liam nodded. 'Absolutely. If the hotel's a bust then I'll do something else. I'll talk to my boss in London and see if I can work remotely. I work on my own most of the time, so worst case scenario I'd have to be in the office one or two days a week.'

'That's a hell of a commute, Liam...'

'It'd be worth it though. And if it gets too much, I'll find something else, something local.'

He was making it all sound so easy, but it was clear he was coming up with things on the hoof. She tugged her hand from his. 'There's no point in talking about this until you know for sure what's happening with the hotel. Concentrate on that for now and if you find a way to make it work and I know you'll be staying, maybe then we can talk about it.'

Liam sighed. 'I suppose I should be glad that one of us can think sensibly about this.' His lips quirked up at one corner. 'Are you sure I can't tempt you to come out with me this weekend? No strings, nothing heavy, it would just be nice to spend some time together.'

Issy couldn't hold back an answering smile. He really was incorrigible and far too charming for his own good. 'I'm helping Kat move into my spare room this weekend. She's having a tough time with her dad and she needs a bit of breathing space.'

'Next weekend, then?'

She laughed. 'Sort things out with the hotel, and then we'll talk.'

14

Liam watched Issy until she disappeared into the rear kitchen before returning his attention to his laptop. What had felt like a daunting task when he'd walked into the café now felt like a challenge he was eager to tackle. Amazing how the right incentive could so swiftly change his mindset. But he wouldn't only be doing this for the chance to explore whether he and Issy might have some kind of future together, he wanted to find a way to make taking over the hotel viable for himself. For Davy too, because surely he deserved some peace of mind after decades of hard work. The hotel might be something of a shadow of its former glory, but it had good bones and a good heritage. A heritage Liam wanted to preserve for the future.

When Issy bought over his food, he was so focused on coaxing the secrets from the numbers on his screen he barely looked up for long enough to smile and thank her. Somewhere in the back of his brain he acknowledged how tasty the soup was, how she'd elevated a simple cheese toastie with the perfect bite of heat and sweet by adding chilli jam, but most of his attention remained focused on trying to chase down a coding anomaly between the handwritten ledger and the electronic records.

He did stop when she returned to clear his plates and set a thick square of Battenberg down in front of him together with a coffee. Liam bent over the cake and sniffed, taking in the sharp-sweet aromas of ginger and lemon. He grinned up at Issy. 'You were definitely thinking about me when you made this, weren't you?'

She rolled her eyes. 'You keep believing that if you want to.'

'I intend to.'

She laughed. 'You are impossible. I'm going to set the Hub up for the after-school club, so give me a shout if you need anything else.'

'Okay.' Once the café filled up with noisy children, there was no way he'd be able to concentrate. 'What time does the club start?'

'Any time after three-thirty.' Liam checked his watch. As though reading his mind, Issy laughed. 'I'll give you a fifteen-minute warning so you can escape before the madness starts.'

'Thanks!'

The bell above the door sounded, drawing Issy away to greet a new customer. He watched her for a moment, admiring the easy way she had with everyone. He didn't think he'd ever find it that easy, but it would be part and parcel of his job if he took over the hotel. Maybe Issy could give him some tips. But that was an issue for another day. Right now he had just over an hour before he had to think about packing up. And he had an error to track down. He turned his attention back to his work. Numbers were much simpler to deal with than people.

* * *

Liam was cursing his earlier hubris when Issy touched him on the shoulder. 'How's it going?' she asked.

'I'm about ready to walk into the sea,' he said with a groan. 'There's an error somewhere in last month's accounts entry between the ledger and what Steve's recorded on the system, but I cannot for the life of me work out what it is.'

Issy tilted her head to one side and frowned at him. 'I thought you were looking at big picture stuff not doing a month end reconciliation.'

Oh shit. Hoping his face wasn't as flushed as it felt, Liam closed his eyes. When he'd realised there was a mistake he'd switched automatically into work mode, determined to find and fix it. 'I've wasted an entire afternoon chasing my tail.'

He opened his eyes to find Issy watching him, silent laughter sparkling in her eyes. 'You can do my books next if you like.'

Liam half-laughed, half-groaned. 'Now you really are flirting with me!' Reaching out, he slapped the lid down on his laptop with a little bit more force than necessary. 'I'd better go and speak to Davy and give him a heads up about this error so he and Steve can sort it out.'

'That's probably a good idea.' Issy bit her lip, and though he should've found it irritating that she was clearly still trying not to laugh at him, all he could think about was how tempting the little red mark she'd left on her lower lip looked.

He pushed his chair back and stood. She'd been standing right next to him, so there wasn't more than a couple of inches between them. 'Are you sure you won't change your mind about a date this weekend?' he asked, keeping his voice low.

'I'm helping Kat move in, remember?' Was it wishful thinking on his part or did she sound a little disappointed about that?

'Oh yeah, well we can make up for it next weekend.'

'I never said I'd go out with you.' Her voice was soft, her eyes bright with amusement and maybe – hopefully! – something more.

He bent down and whispered in her ear, 'You never said you wouldn't either.' Rather than give her the chance to shoot him down, Liam stepped away and began gathering his things. Having shouldered his bag, he turned back to find her still watching him with that sparkle in her eyes.

'What am I going to do with you?' she murmured.

'I'll make you a list.' His heart soared as her merry laughter followed him all the way to the door where he grabbed his jacket from the hook. With his head full of thoughts of Issy, Liam wasn't paying much attention as he pulled opened the door and almost bumped into Ray Evans, who was coming the other way. 'Oops, sorry!' Liam leapt back out of the way, holding the door for the older man.

Ray nodded his thanks as he entered. 'You're looking remarkably chipper compared with the last time I saw you.'

Liam grinned. 'I've got a lot to be chipper about. I hope you won't think I'm rude if I rush off, but having come here to escape Davy I've come across something I actually need to talk to him about!'

'You're seriously giving up on London and moving back here to run it, then?' There was no missing the disappointed set of Ray's mouth.

Not in the mood for a lecture, Liam kept his voice bright and cheerful. 'That's the plan. Now if you'll excuse me, I really need to get going.'

Stepping in front of him, Ray reached out as though he would place a hand on Liam's chest, before he flexed his fingers and dropped his arm again. 'I'd like to have a chat with you when you can spare me the time.'

He really wasn't going to let this go, was he? 'I know you had high expectations of me when you helped with my scholarship, Ray, but the time has come to do what's best for me.' Liam couldn't help casting a look over at Issy, who was busy behind the counter. 'And that's coming home.' With a polite smile, he stepped around Ray. 'I really need to get going.'

'It's not about that,' Ray called after him, but Liam didn't stop. He would always be grateful for the time and effort his old teacher had invested in him, but Liam didn't have to justify his choices to Ray, or anybody else.

The early rain had stopped but the dark clouds overhead held the promise of more to come, so Liam paused to tug on his jacket. He was about halfway along the seafront path when he spotted a man using the zebra crossing ahead. There was something familiar about him but it took until they were almost face to face for Liam to place him. It was the developer who'd spoken to him briefly after the monthly village meeting. 'Still here, then?' Liam asked by way of greeting.

Adam Mountjoy smiled as he paused and offered his hand. 'For my sins. I'm actually down visiting my granddad. He's up at Blue Horizons.' Adam gestured with his head towards the other end of the village where the retirement complex was situated at the base of the promontory on which the castle stood. His smile faded a little. 'He's not been well, though I only found out recently.'

'Oh, I'm sorry to hear that.' They shared an uncomfortable smile at finding themselves in one of those unexpected moments when you've made a connection with someone who is still too much of a stranger. 'So, you're not just here looking for properties, then?'

'Not intentionally. I've had a lot of time on my hands and it's not in my nature to just sit about, so I've had a bit of a nose around. I only showed up at the meeting because I overheard someone talking about it and I didn't have anything better to do.' He shrugged as he gave Liam a charming, quirky smile. 'You seemed like you were in a tight spot when people started challenging you about the hotel, and I've never been one to pass up an opportunity, which is why I gave you my card. I figured it'd be a nice little project to keep me occupied as I'm going to be spending a fair bit of time around here.'

'Well, I'm sorry to disappoint you, but I'm probably going to hang onto it if I can get everything figured out.' If they'd been in a cartoon, a lightbulb would've sprung up over Liam's head. 'I don't suppose you've got time to chat later?' A large raindrop splashed on his cheek and Liam spared a quick glance at the ominous sky overhead. Another drop hit Adam's shoulder, darkening the fabric of his shirt. 'Or we could do it now before the heavens open again.' He pointed down the road towards the Smuggler's Den. 'Too early for a pint?'

Adam raised his eyebrows. 'Want to pick my brains, is it?'

Liam held up his hands in a you-got-me gesture. 'If it's not too much of piss-take after I've just told you I'm keeping the hotel?'

Adam laughed. 'At least you're honest about your intentions, and I like that. It might cost you two beers though.'

Excited at the prospect of being able to talk to someone with the kind of experience and knowledge he was lacking, Liam grinned. 'Deal.'

They settled with their drinks in the same corner booth Liam had shared with Rick – was it really only a week ago? He'd been so close to rock bottom at that point he almost didn't recognise the person he'd been then. Adam took a sip from his drink then set it down and pushed it to one side. 'Right then, show me what you've got.'

A couple of hours later, Liam tore himself away from the hotel blueprints to sort them out a refill. His head was absolutely buzzing with information and he had a daunting list of things he needed to tackle, but Adam had been nothing but generous with his expertise. The pub had started to fill up with people dropping in after work, and though he'd had a late lunch he wasn't sure when Adam had eaten, so he grabbed a couple of bags of crisps while he was at the bar. When he returned, Adam was bent over a tablet, tapping away at the keyboard. He paused, accepting his drink with a smile which brightened considerably when Liam dropped the crisps in the middle of the table. 'Thanks, I'm starving.'

'We can order something more substantial if you want?' The menu wasn't fancy but they had a decent selection of pub staples.

Adam shook his head. 'No, these'll be fine for now. I really need to get up to Blue Horizons in a bit and check in on my granddad.'

'Oh, of course. We can knock this on the head now if you like? You've already been a great help.'

'No, they're not keen on visitors over dinner time, so I've got another hour before I need to head out.' Adam reached for the file Chloe and Anya had put together and began leafing through it again. 'I tried to look up Penrose Duncan Design to see what other projects they've worked on, but their website is quite minimal.'

'They're pretty new,' Liam admitted.

Adam raised an eyebrow. '*How* new?'

'This is the first proposal they've put together.'

The other man raised his hand to rub his forehead. 'And there's a family connection, I assume from the name?'

'My cousin Chloe and her cousin Anya. Her aunt is married to my uncle.' Liam swallowed and decided he might as well go the whole hog. 'I should probably mention that Anya is very close to my brother Rick.'

A burst of exasperated laughter escaped Adam's lips. 'Is your whole family going to be involved in this?'

'Rick has offered to help me navigate the planning side of things because of his work on the local council. And Chloe's dad and brother own a joinery business and I'm hoping to utilise their skills.' He leaned forward and rested his elbows on the table. 'I'd like to use as many local businesses as possible, if I can afford it.'

Adam nodded. 'It would certainly help to get the community onside, plus it might give you some bonus points with the planners in terms of sustainability and benefits to the local area.'

It was a slightly more cynical way of looking at it than Liam had in mind, but he'd been involved in enough big projects to know that even the tiniest advantage could tip the scales in the right direction. 'Rick would be able to help us with that sort of stuff.'

'You'll certainly benefit from his inside knowledge, though he'll have to recuse himself from the formal process.'

'Assuming I even get that far.'

'Don't talk yourself down before you've even got going. There'll be plenty of people along the way who will try and stop you as it is.'

Liam knew he was right but it was hard not to feel daunted. 'I'm doing my best, but leading from the front has never been my strong point. I've always been more comfortable in the background, focusing on the numbers.' He reached for his pint. 'And I'm not even sure how I'm going to make those work yet.'

'You'll need external financing for sure.' Adam raised his own drink and eyed Liam over the top of it. 'Or a business partner with very deep pockets and a lot of useful resources to hand to help keep costs down.'

Liam almost choked on his beer. 'Hold on a minute, I never said anything about bringing a partner on board.'

Adam raised one shoulder in a shrug. 'I told you before, I'm not one to pass up an opportunity either.' He took a long sip then set his pint back down. 'And honestly, I'm a long way off opening negotiations even if you were willing to consider it. There's too much information missing, but I'm interested enough to help you fill in those gaps.'

'Even if I decide I don't want to take on a partner?'

'Even then.' Adam sat back and folded his arms across his broad chest. 'Like I said, I'll be spending a fair bit of time around here over the coming weeks and as lovely as it is, Halfmoon Quay's not exactly got enough going on to keep me entertained.'

Liam stared at the other man for a long moment. Adam had the skills and knowledge he needed as well as the hands-on experience of running this kind of project. Plus it sounded like he was going to be around for a while, so why not take advantage of that? It wouldn't commit either of them to anything at this stage. 'I think I'd better introduce you to my great-uncle.'

15

It had taken most of the weekend to transfer Kat's things from her room at her parents' to Issy's place. Saturdays were the busiest days in their respective cafés, and though Sunday was supposed to be a day off, her father had insisted she work a full shift, claiming another member of staff had called in sick at the last minute. Issy wouldn't put it past Gavin to have made the whole thing up to make things as difficult for Kat as possible. He'd never approved of Kat's friendship group – Chloe in particular, who'd always been the most outspoken – but he saved a special level of dislike for Issy after she and Maud had converted their home into The Cosy Coffee Pot.

The village was large enough to support half a dozen similar businesses, but for some reason he'd taken it as a personal challenge and done everything he could to put a spanner in the works. Maud had kept a lot of the worst stuff to herself, but it had been impossible to miss when Gavin had tried to circulate a petition around the village claiming the change of use would ruin the ambience of the seafront. It was ridiculous given the number of businesses that were already in operation in the same area, and the vast majority of people had sided with Issy and her nan. Embarrassed by her father's behaviour, Kat had tried to avoid Issy until she'd been able to assure her that nothing Gavin did would threaten their friendship.

By the time they'd humped the final box upstairs last night the two of them had been too tired to do much more than make a cup of tea and collapse into bed. Kat had left for work that morning promising she'd finish unpacking as soon as she got home again. Deciding they were going to have a proper house-warming, Issy had got up early and prepared chicken provençale, leaving it in the slow cooker to do its thing.

Issy glanced up at the clock on the wall. Now the lunch rush was over she could do with checking on it. She turned towards her only customer, Ray Evans, who was occupying his usual table by the window. He'd come in a lot earlier than was his habit, and though Issy had noted his break in routine, he hadn't seemed in the mood for conversation, so she hadn't mentioned it. 'I need to run upstairs for two minutes. Do you mind keeping an eye on things for me, Ray?'

The older man glanced up from brooding over a coffee long gone cold. 'I'm not going anywhere.'

There was definitely something up with him, but she would worry about that after she'd checked on dinner. She shot him a grateful smile. 'Thanks. I'll be two minutes and then I'll fetch you a fresh cup.'

Issy tugged off her apron and ran upstairs. The flat smelled delicious and a quick check assured her she could turn the cooker off for now. She was about to head back downstairs when the wine rack caught her eye. With a grin she grabbed a bottle of rosé and placed it in the fridge. *They were supposed to be celebrating, after all...*

When she got downstairs, she was relieved to see Ray was still the only customer and she made haste to wash her hands and tie her apron back on before fixing him a large cappuccino. She added a square of shortbread to the saucer and carried it over to his table by the window where she set it down. 'To say thank you for keeping an eye on things,' she told him when he raised a quizzical eyebrow.

'There's no need for that, I didn't really do anything.' His voice was monotone, the same flatness she'd been noting for several weeks.

'Is everything okay, Ray?'

'Why shouldn't it be?'

The prickly tone should've been warning enough for most, but Issy wasn't so easily put off the scent. 'You don't seem like your usual cheery self, that's all.' That bit of sass at least earned her a bark of laughter.

'Very droll, Isabel, very droll.'

The tiny chink in his armour was enough for her to seize upon and she slid into the chair opposite and rested her forearms on the table. 'You've been in here every week for as long as I can remember, so I reckon I know you about as well as you let anyone get to know you, and something's not right. Is it Denise? Are you missing her?'

Ray huffed. 'When don't I miss her, but no, it's not that. I banged my leg the other day, stupid old codger that I am, and it's been giving me gyp.'

'Have you been to see the doctor about it?'

Ray snorted. 'Don't be confusing me with that fool Davy Penrose. If I thought it was something serious, I'd get myself checked out. It's just a bit of a nasty bruise. I'll be right as rain in a couple of days.' He raised his cup and studied her over the rim. 'So Liam's really thinking about moving back here, then?'

The abrupt change in conversation took her off guard. 'That's something you'd have to discuss with him.'

Ray held her gaze. 'I just assumed you would be in the know. The two of you were always very close.'

A faint stab of old pain made Issy shift uncomfortably in her seat. 'That was a long time ago. Things changed after he went off to school.'

'Yes, they did, didn't they?' Ray set down his cup. 'It was the best thing for him, getting him out of this place and somewhere he could make the most of his potential.' Ray spun the cup around and around in the saucer. It was a strangely nervous gesture, another sign that all wasn't quite right with him. 'I just wish I could've afforded you the same opportunity, but I only managed to get them to consider Liam because I had a direct connection with one of the teachers there.'

Was that what all this was about? It had hurt a lot at the time, and Issy supposed a part of her had blamed Ray for his role in Liam going away, but she wasn't a broken-hearted teenager any more and she understood he'd had the best of intentions. She didn't like the idea he'd been feeling guilty all this time. She reached across the table to pat his hand. 'That's all water under the bridge now, Ray. I'm not upset about it, so neither should you be. I'm content with my lot.' A tinge of sadness tugged at the edges of her mind. 'Besides, if I had gone away to school then I would've missed out on those last precious years with my parents.'

Ray glanced towards the window. 'Such a terrible loss.' His voice was so full of pain she wondered if mentioning it had stirred up his own sadness about Denise's passing. 'If I'd known what was going to happen, I'd have done things differently.'

Yes, he was definitely thinking about his wife. 'We all have regrets, Ray, but at the end of the day we can only do what we believe is for the best at the time.'

He turned back towards her. 'I tell myself that's what I was doing, but the more time passes, the less I'm sure that's enough to assuage the guilt.'

She reached for his hand again. 'Try not to dwell on the past. I know it's easier said than done, and it's advice I'm not always good at taking myself, but I don't like to see you so down in the dumps.'

Ray squeezed her fingers and he sounded a little choked as he said, 'You've a good heart, Isabel. I hope one day you'll find someone who appreciates that, who sees you for the wonderful person you are.'

Issy laughed the compliment off even as it warmed her inside. 'If I find someone who loves me the way you loved your wife then I'll be very lucky indeed.' Her mind strayed briefly to Liam before she brushed the thought away. It was too soon to start entertaining those kind of daydreams. She released Ray's hand and stood. 'I'll leave you to enjoy your coffee now I know you're okay.'

The café soon filled up and Issy only noticed Ray had left when someone asked her to clear away his dirty cup so they could sit down. She gathered it with a quick apology and returned with a cloth and some spray to wipe down. And then she was onto the next person and the next until, before she knew it, it was five o'clock and she was shooing the last customers out the door. She flipped the closed sign and locked the front door, leaning back against it with a long sigh as she surveyed how much clearing up there was still to do. At least the till was full.

A knock on the door startled a high-pitched shriek from her. Clutching a hand to her racing heart, she turned to find a smiling Kat peering through the glass at her. Happiness at seeing her friend chased off any thoughts of tiredness and she quickly unlocked the door and tugged it open. 'Welcome home!'

'Thank you!' Kat darted in and gave her a quick hug. 'Oh my God, Dad has been insufferable all day! I have been counting down the hours until I could escape. And Mum is so cross with me for leaving her to deal with this permanently awful mood of his that she's barely said a word to me all day. I'm not sure which was worse, him snapping every five minutes or her giving me the cold shoulder.' Kat sighed. 'Sorry, I didn't mean to dump all that on you!'

'Nonsense, you dump away anytime you need to, that's what friends are for!' She ushered Kat further inside so she could close the door again. 'You go upstairs and get settled in and I'll be up as soon as I've finished here.'

'Oh rubbish!' Kat scoffed, already unbuttoning her coat. 'As if I'm going to put my feet up and leave you to tidy up. It'll go twice as quick if we both do it.'

Issy could've protested, but honestly the offer of help was a lifesaver. And Kat was right, with two of them on the case they'd have the place sorted out in no time and then they'd have the rest of the evening to relax and enjoy themselves. Heading behind the counter, she whacked the radio up full blast. The pair of them danced and sang their way through the cleaning. Issy had just switched on the dishwasher when Kat wandered over, a plastic carrier bag dangling from one hand. 'Hey, I found this under one of the tables by the window. I had a quick peek inside and it appears to be some sort of box.'

Taking the bag from her friend, Issy opened it. Expecting a cardboard box, she was surprised to see a small plastic chest, the kind of thing a child might keep their treasures in. There didn't seem to be anything else inside it and the bag was from a popular supermarket so could've been brought in by anyone. Issy tried the lid but it seemed to be locked and there was nothing on the outside that indicated who it might belong to. She folded the bag carefully around the box and tucked it on a shelf beneath the counter. 'It'll keep until tomorrow.'

'I wonder who it belongs to,' Kat mused.

'It'll be one of the kids, they're always leaving stuff. At least it's not smelly gym kit this time!' They both laughed. 'I'll put a post on the café's social media pages about it and hopefully someone will see it and can pick it up tomorrow.' Issy cast a quick glance around the room and decided it would do for the night. 'Come on, there's a bottle of rosé in the fridge with our names on it.'

She led the way upstairs and headed straight into the compact kitchen while Kat made a beeline for the bedroom. Issy had turned the heat up on the slow cooker and put some rice on to boil by the time Kat joined her. She'd taken the opportunity to change into a baggy T-shirt and a pair of yoga pants. 'What can I do?'

'You know where the glasses are, why don't you sort out the wine?'

'That's a very good idea!'

While Kat sorted that, Issy rummaged in the drawer where all the stuff that didn't have another home lived. 'I know they're here somewhere... ah ha!' Her fingers latched around a set of keys and she lifted them out. The Hello Kitty keyring they were attached to brought a sad smile to Issy's face as she remembered it being one of her stocking presents on a Christmas morning long past. She shouldn't keep these things hidden away in the backs of drawers. 'Here.' She held out the keys to Kat.

'Oh this is a blast from the past,' Kat said as she held the little white cat's head between her fingers. 'I remember when your room was plastered with this stuff.' She glanced up at Issy. 'Are you sure you're okay with me having them?'

Issy nodded. 'Of course. This is your home now and you need to be able to come and go as you please. And at least we'll always know which is your set – a kitty for Kat.'

Kat laughed. 'Good point. I promise to take good care of

them.' Her fingers closed gently around the keys like she was holding a precious gift. 'You don't know what being able to stay here means to me.'

Issy was sure she had a pretty good idea. She hugged Kat close for a moment before reaching for one of the wine glasses. She raised it towards her friend. 'It's lovely to have you here.'

Kat clinked glasses with her. 'It's lovely to be here.' They both took a sip of the refreshingly chilled wine and let out a pair of happy sighs. 'Do I have time for a quick shower before dinner?' Kat asked.

'Absolutely. Take your wine with you and give me a shout when you're done and I'll hop in afterwards.'

'Great.'

'And I reckon, as it's only us, that PJs are in order, don't you?' Issy called after her.

'Perfect!'

While Kat got herself sorted, Issy pottered around in the kitchen humming to herself. Tired as she was, it was nice to have a bit of company rather than being stuck with her own thoughts night after night. Maybe she should ask Kat's advice about Liam asking her out. Though the sensible part of her knew it would be better to wait until his future plans were clearer, she couldn't deny the way he seemed to occupy more and more of her thoughts.

Issy took a sip from her glass and stirred the pot of rice as it was just beginning to boil. It would be good to talk things over, but not tonight. Tonight was about celebrating her new flatmate.

16

'I assume you've got me up at a hideous hour for something other than the pleasure of my company?' Rick grumbled as he wandered into the kitchen the next morning to join Liam and their father. Like them, he was dressed in gym kit and trainers.

'Something like that.' Liam clapped his brother on his shoulder. 'I bumped into that property developer again last week and we had a very interesting chat. I'm taking him to meet Uncle Davy later on and to have a look around the hotel.'

Jago frowned. 'You're thinking about selling, after all? I thought we'd agreed to talk things out if you got to that stage.'

'No, no, it's nothing like that!' Liam assured them as he led the way out the back door. 'There's just so much I don't know about so I decided to ask him for some advice.'

Jago's shoulders relaxed. 'It makes sense to speak to someone with proper expertise.'

'Exactly. We might end up doing some kind of partnership deal but that's still a long way down the line. In the meantime, Adam's agreed to act as a bit of an unofficial advisor.'

'That seems incredibly generous,' Rick observed as he bent

one leg back and gripped his ankle to stretch out the muscle. 'What's in it for him?'

Liam began his own stretch routine. 'I'm still not quite sure. He said he's going to be around the village for a while; his grand-father lives up at Blue Horizons and isn't too well, apparently. I think he's a bit bored, maybe even a bit lonely, so it gives him something to do.'

'What's his name again?' Rick asked. 'If he's got family here, maybe we know them.'

'Adam Mountjoy. Ring any bells?'

Rick shook his head. 'Not off the top of my head. What about you, Dad?'

'Nope, not a name I'm familiar with. I like to think I know most people around here, but I can't place any Mountjoys.'

'Could be a maternal connection,' Rick pointed out as they finished their stretches and headed down the path. 'Or his granddad might have retired down here and kept himself to himself.'

'Could be. We should invite him round for dinner sometime,' Jago suggested.

Liam shot an amused glance at his father from the corner of his eye. 'So you can check him out, make sure he's not some kind of scam merchant?'

'It's not that! I mean, I always like to get the measure of some-one, especially if he's going to have any dealings with one of you, but you said yourself he seems a bit lonely. And if things aren't good with his granddad – whoever he is – then he's probably a bit upset too. A good meal, a drink or two and some company might go a long way.'

Liam's heart swelled at the sheer generosity of spirit that made him proud every day that Jago was his father. 'I'm only pulling your leg, Dad. I think it's a great idea. I'll ask him later when I see him. In the meantime, I wanted you both here so I can talk through some of the options Chloe and Anya came up with. I'd like a clearer picture in my mind before I speak to Davy.'

They kept the pace slow along the beach as Liam went through each proposal in turn, going through the pros and cons he'd come up with for each of the three options. As he'd known he would, Rick offered him great advice. 'Well, the quick-turn-around sprucing-up one would be the most straightforward,' his brother said. 'You could probably keep the place open over the winter and keep some revenue coming in, as well. Your regulars would prefer that, I'm sure, and it would be the least disruptive to everyone.'

Liam nodded. 'All of those are definitely ticks in the plus column, but as Anya pointed out, a lot of those regulars are older in age. It sounds horribly mercenary, but what happens when they die? I'm not sure the current layout has much to appeal to a younger crowd.'

'Not mercenary, practical,' Jago interjected. 'If this is going to be a long-term project for you, then you need to think about where you want to be in five, ten years' time.'

'Exactly.' Rick added. 'Plus, now is the perfect time to pivot because there's a growing market among people our age for more eco-friendly holidays.'

Liam had been thinking along much the same lines. 'And they're going to want more than a room and a box of cornflakes for breakfast.'

'Yup.' Rick stopped and put his hands on his hips. 'Look, if it was up to me, I'd go the whole hog and really give the place a whole new feel. I took Anya on a date to Port Petroc a few weeks ago and the contrast between the seafront there and what we have here is worlds apart.'

'They have a much bigger population, though,' Jago pointed out. 'And more space to work with.'

Rick nodded. 'That's true, but we're losing out because we're so lacking in options for people in the evening. We've got the pub, which is cheap and cheerful, and the restaurant is amazing but it costs too much for most wallets. We need something in between, something that'll inject a bit more life into the village in the evenings. Nothing rowdy,' he added quickly. 'The kind of thing they offer abroad where you can grab a table and enjoy a drink or a bit of tapas during an evening promenade.'

'Like an outdoor terrace in front of the hotel with a beautiful view out over the water,' Liam said with a grin.

'Just like that. Plus, I could try and do more through the council, get some extra seating installed, maybe look at licensing a couple of mobile catering units.'

Jago frowned. 'I'm not sure Russ Armstrong would be thrilled at the prospect of a burger van parked next to the restaurant.'

'Nothing like that! But imagine a wooden hut on the quayside offering fresh seafood. I've even seen an old VW camper van that was converted into a cocktail bar.'

Liam tried to picture it. It had been a long time since he'd been to Port Petroc; maybe he could take Issy there and they could check it out. It would be interesting to get her perspective, given how much experience she had running a business in the village. 'I could speak to Issy, see if she has any interest in doing something with the café in the evenings.'

The three of them turned as one to stare at the pretty café. 'It's the perfect spot,' Rick agreed.

'I hate to be the voice of doom,' their father said, turning to look at both of them. 'But it might not be as easy as you think. There's a lot of folk around here who are still very stuck in their ways, so you'd best be prepared for some push back, especially from those with properties near the seafront.'

'Don't I know it.' Rick sighed. 'But if we don't change, the community will continue to fracture as more young people leave, and eventually Halfmoon Quay will be nothing more than a glorified retirement home.'

Their father nodded. 'It doesn't mean you shouldn't try, and you'll have my full support. We just need to find a way to get as many people onside as possible.' He turned to Liam. 'Starting with Uncle Davy. He's put his heart and soul into the hotel for as long as I can remember. I know he's said you can do what you want with the place, but you're talking about some big changes here.'

He was right. 'I'll go and see him as soon as I've had a shower and got changed.'

* * *

'So what do you think, then?' Liam prompted his great-uncle.

Davy peered at him over the top of his glasses. 'Give a man a chance to have a proper look, boy.' And with that he returned his attention to the proposal folder he'd already been leafing through in silence for at least twenty minutes.

Liam fidgeted in his seat for another five minutes then stood. 'I'll go and make us a pot of tea, shall I?'

'Good idea.' There was just enough amusement in Davy's tone for Liam to suspect the old devil was deliberately stringing him along. Resisting the urge to sigh, Liam left the office and closed the door behind him.

'How's it going?' Anya asked, swivelling in her chair to face him.

'Who the hell knows?' Liam grumped. 'But his silence is

driving me mad, so I'm going to make us a drink. Do you want one?'

Anya turned back to pick up her mug. 'Just hot water please, if you don't mind.'

Liam returned a few minutes later with three mugs and the teapot balanced on a tray to find Anya laughing with Jim, the village postman. 'Oh, is one of those for me?' Jim asked, nodding at the tray.

'No, but I can make you one if you have time.'

'Only pulling your leg,' Jim said with a broad grin. 'I've got places to go and people to see.' He rummaged around in his sack and pulled out a wad of envelopes, leafing through them with a speed that spoke of long practice. 'Ah ha!' Jim pulled out an envelope and offered it to Liam.

'For me?' Liam set down the tray and took the envelope.

'Well, it's got your name on it!' Jim replied as he tucked the flap back over on his bag and then readjusted it across his body. 'And that's me on my way. See you, Anya. See you, Liam!'

'Bye, Jim,' Anya replied.

'Yeah, bye,' Liam added distractedly, as he frowned at the envelope.

'Bad news?' Anya asked him.

He glanced up, confused. 'Huh?'

'You're staring at that like you're afraid it might bite you, so I wondered if it was bad news, that's all.'

Liam shook his head. 'I'm just wondering who would write to me at mum and dad's when I haven't changed my address on anything yet.' Most of his bills and correspondence were paperless and Caro had agreed to forward the odd bits that arrived at the flat until he'd got himself properly sorted. He felt the corner of the envelope. 'There's something inside.'

'Well open it then!' Anya said with a laugh. 'The suspense is killing me.'

Liam grinned and stuck his finger under the corner of the seal to rip it open. His amusement faded again as he tipped out the contents into his palm. 'It's a key.' It was too small to be a door key, more like the kind you used to open a filing cabinet. He turned it over to check the other side. There was no number stamped on it. Not a filing cabinet, then. A luggage lock, maybe?

'What's it for?'

He looked up at her and shrugged. 'I have absolutely no idea.' He double-checked the envelope, but there was nothing to indicate who the sender was.

'Must be somebody's idea of a joke,' Anya said, though without much conviction.

'I suppose so.' It didn't seem like Rick's sort of thing. One of the twins, maybe? Liam put the key back inside the envelope, folded it carefully and tucked it away in his pocket. 'Hopefully whoever it is will make themselves known to me. In the meantime I'd better get back and see if Davy's got anything to say for himself yet.'

As it turned out, his uncle had plenty to say, and much to Liam's relief it was entirely positive. 'This is all Chloe and Anya's idea?' Davy asked, tapping the front of the folder as Liam set the tray down.

'Yep. They ambushed me with it at Aunty Helen's barbeque the other weekend.' He risked a smile at his uncle. 'I'm glad they've got such good ideas because I was still floundering around over what I would do with the place.'

'It'll be a lot of work.' Davy leaned back and steepled his fingers under his chin. 'A lot of money too.'

Liam nodded. 'I'm still working out the finance side of things. I've got...' He hesitated. It was too soon to call Adam a friend, though Liam certainly got a good vibe from the man even after such a brief acquaintance. '...someone with a lot more knowledge about this kind of stuff coming over in a bit to have a look around. I hope that's okay with you?'

Davy spread his hands wide. 'I already told you, lad. It's yours to do with as you wish.'

Leaning forward, Liam rested his folded arms on the desk. 'I appreciate you want to give me room, Uncle D, but I really would value your opinion. I'd hate to get too far down the line with any plans and then find out you hate it.'

'Just as well you've got no worries on that score then, isn't it?' Davy's grin was so broad his eyes almost disappeared in his wrinkled face. 'My only regret is that I'm not young enough to be doing it for myself.' Standing, he held out his hand to Liam. 'I knew my legacy would be in safe hands.'

Things went from good to great when Adam showed up. He and Davy took to each other like they'd been pals forever, and as the three of them toured around the hotel, it was clear his great-uncle hadn't been paying lip service when he'd told Liam he was happy about the proposed changes. Liam could hardly get a word in edgeways as Davy peppered Adam with a multitude of questions. For his part, Adam seemed happy to answer them all to the best of his limited knowledge and grilled the old man in turn. If he hadn't been busy trying to make notes of everything they discussed, Liam might have felt a bit left out, but this was more than he could've hoped for.

They would've spent the whole day yacking if Maud hadn't shown up and all but dragged Davy off for his afternoon nap. His great-uncle had grumbled he was fine, but Maud had clamped her hands on her denim-clad hips and stared him down until he'd reluctantly admitted to being a bit tired. Liam and Adam had decided to head to the café and check over the notes Liam had made while everything was still fresh in their minds.

Issy was behind the counter and Liam couldn't help smiling as he watched her tug irritably at the scrunchie holding back her black hair. A couple of quick drags of her hands and the silken mass was securely fastened back once more. He gave it about two minutes before the first strands started to escape again. 'You grab us a table,' he said to Adam. 'And I'll sort out some drinks.'

Issy turned away from the sink where she'd been washing her hands and Liam didn't miss the way her face lit up when she spotted him. 'I'm going to have to start charging you rent, you're in here so often.'

'Surely you mean you should be offering me a discount for my frequent visits,' he countered.

'Yeah, yeah. What are you having?'

'Can I get two large cappuccinos and a couple of slices of whatever you recommend, please?'

'Two?' Issy glanced past his shoulder to where Adam was getting settled at the table. 'Who's your friend?'

'That's Adam, he's a developer.'

Her eyes widened as she looked back at him. 'You're talking to him about the hotel?'

He nodded. 'He's letting me pick his brains, and depending on how things pan out, we might come to some kind of partnership arrangement.'

'Then I'd better cut him an extra-large slice of cake.' Issy gave him the ghost of a wink. 'Just to keep him sweet.'

Laughing, Liam dug into his pocket for his wallet while Issy set about fixing the drinks. The envelope he'd tucked in there earlier crinkled beneath his fingers and he pulled it out. 'Hey, Issy?' He tipped the key out onto his palm. 'You don't know anything about this, do you?'

She glanced over her shoulder at him, the coffee machine hissing loudly as she steamed a jug of milk. 'What's that?'

'Someone sent me a key in the post today; I was wondering if it was you.'

'Not me. Just hold on a minute.' He waited until she'd finished making the drinks and had set them on the counter. 'Show me?'

Liam held the tiny key up between thumb and forefinger. 'The only thing I think it might fit is one of those little luggage locks.'

Issy reached out and he let her take it. Frowning, she twisted it left and right. 'I've never seen anything like it bef—' She dropped the key on the top of the counter and bent down.

'Issy?' Liam went up on his tiptoes to try and see what she was doing. A moment later she set a carrier bag on top of the counter, opened the top and drew out a small chest. 'Where did you get that?'

'Kat found it under one of the tables after closing last night. I assumed one of the kids had left it but no one responded to the post I put on the café page. One of the mums shared it in the school WhatsApp group but none of the others know anything about it.' Her eyes were troubled as she looked up at him and then picked up the key. 'What do you think?'

Liam had no idea what to think, but he suddenly had a very bad feeling. 'See if it fits.' The lid popped open the moment she turned the key in the lock and that bad feeling suddenly got a whole lot worse.

'Oh God.' Issy held up an envelope.

Unlike the one he'd received that morning, the writing on the front was sickeningly familiar. His penmanship had never been good, even when he'd made an effort. 'Are those...?'

Issy held up a second, the neat, loopy writing on the front different, nothing like his own spiky hand but almost as familiar.

She stared at him, eyes glistening with tears. 'It's all of them. All the missing letters we sent.'

'Hey, Issy? Can I get a refill when you're ready?' The call from another customer startled them both.

Issy shoved the letters back into the little chest and stowed it back under the counter. 'We can't talk about this now,' she whispered.

Liam wanted to protest, but he knew she was right. The café was full of customers and Adam was still waiting for him to go over their notes. 'I'll come back later after closing.'

She shook her head. 'Kat will be here.'

They couldn't talk privately at his parents'. Well, they could but everyone would be curious. They needed somewhere just the two of them. 'Our place, then. Seven-thirty.'

'Okay.'

17

'You're not really going out in this weather, are you?' Kat asked with a frown when Issy emerged from her bedroom having showered and changed her clothes. Kat had got changed too, only she was wearing a pair of pyjamas covered in cartoon animals who were doing yoga for reasons Issy couldn't fathom, and a cosy fleece hoodie that matched her slippers.

'I won't be long.' Issy opened the narrow cupboard next to the front door and pulled out her raincoat and a pair of waterproof boots. She didn't much fancy going out in the rain but she needed to talk to Liam and try and figure out what the hell was going on.

Kat had turned to watch her, one arm draped along the top of the sofa. 'What's so urgent that it can't wait until tomorrow? You're being very mysterious, Issy. Is everything okay?'

Issy wiggled her foot into her left boot then crouched to lace it up. She looked up at Kat and sighed, knowing there was no point in trying to keep it a secret. 'I'm going to meet Liam.'

'Liam?' Kat scrambled up on her knees, hands braced on the back of the sofa as she leaned so far forward Issy worried for a moment that she'd tumble right over the top. 'Why are you meeting him?' Her eyes widened and a sly smile spread across her face. 'Oh, you're *meeting* him.'

Issy rolled her eyes though she couldn't quite hide her own smile. 'Don't start putting two and two together and making five, it's not like that.'

Kat's enthusiasm deflated like a leaky balloon. 'Oh, that's a shame. I always thought the two of you were made for each other.'

'And I've always thought you were an incurable romantic.' She finished lacing her boots and straightened up. 'I shouldn't be much more than an hour, so why don't you find us something to watch for when I get back, okay?'

'Okay.' Kat's tone was dubious in the extreme but at least she dropped back into her seat again.

Issy was zipping up her coat when she caught Kat pulling out her phone. 'Please tell me you're not thinking of getting on the WhatsApp group,' she groaned. 'I can't cope with Chloe in my ear right now.'

Kat pulled a face like Issy was being a spoilsport, but she lowered her phone. 'Good point.' She rested her chin on the back of the sofa and gave Issy wide, concerned eyes. 'You are okay, though?'

'I am.' Something occurred to her and she spoke without thinking. 'Hey, you know that bag you found in the café yesterday? Can you remember which table you found it under?'

'It was somewhere by the window; I'm not sure which table though.' Kat's expression grew immediately suspicious. 'Why are you suddenly asking me about that now?'

Not wanting to give too much away until she'd had a chance to talk it through with Liam, Issy did her best to give what she hoped was a casual shrug. 'No one's been in to collect it yet, that's all. I've been meaning to ask you since you got home, and kept forgetting.'

'You'd have thought someone would've missed it by now. I'll have a think while you're out and see if I can remember.'

Issy felt a bit guilty for not being completely honest, but she didn't have time to worry about that now. 'Thanks, I'll see you in a bit.'

'See you. Put your hood up or take a brolly. Mine's there on the mat.'

It wasn't like Kat to be bossy and it made Issy smile as she tucked her long hair into the back of her coat and tugged up her hood. 'Yes, Mum.'

The rain had eased a bit and the wind had dropped, so at least she wasn't fighting with her hood as she hurried along the street in the opposite direction to the beach. A handful of cars passed by, their tyres swishing as they sent up spray from the wet road. Issy huddled on the edge of the path closest to the sea wall to avoid getting splashed. The setting sun was barely a red smudge on the horizon and the orangey tinge on the clouds overhead was mostly from the street lamps glowing into life around the village. The light continued to fade as the number of buildings and houses reduced and by the time she reached the well-worn path towards the sand dunes, she needed the torch on her phone to check where she was walking. The steady climb soon had her breath misting but it wasn't long before it levelled off and she found herself in the quiet depths of the dunes. It was like stepping into another world, the tall banks of sand and their curtains of long grasses protecting her from the worst of the wind, which had begun to pick up as she'd climbed the hill. A moving light ahead caught her eye and she quickened her pace as much as the uneven terrain and the rapidly fading light would allow.

'I thought you might have changed your mind,' Liam said by way of greeting as she ducked under the roof of the sheltered bench seat a couple of minutes later. It was one of a number dotted along the coastal path, offering a place of rest for weary walkers – and a prime make-out spot for teenagers who wanted to be alone. He was seated on the long bench that lined the back of the shelter, his face illuminated by the glow of his phone screen. 'I was going to call you and say not to come out in the rain, but I realised too late that I didn't have your number.' He fiddled with his phone and the torch came on, filling the immediate area with light. He set it down beside him.

Issy sat on the bench near but not quite next to him. 'Yeah, I was going to call you but I ran up against the same problem.' She turned on her own torch and set her phone next to his.

They both fell silent, listening to the rain tap-tapping on the roof and walls of the wooden shelter, the roll and wash of the sea below a distant backdrop. Further away still, Issy could hear the faint crash of the waves against the rocks that lined the base of the dunes. 'I haven't been up here in a long time.'

'Me neither, not since...' His voice trailed off into a sigh. 'I still don't know what to make of the letters turning up like that.'

'Well, at least I know it definitely wasn't my parents.' Issy hadn't known she was capable of such black humour, but it actually felt good to be able to joke about anything to do with them.

Liam snorted then shifted on the bench so he was facing her, his right leg raised so the foot rested on his left thigh. 'I don't like that someone is playing games with us.'

'Either that or you returning to the village has pricked someone's conscience.'

His expression turned thoughtful. 'I hadn't considered that.'

Issy rested her head back against the wall with a sigh. 'I've been going over and over it and it's the only thing that makes sense. If whoever it is was simply making mischief they could've kept quiet about it.' She paused for a minute as she tried to find the right words to express what she was thinking. 'It almost feels like someone is trying to make amends, don't you think?'

'In what way?'

'By sending me the chest and you the key, it's almost like they were trying to bring us together.'

Liam shook his head. 'I don't know. It seems a bit random, especially when they didn't give us any clues. How were they to know we'd even found out what the other person had received?'

Okay, maybe her theory had a flaw or two in it. She tucked her feet up on the bench and rested her chin on her knees as she continued to ponder the strangeness of the whole thing. 'What we do know is that whoever it is must know us well enough to have wanted to break us up in the first place.'

'Hmm, that's true.' The corner of his mouth quirked up. 'You seem to be on a roll, Sherlock, let's see if you can figure the rest out.'

Issy poked her tongue out at him. 'So, therefore, they know how closely we're connected through family and friends. They might not have expected us to link the chest and the key as quickly as we did, perhaps...' She fell silent again as she mulled it over. 'I need to figure out who was in the café yesterday... I wish Kat could remember which table the bag was left under.'

'We could make a list of who came in,' Liam suggested.

'I can try, but the busy times are always a bit of a blur. So many people come in every, or nearly every day, it'd be easy to get confused about who I did or didn't see.' She rubbed her forehead as another thing occurred to her. 'It was a kids' club afternoon as well, that's why I assumed it was one of the children who left it behind.' She sat up straighter. 'I'll have a list in the café of the people who had lunches pre-ordered, but most of them are in and out. And I can rule out the regulars like Betty and Ray who come in for a bit of company.' She sat up straight, feet thudding to the floor. 'Ray didn't come in today.'

Liam frowned. 'We're not talking about today, though; the chest was left yesterday.'

'You don't understand. He comes in every afternoon at three-fifteen. I can practically set my watch by him, but I didn't see him today.' He'd definitely been out of sorts recently. 'I hope he's okay. He was telling me the other day he'd hurt his leg, but he promised it wasn't anything serious.'

'Maybe he didn't come in because he's got something to hide.' Liam's brows drew together. 'You said yourself you thought the chest and key might be from someone with a guilty conscience.'

Incredulous, Issy looked up at Liam. 'You can't be serious.'

'He was the one who wanted me to go away to school.' Liam tapped the little finger on his left hand with his right index finger like he was counting off a list. 'He persuaded Mum and Dad.' He tapped his ring finger next. 'He had contacts at my school because he knew all about how their scholarship scheme worked.' Middle finger tap.

She reached out and closed her hand over his. 'Stop it. I can't believe it's him, he's never been anything other than kind to us.'

Liam turned his hand so they were palm to palm. 'When I bumped into him last week as I was leaving the café he said he wanted to talk to me about something. I assumed it was to have another go about me taking over the hotel, so I brushed him off, but he called out after me and said it was something else.' He shook his head. 'I don't want to think him capable of it, but he has to be up there near the top of the list. I'll speak to him tomorrow.'

Issy was struggling to get her head around it. 'You'll need to tread carefully with him.'

'I'm not going to put him in a headlock and demand answers!' Liam's tone was exasperated.

She linked her fingers between his and squeezed gently. 'I wasn't suggesting for a minute that you would, but you haven't been around to see how much he's declined recently. Ever since his wife passed away, it's like the energy's been slowly draining out of him. If you accuse him of something he hasn't done, I'm worried about what it'll do to him.'

Liam tugged his hand free and shoved to his feet, his entire body practically vibrating with frustration. 'What about what's been done to us?' he demanded. 'Don't you want to know the truth?'

'Of course I do!' Standing, she placed a hand on his chest. 'The one thing I don't want is for us to fall out over this.' Away from the torches on their phones it was hard to read his expression. Reaching up gently, she cupped his cheek. 'We've only just stopped being angry with each other, and I'm not in any hurry to revisit that, are you?'

She felt his flesh curve beneath her fingers and was relieved she'd managed to at least make him smile. 'No, absolutely not.' She lowered her hand but he caught it on the way down and interlaced their fingers again. 'I hope we'll never be angry with each other again.'

He sounded so sincere, it warmed her deep inside. 'That might be taking things a step too far.'

'So, what do you suggest we do?'

She wished she knew. Tugging him by the hand, she led him back towards the bench and they sat down again. He didn't seem inclined to let go of her hand and she wasn't either. There was a comfort in that connection, a rightness that kept her grounded. 'I don't know. Maybe we can hold fire for a couple of days and see if anything else comes to light. If it's not Ray then challenging him with accusations could cause him untold hurt.'

'And if it is him?'

Issy sighed. 'If it is him then perhaps the chest and the key are just the first step. You said yourself he's already tried to talk to you. Maybe he's trying to build up the courage to explain himself.' The more she thought about it the more it made sense. 'He apologised to me the other day for not being able to help me in the same way he helped you.' She closed her eyes as the rest of the conversation came back to her. 'Oh God, he even mentioned that connection to one of the teachers at your school.'

'Still think he didn't have anything to do with it?' Liam's tone said he'd already made up his mind.

Issy had to admit the odds were definitely not in Ray's favour. 'Probably not,' she admitted. 'But I'd prefer to wait and see if he comes to us. Confronting him might make him clam up completely, and then we'll never learn the truth.'

'A couple of days, but no more.' She could tell by Liam's sceptical expression he didn't see the point in waiting, but he seemed calmer, and that was more than enough for now.

'Thank you.'

'So what do we do in the meantime?'

She looked down at their connected hands. His touch was so familiar and reassuring, it was like a piece of her had slotted back into place. She turned his hand palm up and began tracing circles. His skin was different to that of her distant memories – harder and calloused in places. The lines were deeper and she followed one with her thumb to the point where it reached the top of his palm between his index and middle fingers. His life line, maybe, or was it his heart line?

Once upon a time she'd known, but the information was lost to her now. There'd been a summer she and the girls had been obsessed with palmistry after an article in a teen magazine had promised they'd be able to find their true love once they unlocked the secrets of it. She folded his fingers into a gentle fist and tilted it to one side, looking at the creases next to his little finger. Hadn't there been something about them predicting how many children someone would have? There were two on Liam's hand and she quickly closed her own hand and checked it. Two for her. Just as well it was all silly, superstitious nonsense.

'What are you doing?' His voice was patient and amused and when she glanced up he was smiling down at her.

'Nothing.' There was no way she was letting him hop alongside her on that train of thought. 'We were talking about what to do while we wait to see what happens.'

'And what do you suggest?'

'Well it seems like everything with the hotel is starting to fall into place.'

'There's still a long way to go, but I think it's safe to say things are on the right track,' Liam agreed, in that amused and bemused tone. 'Where are you going with this?'

Issy took a deep breath and spoke the truth of what was in her heart. 'You said you wanted to focus on the future.' She swallowed under the sudden intensity of his eyes. 'Our future.'

18

All thoughts of Ray and the letters vanished from Liam's head the instant she spoke those words. 'Are you serious?'

'Yes. I think so.' A little nervous laugh escaped her pretty mouth.

That was good enough for him. 'Where shall we go on our first date? Paris? New York? Rome?' He was joking of course, anything to make her laugh again because each time he heard it another flood of happy memories enveloped him like a warm hug.

His efforts were duly awarded with another bright burst of pure joy and the sound fizzed through his veins like the finest champagne. 'I was thinking more along the lines of dinner in Port Petroc, or a trip to the cinema!'

Liam shook his head. 'What happened to that adventurous spirit of yours? I still remember that map of the world you had on your bedroom wall. It was covered in little pins marking the places you were going to visit.'

'Oh goodness, I haven't thought about that map in a long time!

I don't even know what happened to it. It's probably up in the attic somewhere.'

'Where would you go first?' When she laughed and shook her head, Liam tapped her foot with his. 'Hey, we're just playing hypotheticals here.'

He tried to think back to that map on her bedroom wall. How many times had he stared up at it as they lay side by side on Issy's bed, his arm around her, her head on his shoulder as they talked about their hopes and dreams. Back then, Liam had pictured himself working for his dad in the harbour master's office, or maybe persuading Pa to teach him about boat building. Lots of the usual touristy places had been marked by pushpins – Paris, Rome, Egypt to see the Pyramids, India to visit the Taj Mahal. But there was one place she'd talked about above all, somewhere the complete opposite of sleepy Halfmoon Quay. 'New York,' he guessed.

'I can't believe you remembered that.'

I remember everything. He swallowed the words down. After living in London he wasn't in any hurry to explore another metropolis, but this wasn't about him. 'You had a whole list of things you wanted to do there.'

Issy's smile was wistful as she pulled her knees up and rested her chin on them. 'In my travel journal. I guess that's up in the loft somewhere with the map.'

'You should dig it out sometime.'

Her smile fell. 'What would be the point? I'm tied to the café. Nan does brilliantly for her age, but I couldn't leave her to cope with it on her own.'

'We could go out of season. Shutting for a week wouldn't do any harm.' He didn't know why he was pushing the point, only he hated to see the way Issy had completely given up on something that was once so important to her.

Her snort was soft but dismissive. 'Maybe not if you're earning big money, but I don't have that kind of cash to chuck away on a holiday.' She dropped her feet to the floor with a sigh. 'Look, I'm not living hand to mouth, but the savings I have are tucked away for a rainy day. I'd probably get through one washed-out summer, maybe two, but after that...'

Liam hadn't factored that into his thinking because in his head the sun shone in Halfmoon Quay all summer long. It was yet more proof of how disconnected he was from the village. 'I haven't picked up an appreciable dip in income going through the last few years of the hotel's accounts.'

'We've been lucky with the weather recently, but there was an awful year not long after we opened when Nan and I weren't sure we'd survive. It's one of the reasons I've worked hard to diversify, make sure I'm focused on the people who live here with things like packed lunches. I've even catered for a few parties.'

'So, in theory, if I was to reopen the kitchen at the hotel, would that cause you a problem?' It was one of the things he and Adam had discussed with Davy. At the moment all the hotel offered was a basic cold breakfast buffet for guests in the small dining room – individual cereal boxes, fresh fruit, toast and toppings and a self-service coffee machine, but that was all.

'Depends what you planned to do, but no I don't think so.' Issy folded her arms, her brows drawing together as she mulled it over. 'The more options we can offer people the better, and besides, you wouldn't be in direct competition with me. I might lose a few people wanting breakfast, but not enough to cause an issue. We could work on some ideas if you like? And I'm sure if you had a chat with Harry he'd have some great suggestions. He might even know of someone looking for work.'

'I don't think I'd be looking at opening up the kitchen at the hotel full time, not at first anyway, but I'd like to make better use of it. Improve the breakfast offering a bit, maybe some bar snacks in the evening.'

'Don't you need a bar for that?'

'Funny you should mention that!' he said with a grin. 'Adam's going to help me sort out a proper structural survey, but Chloe and Anya have come up with a design to completely revamp the reception area. There's a lot of wasted space and we really need to improve access. If we convert the kitchenette next to reception into a bar and knock through into one or two of the adjacent bedrooms we can turn the entire area into a lovely airy space for guests to relax. If I can get the planning permissions sorted, they'll be a terrace out the front for people to sit in the evenings.'

Issy nodded thoughtfully as though she could picture it. 'The view would be spectacular in the evenings, especially if it was enhanced with a cocktail and a few nibbles.'

'Exactly.' He thought about the little seating area in front of the café. 'What about you? Have you considered opening in the evenings?'

She sighed. 'I've thought about it, but I already do such long hours. I did wonder about getting someone else in, but I'm not sure how easy I'd find it to relax.'

Liam laughed. 'You always did like to be in control of things.' He leaned back against the wall. 'Remind me next time you're in the café and I'll show you the plans for the hotel. Who knows, it might spark a bit of inspiration.'

'Inspiration my finances might not be able to live up to!' She said it with a laugh, but he could sense the frustration behind it too.

'Maybe you should have a chat with Adam.'

'The developer who was with you this afternoon?' Issy frowned. 'I'm not sure he'd be interested in something as small as my café.'

'Maybe not, but you won't know if you don't ask him. He's been very helpful to me already and I get the impression he's going to be around a fair bit, so he might even be willing to just act as a sounding board.'

Closing her eyes, Issy shook her head. 'You need to stop filling my head with all these dangerous ideas, Liam.' She was smiling though, and he could tell the cogs were already whirring away in her brain.

Not wanting her to get too distracted, he raised a finger and gently touched her cheek. 'This is fun, hey? Us making plans for the future, just like the old days.'

Her smile was sweet and just a little sad. 'We were only kids back then. We had no idea what we wanted out of life, not really.'

He'd known, and deep down he was sure Issy had known too. 'Remember the day you promised to marry me?'

Her shocked burst of laughter echoed around the shelter. 'We were five years old!'

'A promise is still a promise,' he said in the most solemn voice he could manage. 'I gave you a ring and everything.'

'It was a plastic one out of the bubble gum machine outside the newsagents and the flower snapped off the top after a week.'

'I'll get you another one.'

'Last of the big spenders.'

'I didn't mean from the machine.'

Issy's eyes widened. 'We are *not* getting married, Liam Penrose. We've barely even spoken to each other for fifteen years, never mind anything else.'

'I didn't mean tomorrow.' Though his heart was so full right then, if she'd wanted to do something crazy like jump in the car and drive to Gretna Green, he might just be up for it.

'We don't even know each other.'

'Your favourite food is pasta, your favourite colour is green, you love those old eighties movies you used to watch with your mum.'

She shook her head. 'That's the girl I used to be, not the woman I am now.' Her voice was gentle as if she was trying to let him down nicely. 'None of those things apply any more.'

He reached for her hand. 'So you can teach me all your new favourite things.'

'You make it all sound so easy.'

'Why shouldn't it be?' Releasing her hand, he picked up his phone and selected a track that had always been at the top of his playlist even throughout all the years they'd been apart. The first delicate piano chords of Elton John's 'Your Song' filled the air. He'd been obsessed with the Ellie Goulding cover version after he and Issy had slow danced together at a school disco, and he'd played it endlessly. His dad had heard it one day when he'd been passing Liam's room and stopped when he'd recognised the lyrics. With a laugh, he'd told Liam he needed to introduce him to the original. Liam had played it for Issy and from then on 'Your Song' had become their song.

He stood and offered her his hand. 'Dance with me?'

She stared up at him for a long moment. 'God, Liam, what are you doing to me?'

'Anything you want me to. Tell me how to make you happy, Issy, and I'll spend the rest of my life trying to make it come true.'

'Dangerous, dangerous man.' She rose and closed the short distance between them, her soft body curving against his in ways it had never done when they were a pair of shy, fumbling teenagers. He closed his eyes, his arms going around her as her hands found their way to the base of his spine and they held each other, swaying gently in time to the music.

It was like coming home, and yet so much more.

His heart beat so hard in his chest he could feel the pulse of his blood throbbing in his ears. 'Can I kiss you?'

'Please.' They both moved so quickly they bumped noses and by the time their lips made contact they were both laughing softly at the momentary embarrassment of it.

He took her laughter into his mouth, breathed it in, breathed her in until she filled all the cold and lonely places deep inside. It didn't take long to find an old familiar rhythm of mouths and tongues, nor to shift right past that into a richer, deeper motion as the delicious taste of her stoked a primal hunger. In a fit of super-human willpower, Liam broke the kiss and gasped for air. 'We need to stop before I drag you into those dunes.'

Her soft, husky laugh was almost enough to undo his good intentions and he buried his face in the side of her neck to prevent himself from seeking out the tempting sweetness of her mouth again. 'I don't remember it being like that,' she said, her fingers still playing with his hair.

'I'm trying to be good here, Is,' he grumbled against her neck.

She laughed again. 'How's that working out for you?'

'Let me show you.' He found the jumping beat of her pulse, pressed a kiss to it, then another before following the slender column of her neck with his lips until he located the spot just beneath her ear that had always made her squirm. When she gasped his name and arched her body into his, Liam felt a ridiculous amount of satisfaction.

'Dangerous,' she murmured, her voice languid and dreamy, but she made no effort to move away, so Liam didn't see any reason to stop what he was doing. Issy, it seemed, had other ideas as she pressed her hands against his chest. 'We really should think about getting back. I told Kat I'd only be an hour.'

He knew she was right, but he wasn't ready to let her go. Not now, maybe not ever. 'Five more minutes,' he murmured as he ducked his head to press a kiss against her racing pulse.

She tugged at the curls in his hair, not hard enough to hurt but enough to make him raise his head. 'And what'll be after that? Another five minutes?'

Five minutes or an hour, it was never going to be enough. He raised his hand and cupped her cheek. 'There isn't enough time in the world for all the things I want to do with you, Isabel Kernow.'

19

'No, she didn't say where she was going, only that she'd be back in an hour and that was nearly two and a half hours ago.' There was no mistaking the worry in Kat's voice as Issy let herself in through the front door. She'd hoped to slip past to her room unnoticed but there was no way that was going to happen, so she'd have to brazen it out.

'Sorry,' she said in her brightest voice as she closed the door and began to unzip her coat, the movement dumping what looked like half the bloody beach on the doormat. Damn Liam and his persuasive kisses. She struggled out of her coat and yanked open the cupboard door to hang it up. 'I must've lost track of time.' Issy made the mistake of glancing at the mirror hanging on the back of the cupboard door and winced at the state of her reflection. Her black hair was a soggy, dishevelled mess, and as she reached out to remove a piece of grass what looked like the other half of the beach tumbled out of the knotted strands, leaving a telltale scattering of golden-white across the front of her black top.

Five more minutes, my arse.

When she got hold of Liam again... Her mind fritzed into

images of exactly what she might do next time she got hold of him and her cheeks flamed. Unable to meet her own reflection while thinking those kind of things, Issy slammed the door shut and bent over to tug at the laces of her boots.

'Oh, thank goodness you're back, I was worried. She's back.' The last was directed at the phone in Kat's hand as she jumped up from the sofa and hurried over.

'So I hear.' Chloe's dry tone was unmistakable. 'If the drama's over then I'm going to finish running my bath.'

'What happened to you?' Kat gasped as she took in the state of Issy. 'You look like you've been dragged backwards through a sand dune.'

Not quite, but close enough. 'We were walking back from the cliff path and I, uh, I lost my footing in the dark. Don't worry, I'm fine. I need to have a quick shower, though.' She edged towards the bathroom but Chloe's voice stopped her.

'Not so fast! Kat said you went to meet Liam. What happened? Let me look at you!'

The glare Issy shot at Kat at least earned her an apologetic shrug as she offered Issy the phone. With a sigh she raised the screen and looked at Chloe. 'Nothing happened, I'm fine.'

Chloe's eyes widened and then she began to laugh. '"Nothing happened," she says with a face covered in stubble rash! You must've fallen right into Liam's face when you "lost your footing".' Her friend crooked her fingers like speech marks as she said that.

Issy bared her teeth. 'I don't know what you're talking about. I need to take a shower.' She thrust the phone at Kat and hurried to the bathroom.

There was only so long she could hide in there even after washing her hair twice and combing through her best condi-tioner to get all the knots out. Yes, and applying what claimed to be a skin-soothing face mask while she was at it. She finally exited the bathroom ready to make the two-step dash to her bedroom only to find Kat busy with the hoover.

'Just picking up the sand.'

Feeling her cheeks flame once more, Issy nodded and ducked into her bedroom. Ten minutes later her hair was towel-dried and fixed up on her head in a loose bun and she'd put her pyjamas on. With her clothes bundled as best as she could to try and avoid dropping any more sand, she emerged to find a grinning Chloe sitting next to a sheepish-looking Kat. 'You didn't think you were getting away with it that easily, did you?'

Issy considered retreating into her room and locking the door before submitting to the inevitable with a sigh. 'I hope you at least brought some wine with you,' she grumbled as she stomped across to the kitchen and shoved her clothes in the washing machine.

'When have I ever shown up empty handed?' Chloe called out, her obvious amusement at the situation clear in her voice.

It was late by the time Issy had managed to satisfy both Kat and Chloe's curiosity. Though Chloe had protested she was fine walking home, they persuaded her to sleep on the sofa. Issy was woken the next morning by a tap on her bedroom door. She sat up and immediately regretted the swimmy feeling in her head. Two bottles on a school night was a very bad idea, especially when all she'd eaten was crisps raided from the cupboard. The door creaked open and Chloe peeked around it. 'Morning,' she whispered. 'I just wanted to let you know I'm heading home for a shower before work.'

'You can come in,' Issy said as she shifted her legs to the side to make room on the bed for Chloe to sit down.

'Just for a sec, then, because I really need to get going.' Chloe sat and tucked one knee up to rest her chin on it. 'I'm sorry I barged in like that last night. All this stuff with Liam must be a bit confusing for you.'

Issy rested her head against her pillows and sighed. 'It's all just so unexpected and I think we both got a bit carried away in the moment.'

'Morning-after regrets?' Chloe's expression was nothing but sympathetic understanding.

'No, nothing like that!' She and Liam hadn't gone much further than kissing, and even if they had, she wouldn't have regretted it. The attraction that had always been there between them had rocketed to heights she'd never dreamed possible now they were adult enough to understand what was happening between them. 'It's scary how quickly I'm finding myself falling for him again.' Scary, but exciting too. He was like an addiction she'd thought she'd quit long ago, but a few kisses and she was craving him. 'Do you think we're making a big mistake?'

Chloe shook her head. 'I think the two of you are finally getting a chance at the happiness you've always deserved. I know he's been away a long time, but deep down Liam's the same person he's always been. I know I'm a bit biased, but we make them good in the Penrose family.'

Issy grinned as she held out her hand to her friend. 'And you're the best of the lot.'

Chloe laced their fingers together. 'So I'm forgiven for barging in last night?'

'Of course. And you know there's no way I would've kept any of this to myself for long.' She squeezed Chloe's hand. 'I'm relying on you to stop me from doing something stupid. Liam's got me turned upside down and all around, so I need you to be honest with me if you think there's any danger I'm going to make a fool of myself.'

'I promise. And look, don't let what I think influence you. If you start down this path with Liam and find out it's not what you want after all, don't be afraid to say something. He might be my family, but you'll always have my unwavering support. Friends first.' She twisted her hand so their pinkie fingers were linked together.

'Friends forever,' Issy finished their childhood pledge.

'Damn straight!' With a grin, Chloe leaned forward and pecked a kiss on her cheek. 'I've got to run. Message me later, okay?'

'Okay.'

After Chloe closed the door behind her, Issy sank back against her pillows. Though she knew deep down she could rely on her friend – on all three of them – through thick and thin, it was still a relief to have heard her say it.

Making plans with Liam last night had been wonderful, but there was a tiny cloud on the horizon that whispered she should be careful. She knew better than most how quickly things could change, how easily happiness could be stolen away. It would be simple enough to back away now. Let Liam down gently and tell him they'd got a bit carried away. It would certainly be the safest option.

But Issy had spent too many years guarding her heart from any more hurt. She wanted to be happy, to have all the things everyone else enjoyed. A partner to share the joys and burdens of life with. Someone to love and be loved by. Maybe even someone she could build a new family of her own with one day. *Dangerous thoughts*, the little cloud of doubt whispered.

Maybe so. But wonderful thoughts. Exciting, exhilarating thoughts.

20

The café was ticking over nicely with people out and about making up for being kept in by the rain the day before. The weekly craft club were settled on comfy chairs in the Hub, their knitting, cross-stitch and crochet projects taking second place to the opportunity for a natter and a catch-up. Maud was there, needles flashing almost as quickly as her mouth as she gossiped with her friends.

The door opened and Issy hurried over to help Shelly Dean wrestle her double-buggy over the threshold. They'd known each other since school, though hadn't always been close. Things were improving on that front since Anya had moved to the village, as Shelley's eldest was the same age as Freya and they'd both recently started at the local school. 'What can I get you?' Issy asked once Shelly was settled at a table.

'The largest, strongest coffee you've got please. These two had me up half the night.' She nodded to the two sleeping children in the buggy.

With their golden heads tilted towards each other they looked like a pair of sweet angels. Issy knew what they could be like when they were awake though. 'They look completely zonked out,' she said, making sure to keep her voice down.

'Let's hope they stay that way for a few minutes,' Shelly replied, raising her crossed fingers. She looked absolutely knackered and her hair had that slightly dull tinge that said it was a day past needing a wash. With three small children to wrangle and her husband, Jason, working away for long stretches of time due to lack of work for him locally, Issy wasn't surprised if Shelly was struggling to make a bit of time for herself.

'I'll be right back with your coffee. Do you need something to eat?'

Shelley wrinkled her nose. 'I'm starving, but it's too early for cake.'

Issy wasn't sure it was ever too early for cake, but she knew what Shelley meant. 'Toast, then, or a bit of cereal?'

'Toast would be great. I don't suppose you've got any Marmite?'

'I keep some in the back for weirdos like you,' Issy teased with a grin. 'Give me a couple of minutes and I'll have you sorted.'

She was as good as her word and soon Shelly was wolfing down toast like she hadn't eaten in a month. Thinking she might pop another couple of slices in just in case, Issy did a quick circuit of the café to check everyone was okay. When she stopped by the crafters, Maud leaned over and gave her a hug around the waist. 'Everything all right, lovely?'

'Yes thanks, Nan. How about you ladies? Another pot of tea?'

'Keep it coming!' Amy Penrose said, smiling up at Issy over her crochet.

'Yes, ma'am.' Issy nodded at the pretty primrose yellow yarn on Amy's lap. 'What are you making?'

Amy held up a square of neat, even stitches. 'It's a cardigan for our Freya. She's growing so fast it's hard for Anya to keep her in anything that fits for more than five minutes.'

Our Freya. Issy loved the way Amy said it with such posses-siveness. She and Ron had been a wonderful help to Anya since she'd moved to the Quay. They babysat for Freya several times a week, and had embraced the little girl from day one. 'It's very pretty, I'm sure she'll love it.'

'Oh look,' Maud said, nodding towards the window. 'Here comes your Liam!'

Issy spun around to face her nan. *How on earth did she know?* Thankfully, before she could make an utter fool of herself, the bell above the door rang and Amy had set aside her crochet to wave towards her grandson. 'Hello, darling!'

Grinning broadly, Liam paused only long enough to dump his messenger bag on what had become his usual table by the window then strode over to envelop Amy in a massive bear hug. 'Hello, Ma! You're looking beautiful as ever.'

'Such a charmer.' Amy patted his cheek, smiling up at him fondly. 'What are you up to, today?'

Still smiling, Liam released her and stepped back so he was standing next to Issy. 'Working on plans for the hotel.'

Eyes bright with interest, Maud gave him a studying look. 'How's it going?'

Liam nodded. 'Really well, thanks.'

'You're going to take it over then?' one of the other women in the group asked, leaning forward, eager to catch the latest gossip.

Liam's expression shuttered immediately, but before he could say anything, Amy turned on her friend and wagged a finger right under her nose. 'Leave the boy alone, Beryl, and mind your business.'

Beryl shifted her shoulders like a ruffled hen settling back on its nest. 'I was only asking, and I'm not the only one who wants to know.'

'Well you can tell them to keep their beaks out and all. This is Penrose business.'

Beryl tutted but didn't say any more.

Apparently satisfied she'd made her point, Amy turned back to Liam. 'Now then, when are you going to come and visit me and Pa? I've hardly seen you since you got back.'

'I'll go and fetch that pot of tea,' Issy said, suddenly conscious of how long she'd been standing there gawking.

Liam turned and smiled down at her. 'Will you grab me a cappuccino while you're at it?' He gave her a ghost of a wink and managed to brush his hand against hers as he turned back to speak to his grandmother.

'Of course,' Issy managed to say as her fingers closed around whatever it was Liam had pressed into her palm. Thankfully everyone's attention was fixed on Liam and they hadn't noticed the sneaky handoff. As Issy turned away, Maud caught her eye, deliberately looked down at Issy's clenched fist then turned back to her group with a secretive smile on her face. Oh dear.

Issy hurried back behind the counter and only once her back was turned did she dare uncurl her fingers and look down. Lying across the centre of her palm was a rainbow striped lollipop, one of the sickly sweet ones they kept in a jar on the counter of the hotel. It was such a silly thing, yet Issy's heart did something funny in her chest.

Rainbow, bring my granddaughter a love to last a lifetime. Maud's words drifted into her mind and Issy clenched her fingers tightly over the lolly before slipping it into the pocket of her apron for safekeeping. If she wasn't careful, she was going to find herself in big trouble. Rather than be worried, Issy found herself looking forward to it.

Liam Penrose was the best kind of trouble.

21

Liam escaped his grandmother after promising to have lunch with her and Pa in the next couple of weeks and had just finished unpacking his laptop when Issy stopped at his table with his requested cappuccino and a slice of the lemon and ginger Battenberg. 'I don't remember asking for that,' he said with a smile.

'I can take it away if you want?' Issy reached for the plate and he quickly snatched it up out of her reach.

'No, no, I'll keep it, thanks.' Their eyes met and he couldn't stop thinking about how soft and warm and perfect she'd felt against him as they'd cuddled in the dark amongst the dunes. Leaning closer, he lowered his voice. 'Can I take you out on Friday?'

'Depends where you're planning on taking me. It took me forever to wash the sand out of my hair last night.'

'That's not a no.'

Her lips quirked. 'Find somewhere nice to take me and I'll consider it.'

'Challenge accepted.'

He watched her walk away, marvelling at how perfectly her

bottom rounded out her jeans. His fingers itched in remembrance of how fantastically her curves had filled his hands, like her entire body had been shaped to fit them. It had kept him awake half the night and when he had finally managed to close his eyes, the dreams he'd had were little short of spectacular. And if he played his cards right he might just get the chance to make one or two of them come true.

Somewhere nice.

Mild panic hit as he realised that he had no idea where to take Issy. Other than the odd night out to the pub, the only other place he'd been recently was his brother's restaurant. Digging out his phone, he fired off a quick text to Harry.

> Any chance of a table for two Friday night?

The reply came back a few moments later.

> Are you taking the piss? We're booked up every weekend for the rest of the year.

Damn, he should've thought of that. Russ Armstrong had such an amazing reputation, he knew friends back in London who'd driven down specifically to eat at his restaurant. Foolish of Liam to think he could walk in last minute. The dots on the screen danced and then another message popped up.

> Hold on. Table for two? You and???

Liam sighed. There was no point in being coy about it. If Issy hadn't said anything to Chloe or her other friends yet it surely wouldn't be long, and once Chloe found out it'd be round the rest of family like wildfire.

> Issy.

Harry's response was a GIF video clip of a man staring wide eyed as he shoved popcorn into his mouth, which made Liam laugh.

> Shut up. Any recs on alternative places I can take her?

It didn't take long for Harry to reply.

> Oh no, you are not going ANYWHERE else. I'll see you BOTH at 7.15 on Friday

The GIF that followed was a man staring through binoculars and waggling his tongue in a frankly disgusting manner. Liam was already regretting asking, but it was too late to back out now. He tapped on the GIF option and typed Eww in the search bar, sending the first three that popped up to Harry. All he got back was a row of laugh-crying emojis. Shaking his head, Liam put his phone away and pulled his laptop closer.

He was busy making a list of the final couple of things he wanted to chat through with Davy when Issy stopped next to his table to collect his empty plate and cup. 'Do you want something else?'

'No, I'm fine thanks. Oh, we're all sorted for Friday night. I'll call for you just after seven if that's okay?'

She raised her eyebrows in amusement. 'That was quick, but I'm expecting more than a pint and a pickled egg at the Smuggler's, you know.'

Christ, he couldn't think of anything worse. 'It's somewhere special, I promise.'

'So I should wear something nice, then?'

He grinned up at her. 'You look lovely in everything.'

'Ha! Ma wasn't kidding about you being full of charm. I'll see you Friday, Casanova.'

* * *

It was too much to hope he'd be able to sneak out of the house unnoticed on Friday night, though Liam gave it his best shot. He was about two steps from escaping out the front door when his mother called out from the kitchen, 'Is that you, Liam, love?'

Busted, he had no choice but to divert in that direction. He poked his head around the door. 'I'm off out for the evening, don't wait up.'

'Come in here and let me have a look at you,' his mum insisted. With a sigh, he stepped fully into view. 'Oh, darling, you look so smart. I can't remember the last time I saw you in a suit. Going somewhere special, then?'

'Leave the poor lad alone, Rach,' his dad said, rolling his eyes as he grinned at Liam. 'He's nearly thirty, not thirteen.'

'I was just saying he looks nice, is all,' his mum said, sounding all huffy. 'I wasn't prying.'

'Course you weren't, love.' Jago leaned over and put his arm around Rachel's shoulders and kissed her cheek. 'With Liam going out wherever he is and Rick over at Anya's, you realise we've got the place to ourselves tonight?' He waggled his eyebrows in a suggestive manner that Liam feared he'd never be able to unsee. He loved how much his parents still clearly loved each other, but he preferred to think about it in the abstract.

'Behave yourself.' Laughing, Rachel pushed Jago's face away, but Liam didn't miss the way her hand lingered on his father's cheek.

'And that's my cue to leave. I've got my key.'

'Okay, son. Have a good night,' his father said, though his eyes were only for his wife.

Definitely time to leave. He got halfway out the door when his mother called him back. 'About your birthday next week: I thought we'd have a bit of a get-together.'

'Oh, there's no need for that, Mum.'

Rachel's face fell. 'Well, if you'd rather not bother, I just thought it would be nice to celebrate, seeing how long it's been since we were able to share your special day with you.'

Damn, there was no guilt guaranteed to strike harder than rejecting a mum trying to do something nice, was there? 'Sorry, Mum. I only meant you didn't need to go to any trouble, but if you want to have a few drinks or something, that'd be really nice.'

She brightened instantly. 'Great! I'll text Helen now.'

Jago sighed and got up from the table. 'There go my plans for the evening.'

Liam raised his hands in a don't-blame-me-I-tried gesture and beat a hasty retreat before his mum could rope him in any further.

It was dead on seven when he pressed the intercom button for Issy's flat. 'She'll be a couple of minutes,' Kat's voice echoed through the speaker.

'No rush,' Liam replied. 'I'll be waiting by the sea wall when she's ready.'

He circled around to the front of the café and tucked his hands into his trouser pockets as he strolled slowly along the path. There were a few people out and about enjoying the evening. Noise and laughter drifted across from a group of people waiting outside the front of the restaurant on the opposite side of the road. Deciding to join the wanderers, Liam strolled along the seafront, trying to see it through fresh eyes. It had its plus points – the immaculately clean beach, the long straight path that led walkers through the village and up to the heights of the dunes, the restaurant, the café, other well-maintained businesses. He paused beneath the folded awning of the newsagents, noted the fresh coat of paint on the external woodwork, the effort to put an eye-catching display in the window. The old gumball machine sat next to the front door and Liam fished out a pound coin from his loose change, popped it in the slot and twisted the handle. A plastic ball rolled down to sit in the collection tray and he picked it up and tucked it away in his pocket before strolling on.

It didn't take long to reach the hotel. A few windows were lit behind the curtains and shades, but it was silent compared to the lively bustle outside the restaurant. The grass out the front was dry and worn in places. It really was a wasted space, without even a flower bed to brighten things up. Squinting, he tried to superimpose the sketch Chloe had included in the most ambitious of the three options she and Anya had produced. In her vision, the scrappy grass had been replaced by a large terrace and the entrance porch had been refurbished and extended to shelter the back of the terrace. Colourful parasols provided shade for the tables nearer the front and smiling people had been relaxing at each one with drinks and little bowls of snacks.

It was hard to visualise everything, being so close, so he crossed the road again and rested against the sea wall, letting his eyes rove over the entire edifice of the building. It had so much potential – a bit of loving care and a lot of hard work and it could once more be a highlight of the village.

'There you are!'

Liam turned at the sound of Issy's voice and froze at the arresting sight of her. Her usual uniform of jeans and T-shirt had been replaced by a pair of red wide-legged trousers that shone like they were made of some kind of silky material, and a black vest top with a gold-chain detail on the shoulder straps. The front of the top draped in a way that hinted at rather than showed off her cleavage. Her hair was pinned up on one side with a red flower on a clip. Whatever she'd done with her make up, it made her beautiful eyes even more mesmerising than usual. Liam didn't feel worthy. 'You look incredible.'

She lowered her head a little, a shy smile playing around her lips. 'I wasn't sure how dressy I needed to be. I hope I judged it right.'

'You're perfect.' He'd meant to say she looked perfect, but hey, that was true enough.

Issy glanced around. 'I didn't see a car by the café, did you book a cab?'

Shaking his head, Liam offered her his arm. 'We don't need one. Come on.'

She gave him a puzzled look but allowed him to walk her back in the direction they'd come. 'You were very deep in thought back there,' she said as they strolled side by side.

'Just imagining how the hotel might look this time next year. But I don't want to talk about that now. I want tonight to be special.'

'Well, I guess that depends on where you're taking me,' she said, with a laugh that trailed off when he pointed across the street to Russ Armstrong's restaurant. Her sea-glass eyes were round as saucers when she stared up at him in amazement. 'There's no way you got us a table there. Not at such short notice.'

Feeling thoroughly pleased with himself, Liam grinned down at her. 'Hey, sometimes it pays to have connections.'

She drew her brow down for a second before her face lit up. 'Harry!'

Liam nodded. 'What's the point in having annoying little brothers unless you can exploit them now and again?'

'I'm not going to complain about that if it comes with these kind of perks. I hope you wangled a family discount at the same time, because dinner here has been on my wish list for years and I intend to make the most of this opportunity!' Reaching down with her free hand, Issy plucked at the side of her trousers to extend the waistband. 'Just as well I put on my eating trousers.'

Liam laughed. 'I love a woman with a good appetite.' Honestly, he was starting to remember what it was like to love everything about this woman. It was an exhilarating feeling, like the tremor he always got in his stomach when a roller coaster slowly clanked its way to the top of the first climb. He had a feeling that he was in for the ride of his life, and he was strapped in and ready to go.

22

Issy hardly had a chance to get her head around what Liam had managed to pull off before he was opening the door to the restaurant and Russ Armstrong himself was there to greet them. He was a barrel of a man, not overweight but solidly built like a power-lifter. He was always shorter in person than when she pictured him in her mind, just a couple of inches taller than her, but there was a presence about him, a charisma and confidence that made him seem larger than life. He had a voice to match his build, a booming bass that always held a hint of laughter, like life was one glorious joke and he wanted everyone to be in on it with him. Russ held his arms wide. 'Isabel, Liam, it's a pleasure to welcome you both tonight.'

'Thank you, Russ, it's incredible to be here.' Issy offered him her hand and he took it and pulled her in for a quick hug before releasing her and doing the same to Liam. As they embraced, Issy cast a quick glance around the packed restaurant. There wasn't a table free and she wondered if they'd have to sit at the bar and wait for a space. She wouldn't mind if they did, of course, not when Russ was obviously doing them – or Harry at least – a favour.

'Yes, thanks, Russ, and sorry for the short notice,' Liam said.

'Hey, it was no trouble at all. Anything for family, right?' Russ put an arm around each of their shoulders and steered them through the packed restaurant towards the door marked Staff Only. 'Come on, I've put you through here.'

'Through here' turned out to be a small private room with a single table for two in the middle. A desk had been pushed up against the window and the shelves on the walls were full of ring binders, dozens upon dozens of recipe books and an impressive collection of terrible holiday souvenirs. Issy hesitated at the threshold. 'Is this your office?'

'Not tonight,' Russ replied, with a laugh and a wink. 'Come on now, have a seat and make yourselves at home.'

He walked to the table and pulled out one of the chairs and Issy had no choice but to take it and let him settle her. 'You shouldn't have gone to any trouble,' she protested.

'Ah, it's no trouble at all,' Russ said as he whipped a napkin from the table, shook it out and draped it across her knee. 'Who doesn't love the chance to play Cupid now and again?'

Issy tried to ignore the heat rising on her face as she looked at the table. It was beautifully laid with an immaculate white cloth, spotless silver tableware and a cut-glass crystal bud vase containing a single red rose. 'Thank you.'

Russ offered Liam his own napkin then clapped his hands together and beamed at them. 'No menus tonight, folks, as we've put together a tasting selection for you. I'll give you a few minutes to get settled and then someone will be in to sort out your drinks.'

He left the room and they looked at each other. 'Well, this wasn't quite what I was expecting,' Liam said, shaking his head as he looked around them.

It should've felt weird being surrounded by what were obviously Russ's personal effects, but they added an intimacy to the space, like they'd been given a glimpse behind the scenes. 'You're going to owe Harry for this.'

'He sure is!' Harry swept in, looking every inch the professional in his chef's whites, a black bandanna tied around his head to keep his hair covered and out of the way. 'Issy, you look gorgeous!' He bent down and pecked a kiss on her cheek. 'Far more beautiful than Broomy here deserves.'

'No!' Liam said, pointing a stern finger at his brother. 'You can tell that idiot twin of yours that is not happening, do you hear me?'

Harry pulled a hangdog face. 'Oh, you are such a spoilsport. What's the point in having you back home if we can't take the piss out of you?'

'Don't you have some cooking to do, or something?' Liam did his best to glower at his brother, but there was a telltale twitch of his lips that said he was amused by Harry's antics.

'Indeed I do! I hope you brought your appetites with you.' He turned as a young man entered with a bottle of champagne and two slender glass flutes. 'Ah, perfect timing, Thomas.' He took the bottle and deftly opened it while the young man placed the glasses on the table. Filling one with the pale gold champagne, Harry handed it to Issy. 'There you go.' He filled the second and passed it to Liam. 'Compliments of the house.'

Liam accepted the glass. 'Thank you.' He set it down and offered his hand to Harry. 'Seriously, thank you.'

Harry shook hands. 'It's my pleasure, bro. It's just so good to have you home. Right, I shall leave you love birds to it. First course will be with you soon.'

Issy watched Liam as his gaze followed his brother out of the room. 'They're really happy to have you back.'

Liam's expression was a little misty as he turned his attention back to her and smiled. 'Yeah. It's funny, you know, all the time I was away I was only focused on how much I was missing everyone; I never really thought about anyone missing me in return.'

'You were missed.' Issy reached across the table and held out her hand to him. 'I missed you, Liam.'

He clasped her fingers and squeezed them tight for a second. 'I missed you too. More than I have words for.' He released her hand and reached for his champagne. 'To you, Issy. I'm still not sure how this happened, but there's nowhere in the world I'd rather be right now than here with you.'

She raised her glass, her hand a little shaky as she tried to work out how things had changed so quickly. 'To us.'

The food kept coming, each dish accompanied by a complementary wine, though Issy preferred to stick with her champagne. Every course was somehow more delicious than the last. In between bites they talked about anything and everything. Though he was reluctant to at first, she persuaded him to talk about his life in London, including his time with Caro. 'Are you sure you want to know?'

'Yes, because it's a part of who you are. I know my old Liam and I want to connect those memories to who you are now. I'm not a child any more to be jealous of you being with somebody else. She was a big part of your life that I know nothing about and I'm curious.'

He pushed his chair back slightly, turning it sideways to make room to stretch out his long legs to the side. He toyed with the wine in his glass for a moment, swirling the ruby red liquid as he seemed to gather his thoughts. 'She wasn't like anyone I'd ever met before. I mean, she was a lot like the boys I was at school with in terms of her background, but she wasn't stuck up like them.

She just seemed to carry this confidence with her, like she was so sure of her place in the world. I think that's what attracted me to her more than anything. I'd been adrift for so long and she was an anchor point. I didn't know who I was at that stage, or at least I didn't know who I wanted to be, so it was nice to be around people who seemed to have it all figured out.'

She'd always wondered what he'd seen in Caro, beyond the woman's obvious attractiveness. Issy had been aware of her, of course, on the few occasions the pair of them had come to visit Liam's family, but what bit she did know of her had been second-hand opinion from Chloe, who hadn't been impressed at all. It made more sense now, hearing him talk about her. 'You had a good time together?'

Liam's smile was fond. 'We did. She exposed me to a lot of things I never would've explored on my own. Films, music, live theatre.' He laughed. 'Before her, the only time I'd been to the theatre was when Ma and Pa took us to the pantomime one year.'

'You won't get much of that back here,' Issy said with a grin. 'The best we have to offer is the summer shows at Port Petroc and the odd tribute band in the pub.'

Perhaps that was something they could think about changing in the future. 'I've been thinking all day about how I can improve things at the café. I don't want to commit to opening regularly in the evenings, but maybe I could trial slightly different hours during the quieter months. Close a couple of afternoons and open in the evening instead.'

Liam leaned forward, expression open and interested. 'Sounds good. What would you do?'

Issy shrugged. 'A bistro night, maybe? I could offer a set menu and accept pre-bookings only, so I'd know in advance how many covers.' It would keep the costs down and avoid wastage. She gestured at the beautifully laid table between them. 'It's amazing what something as simple as a tablecloth can do. I'd have to speak to the council, apply for an alcohol licence—' She cut herself off with a laugh. 'Sorry, I'm talking shop when we're supposed to be out on a date.'

'No, no, this is great! There's all sorts of things like that we could do that wouldn't break the bank. A cheese and wine-tasting evening could be fun. I reckon Mum and Dad would be up for something like that.'

Excitement bubbled inside her as the possibilities raced through her mind. 'I could speak to Gio and Angie at the deli about supplying it.'

'Brilliant!' Picking up his chair and his drink, Liam carried them around to her side of the table. Sitting down beside her, he pulled out his phone and opened the notes app. 'Let's start making a list.'

They put their heads together and it didn't take long before their conversation branched away from the café towards a more general list of the things they currently had to travel outside the village to do. Some immediately went on a can-do list, while others verged on the outrageously ambitious, like hosting a literary festival weekend. Though she'd only drunk one glass of champagne, her head was spinning like she'd downed the bottle. 'It'll take us years to get through all these ideas!'

Liam glanced up from the list, his smiling face just a few inches from hers. 'We've got time.' His smile softened and his eyes darkened as the pupils expanded. 'We've got all the time in the world.'

Like she'd developed a magnetic attraction to him, Issy found herself moving forwards to close the small gap and their lips touched. *Who needed champagne when one brush of his lips could make her feel like this?*

'Are you ready for desser—oh sorry!'

They broke apart and turned to find poor Thomas standing in the doorway, holding two glass plates filled with tempting little bites of pudding.

'It's fine.' Liam jumped up, grabbed the back of his chair and returned it to the other side of the table. 'Please, come in.' He gave Issy a look that promised they would pick things up later before returning to his seat.

'Umm, okay.' Face still blazing like it was on fire, Thomas hurried over and set the plates down in front of them. He stepped back, took a deep breath and began to babble. 'Chef Armstrong specialises in classic desserts and familiar favourites with a twist of sophistication. There's a lemon posset with freeze-dried raspberry dust, a Belgian chocolate cheesecake with sour cherries and amaretto cream, and an apple and juniper berry miniature crumble with crème anglaise.'

The poor boy looked mortified and Issy bit the inside of her cheek to stop herself from giggling at his obvious discomfort. 'Thank you, Thomas, this all looks wonderful.'

'Do you need anything else?'

'No, Thomas, this is perfect, thank you,' Liam said, also clearly amused at the lad's plight.

'Okay, well, please enjoy your desserts.' Thomas didn't quite flee the room, but it was close.

'Oh dear, I hope we haven't scarred him for life,' Issy said, letting out the laugh she'd been holding in.

'He'll get over it.' Liam picked up his fork and spoon. 'I'm not sure where to start.'

Issy shrugged. 'Me neither, and honestly, as amazing as this looks, I'm not sure I'll manage to eat it all.'

'I thought you'd put your eating trousers on,' he teased her.

It was true the silk palazzo pants had a generous elasticated waistline, but she was testing them to the limit. 'I don't think it's the trousers,' she said with a laugh.

She did better than she'd expected, leaving only half the crumble because she literally couldn't put another forkful into her mouth. 'That was so good.' She pushed her plate away with a sigh and sank back against her chair.

'You're not leaving that bit, are you?' Liam was eyeing her plate, fork raised.

'If you can finish it, then help yourself!'

Liam scooped up the crumble and wolfed it down like he could eat the whole thing again. It was only when he laid his fork down and slumped back in his own chair that she realised he was just as full as she was.

'I might not eat again until next week,' she said, shifting in her seat to try and find a comfortable position.

'Are you okay?'

'I don't know.' She laughed. 'I'm fine, really. It was unbelievably good, I'm just so full.'

'Not too full, I hope,' Liam said as he shifted onto one hip and pulled something out of his pocket and offered it to her in a closed fist.

She shook her head. 'If it's a lolly from that damn jar on the hotel reception desk, I think I might be sick.'

'It's not that,' he assured her with a smile. 'Take it.'

With a sigh, she held out her hand and he turned his over and opened his fist. A plastic container she recognised dropped into her palm and she laughed. 'Bubble gum? That's even worse than a lolly!'

He shook his head. 'Forget the gum and open it; who knows what it might contain. Could be a ring, again.'

Her heart suddenly fluttered beneath her ribcage and it took her a couple of goes to prise the edges of the plastic ball apart. Nestled beside a bright red gumball was a little plastic hair slide with a yellow butterfly on it. She wasn't sure to be relieved or disappointed as she took it out and clipped it into her hair.

'Ah well, there's always the next time,' Liam said with a grin. 'It looks cute on you, though.'

Issy was still trying to figure out if Liam was joking or not when Russ came in. 'Everything okay?'

'I ate too much,' Issy said with a laugh. 'It was impossible not to.'

Russ grinned. 'That's music to my ears. I'll get someone to clear your plates, and then we'll sort you out some coffee.'

Liam set his napkin aside and stood. 'I think we might skip coffee, if you don't mind.'

'Not in the least, but there's no need to rush off. Take your time and relax.'

Issy pushed her chair back and Russ was there in an instant to hold it as she stood. 'Oh, that's better.' She rested a hand on her stomach. 'I hope you don't think we're being rude or ungrateful if we leave, but I really could do with some fresh air.'

Russ settled his hands on her shoulders and gave them a gentle squeeze. 'Not at all, my dear. I'm delighted you enjoyed everything.'

She raised a hand to pat one of his, smiling up at him over her shoulder. 'It was perfect, honestly.'

'Wonderful.' Russ stepped back and ushered them out into the main part of the restaurant.

Harry joined them while Liam was settling the bill. 'All good?'

'Fantastic, thank you.' Issy leaned up and kissed his cheek. 'Thank you for giving us such a special night.'

Harry grinned and he looked like the sweet little boy she

remembered, not the gruff, slightly cynical man he'd grown into. 'Anything for you, Issy.'

'Hey.' Liam tucked his wallet away and hooked an arm around his brother. 'Stop being charming to my girlfriend.'

'Girlfriend, is it?' Harry raised his eyebrows as he looked between them.

Issy looked up at Liam and something settled inside her. She nodded. 'That's right.'

Liam's grin was wider than the Cheshire Cat's as he tugged Harry into a quick hug and kissed his cheek. 'Thanks, mate.'

Harry squirmed away, but Issy didn't miss the way he reached out to smooth the front of Liam's jacket where it had wrinkled when they'd hugged. 'It's my pleasure.'

They strolled hand in hand along the seafront for a few minutes. The fresh air felt good, but the temperature had dropped and Issy was regretting not bringing a cardigan with her. She shivered and Liam let go of her hand to remove his jacket and drape it over her shoulders. It was like being instantly enveloped in a warm hug, one that smelled deliciously of Liam's aftershave. 'What about you?' she asked as he took her hand again.

'I'll be brave,' he said with a grin. 'And if I get too chilly, I'm sure you'll find a way to warm me up. Come on, let's get you home.'

They lingered in the shadow of the café for what seemed like hours, chatting and laughing and kissing. It was like being a teenager all over again, finding a secret spot to sneak away where no one would catch them. Though Issy knew she'd done the right thing by asking Kat to come and stay with her, she began to regret her altruism as Liam pulled her close and whispered in her ear all the things he wanted to do with her.

'Behave yourself,' she gasped, even as she pulled him closer against her. She could feel the evidence of his obvious desire and it only served to heighten her own.

'I can't,' he groaned against her cheek. 'Let me take you out again soon, Issy. Somewhere away from the village, somewhere we can be together. I'll book us a nice hotel, what do you say?'

'Yes.' She locked her arms around his neck. 'Yes, please, and soon.'

23

Issy was still flying high from Friday night all weekend and into Monday morning. She hadn't seen Liam over the weekend as he'd been back at Matt and Ed's cottage helping them with the refurbishment, but he'd messaged her. A lot. They'd arranged to go for a walk on the beach after she'd finished work and she was counting down the hours.

Nothing bothered her as she went about her day, not the knocked-over cup that sent sticky caramel latte splattering across the front of the display counter and all over the floor. Not the desperately apologetic call from Chloe asking if she could cater for the monthly partners lunch meeting at the solicitor's office because the person who'd been supposed to organise the food had completely forgotten. Not even when a customer put salt in their coffee instead of sugar and then acted like it was Issy's fault.

Chloe rushed in at ten to twelve with her very crestfallen and apologetic colleague in tow. 'I'm so sorry, Issy!' Chloe said for the umpteenth time.

'It's fine, it's fine,' Issy assured her. 'It's all sorted. Let me just grab the stuff from the fridge.'

'You are a miracle worker!' Chloe exclaimed, pecking a quick kiss on Issy's cheek once she was loaded up with clear plastic boxes full of sandwiches, mini quiches and sausage rolls and a selection of cakes and biscuits. 'I'll put these through the dishwasher and drop them back tonight.'

'Don't worry about washing them, I can just stick them in overnight.'

'As long as you're sure? Right, I must dash. Email an invoice and I'll make sure you're paid ASAP. Billy, come on, we haven't got all day!' And with that, the whirlwind of energy that was Chloe whipped out the front door with her hapless colleague once more in tow.

A tall, broad-shouldered man was waiting patiently at the counter and Issy hurried over with an apologetic smile. 'Thank you for waiting, what can I get you?' Now she had the chance to get a proper look at him, she realised who he was. 'Oh, hi Adam!'

A frown creased Adam Mountjoy's brow. 'You seem to have me at a disadvantage.'

Blushing as she realised they hadn't actually been introduced, Issy laughed. 'Oh, sorry. I'm Issy, Liam's friend, girlfriend actually.' It felt strange to say it out loud, but she'd claimed the title on Friday night and it felt right to use it. 'He's been telling me about some of the work you've been doing together on the hotel.'

Adam's expression brightened into something friendly and open. 'Oh, hey! It's great to meet you.' He offered his hand then took it back with a laugh. 'You probably don't want to be shaking hands with anyone when you're handling food all day.'

'Not really, especially with how many times I end up washing them as it is.'

'I get it.' His smile assured he took no offence. He glanced back at the door before turning back to Issy with a speculative expression. 'You do catering as well?'

'When the opportunity arises. Especially now we're out of the main holiday season. Now, what can I get you?'

'Umm, I'll take a slice of that caramel shortbread and a large flat white to go with it, please.'

'Grab a seat and I'll be over in a minute.'

There were no new customers in the time it took to fix his coffee, so Issy remained next to his table, keeping one eye on the door. 'So how are you finding the Quay? Liam mentioned you're spending a bit of time down here visiting your grandfather.' When Adam blinked at her in surprise, she gave him a slightly embarrassed smile. 'Halfmoon Quay is a small town and word travels fast. Sorry, I didn't mean to pry.'

Adam's shoulders relaxed. 'No, it's fine, just takes a bit of getting used to, that's all.'

'Forget I said anything. Enjoy your coffee and give me a shout if you need anything else.'

He held out his hand to stop her. 'No, really. If you're not too busy I wouldn't mind picking your brains a bit about the village and how things work around here. I was going to chat to Liam, but he's been living away for quite a long time and I thought you might have your finger on the pulse.'

'Sure.' Issy slid into the seat opposite him. 'But fair warning, I might want you to return the favour.'

'I'm not sure what there is in my brain that would be of help to you, but fair enough.'

'So, what did you want to ask me about?'

'What's the housing market like here?'

The question took her by surprise. 'I know you're some kind of property developer, but I assumed from your interest in the hotel you dealt with commercial not private.'

Adam shook his head with a laugh. 'Oh no, this is personal not business. I'm staying in an Airbnb place at the moment. It's nice enough but the owner's already indicated they don't want to get locked into a long-term rental arrangement, plus ideally I'd prefer somewhere I can make my own.'

'You're looking to stay in the village?' Issy put an apologetic hand over her mouth and smiled behind it. 'Sorry, there's me going into busybody mode again.'

'It's fine,' he repeated. 'And I'm not looking to relocate here permanently, but with the way things are with my granddad, it could be quite a while. If I have my own place I can set up a proper home office and what-have-you.'

Which all made perfect sense to Issy. 'You'll struggle to get a long-term rental. It's one of the reasons we lose a lot of younger people. Salaries around here aren't what you can earn elsewhere, which makes saving for a deposit nigh on impossible. Even if you can save enough, the external demand for properties puts the cost out of reach.'

'Hmm. So buying somewhere is likely to make me unpopular with the locals, then,' Adam mused.

Issy shook her head. 'Maybe with a few, but Halfmoon Quay prides itself on making people feel welcome. If people didn't want to live here or come on holiday here then the village would die.'

'Sounds like the council needs to sort out some kind of affordable housing scheme.'

Issy scoffed. 'Sure, right, after they find the funds to repair the roads, put a new roof on the school and upgrade the street lighting.'

Adam at least had the good grace to look a little embarrassed as he nodded. 'Of course. There's a lot of pressure on coastal communities, I understand that.'

She wasn't sure he did, wasn't sure anyone did unless they lived with the push–pull reality of needing the tourist industry to survive while paying the price for the damage it did. 'Sorry, I'll climb down off my high horse.'

'No, no, you're right and I don't want the fairy-tale version, I want the unvarnished truth. It's a tightrope to walk for the community.' His expression grew thoughtful, his eyes slightly unfocused as he disappeared off into his thoughts somewhere. Issy was just wondering if she should leave him to it when he spoke again. 'If it's not a priority for the council, perhaps there's a gap in the market for some private investment.'

'I'm sure that's something you'd know more about than me,' she replied with a knowing smile. 'As for buying property, a few things go up on the usual internet sites, but most people stick with the local estate agent.'

Adam sighed. 'Yeah, I had a look in the window but there's nothing suitable.'

'Well, if I hear anything on the grapevine, I'll give you a heads up.' Issy stood. 'The only thing I can think of off the top of my head is the Nicholsons' cottage, but that won't be on the market until after Christmas from what Chloe said.'

'The Nicholsons?'

Issy nodded through the window towards their shop. 'They're planning on retiring at the end of the year and are looking to relocate.'

Adam stared over his shoulder for a long moment. 'So, they'll be looking to sell the shop as well then...'

She laughed. 'You weren't kidding about always being on the lookout for an opportunity! Right, I shall leave you to it for now.'

He smiled at her. 'Thanks for the chat, Issy, I appreciate it. Now, didn't you say you wanted to pick my brains about something?'

'Another time. It sounds like you're going to be around for a while.'

Issy was too busy for the next hour to pay much attention to anyone beyond making sure they were served quickly and the tables stayed clean. Adam Mountjoy was on the phone when she approached his table to collect his empty plate and cup. He looked completely different to how he'd been during their friendly, easy chat earlier. His thick eyebrows were drawn down and his lips were narrowed as he tapped a pen on the table in a rapid, irritated beat. Not wanting to intrude, she caught his eye and pointed at the cup, asking silently if he wanted a refill. His expression brightened for the brief moment it took for him to nod, before the grim set to his mouth returned.

As she walked away she heard him say something that stopped her in her tracks. 'Look, Dad, you might not give a shit about him, but this is important to me, okay?' Issy cast a quick glance around. Though Adam seemed to have forgotten where he was for a moment, no one was sitting close enough to have overheard his angry outburst. Not wanting to encroach on his privacy any more than she already had, Issy hurried off, but not before she caught him saying, 'Well it's just as well I'm too old to need your permission, isn't it?'

The rest of the afternoon followed its usual pattern, apart from one thing. Ray still hadn't made an appearance. Though she'd so wanted to give him the benefit of the doubt, Issy was starting to wonder if what Liam suspected could have possibly been true. As she stood beneath the shower and let the hot water pound away the aches and pains of a day spent on her feet, she considered keeping Ray's disappearing act to herself. Part of her wanted to forget all about the blasted letters, hating the way they hung over her head like a shadow. They couldn't change the past and what did it matter who'd been responsible, because they hadn't succeeded in ruining her and Liam's chance at happiness, only delayed it. As she wrapped a towel around her, Issy caught her reflection in the steamy mirror. It was little more than a blurred outline, but if she'd been able to look herself straight in the eye she'd have recognised the truth. They needed to get to the bottom of everything so they could move past it. If they didn't find out, it would begin to eat away at Liam. At them both.

She'd just finished getting changed when the buzzer sounded and she left her room to find Kat curled up on the sofa. 'I won't be long, not more than an hour.'

'You said that last time,' Kat replied with a knowing grin. 'Try not to get sand in your hair.'

Issy was still laughing when she reached the bottom of the stairs and opened the door to find Liam waiting. 'You're a sight for sore eyes,' he declared as he swept her into his arms and kissed her.

When he finally let her go, she reached up to wipe a smear of her lipstick from the corner of his mouth. 'Well, putting that on was a waste of time.'

With a grin, he turned his head to kiss her palm. 'I can't help it if you're irresistible.' He cast a glance over her shoulder up the shadow of the stairs. 'Kat's home, I take it?'

'She is, so you can get that thought out of your head.' Issy tugged the door closed behind her. 'Come on, I've been stuck inside all day and I could do with some fresh air.'

They had the beach to themselves apart from someone walking their dog off in the distance. Issy watched for a minute as the owner extended their arm and tossed a stick into the shallows and the dog leapt into the sea with an excited bark. He bounced around, chasing the stick through the gently undulating waves before snatching it up in his teeth and splashing back to drop it at his owner's feet.

'Fancy a paddle?' Liam's voice was soft and amused at her ear.

Issy turned away from the idyllic view with a sharp shake of her head. 'No.'

'What's the matter?'

She raised her eyes and met his concerned gaze. 'Nothing, I'm just not in the mood to get my feet wet.'

She tugged his hand to try and lead him in the other direction but he didn't move. 'Issy?'

'I'm just not a fan of the sea, that's all.'

His eyes narrowed in confusion for a second and then he looked at her with such sympathy it made her want to cry. 'I'm sorry, I wasn't thinking.'

Issy let him gather her into his arms, taking comfort in the broad strength of his chest. 'I know it's silly but I haven't been in the water since they died.'

'Oh God, Issy, I had no idea!' Liam hugged her tighter and she clung to him for a long moment as the loss that was never far away swept through her. 'I should've been here,' he murmured against her temple. 'I *would've* been here.'

At the sudden anger in his tone she pulled back and looked up at him. 'No, Liam. There's nothing you could've done.'

Frustration darkened his eyes to wet slate. 'I could've taken care of you, held you and comforted you.'

She cupped his cheek. 'It's enough to know you'd have been there if you could.'

'Is it?' He shook his head. 'Then you're a better person than me, because I'm not sure I could be so generous in your shoes. I let you down, Issy. I let my childish pride get in the way, focused on my own petty hurts instead of putting them aside.' When his eyes met hers, the frustration and anger had been replaced by pain. 'I don't know how you can forgive something like that.'

'Oh, Liam, no.' She flung her arms around him and hugged him close. 'Don't do this to yourself. There's nothing to forgive.'

When he pulled back to look at her, she smiled up at him through tears. 'Please, Liam, let it go.'

His throat bobbed around a hard swallow and the nod of his head carried more than a little reluctance. 'Okay.' He reached up and brushed away a strand of hair that had stuck to the wetness on her cheek. 'I'm going to spend the rest of my life making it up to you.'

She let him gather her against his chest again, and as he held her tight, she looked out over the water. The sun had begun its slow, inexorable journey to the edge of the horizon casting a band of shimmering gold down the centre of the gently rippling blue. It was the kind of image reproduced on the postcards visitors bought by the hundreds. It looked so beautiful that it was hard to remember the danger that lurked there. A shiver ran through her as the old familiar fear inched up her spine. Unlike the grief, which she would always accept because it was the price she paid for having loved her parents, she wished there was a way to be finally rid of it.

It had held her back from so many things over the years, tainted the happiest of memories with its ugly shadow. 'I'm so tired of it.'

Liam pulled back. 'Tired of what?'

'Of being afraid.' She glanced away from him and back towards the water and a sudden determination straightened her spine. 'I want to go paddling.'

Liam shook his head. 'I was only kidding when I suggested it, and besides, the water will probably be freezing.'

'I don't care.' She looked up at him. 'I don't want to let this fear rule my decisions any longer.'

He stared at her for a long moment then sank to his knees in the sand before her. Before she could ask what he was doing, he tapped his thigh. 'Give me your foot.'

Tears prickled her eyes as she raised her right leg and let him guide her foot. As he began to gently unlace her trainer, she gripped his shoulder to keep her balance. In silence he removed her shoes and socks then rolled up the legs of her jeans to mid-calf. Task complete, he straightened enough to kick off his own trainers and in a matter of moments they were standing barefoot in the sand. It was chilly beneath her soles, a warning of what was to come. Before she could let the fear take hold again, she grabbed his hand and tugged him towards the water. She let out a shriek of shock as the first icy wave washed over her toes. 'It's freezing!' she cried, dancing back out of reach.

'It's not that bad.' Liam took a couple of short strides until he was standing ankle deep. Issy shot him a dubious look but she inched closer until the water lapped around her feet. It was still cold, but not as bad now she knew what to expect. Liam held out his hand, his smile full of encouragement. 'Come on, I've got you.'

Even though he hadn't moved, he suddenly felt a long way away. 'I think I'm okay where I am, thanks.'

'One more step.' He wiggled his fingers towards her. 'You're safe with me, I promise.'

Knowing it was true, she gathered her courage and took a step forward, then a second and then his arm was around her waist and the niggling fear faded far enough into the background that she could ignore it. Liam curled his other arm around her and smiled into her eyes. 'I'm so proud of you.'

Bracing a hand on his chest, she reached up and kissed him. 'Thank you for doing this with me.'

'Anytime.'

He kissed her back for a long, lingering moment and she almost managed to forget about the cold until a larger wave washed up her legs and soaked the bottom of her rolled-up jeans. 'Bloody hell!'

Laughing, Liam grabbed her hand and they sprinted out of the water. The sand she'd thought was chilly felt gloriously warm after the frigid water. Liam tugged off the sweatshirt he was wearing and went down on his knees again to rub her ankles and feet dry before doing the same to his own. He tied the damp top around his waist then bent again to gather their shoes. Issy tucked her socks into her trainers then hooked two fingers into the back of the footwear to carry them. Hand in hand they began to stroll along the beach.

It might have only been a couple of steps but it was an important start. She wished she hadn't waited so long to face it. Knew it was time to face something else. 'Ray didn't come in again today.'

Liam nodded as though he'd been expecting it. 'I'll speak to him tomorrow. I'm going to the hotel anyway, so I'll call in on him while I'm there.'

'I really hope we're wrong about this.'

'Me too.'

24

With something of an air of dread the next morning, Liam raised his fist and knocked a couple of times on the door of Ray's room. There was no answer at first and Liam wasn't sure whether to knock again or leave when the door finally opened and Ray greeted him with a single nod. 'Ah, I was wondering how long it would take before you came calling.'

Right up until that moment Liam had nurtured a faint hope he and Issy had made a terrible mistake. 'Why, Ray?'

The older man stepped back, opening the door wider in invitation. 'You'd better come in.'

The room was plain to the point of being austere. The white walls were bare, lacking even the generic floral prints Liam had seen decorating the other bedrooms. The bed was neatly made, the tightly tucked corners reminding Liam of the hours he'd been forced to make his narrow single bed at school until it met whatever impossible standard his housemaster had deemed acceptable. He'd been told it was an exercise in discipline and perseverance; looking back, Liam was convinced it was simply another petty rule that existed for the sake of it. The only concession Ray seemed to have made was a single photograph on the bedside table of him and Denise. They were dressed up for a wedding or some other celebration. Denise was laughing as she looked at the camera while Ray watched her with a fond smile. 'What made you move into the hotel after she died?'

Ray followed Liam's gaze towards the photo. 'I couldn't bear to be in the house surrounded by all her things, all those memories.' He crossed to the cabinet and picked up the photo. 'By the time I was over that first desperate onslaught of grief and anger it was too late to realise they might eventually be a comfort to me.'

Liam hadn't come expecting to feel sorry for the man, but there had to be a middle ground between a house full of love and memories and this... monk's cell. 'Did you ever speak to Davy about decorating or moving in your own furniture?'

'To make it more homely, you mean?' Ray shook his head. 'What would be the point? It wouldn't matter what I did with the place, it could never be a home – not without her.'

Liam's heart ached for the sadness in the other man's tone. 'You must miss her very much.' To have known a love like that and still be capable of tearing apart another relationship full of the same potential simply didn't make sense.

'More than I have the words to express, but you didn't come here to talk about that, did you?'

'No, no I didn't.' Liam raised his head and sent Ray a look of direct challenge. 'You had no right to do what you did.'

He expected push-back or a long string of excuses, so it surprised him when Ray nodded and replied, 'No, I didn't and I owe both you and Isabel an apology for my actions.'

Feeling a little nonplussed, Liam took a step back and leaned one shoulder against the wall. 'That's it?'

Ray sank down on the side of the bed, his usual ramrod stature collapsing, leaving nothing more than a tired old man. He clasped his hands between his spread knees and stared down at the dark blue carpet. 'I didn't think you'd want to listen to me try and justify what I did.'

'There's no justification for what you did, not that I can see, but I would like to understand your thought process at least.'

Ray lifted his head and stared up at him. 'We were concerned about how hard you were finding it to settle in.'

'We?' Liam jumped on the word.

'Charles and I.' When Liam frowned at the unfamiliar name, the corner of Ray's mouth twitched. 'I suppose you'd still think of him as Mr Pritchard.'

Liam's housemaster.

The pieces fell rapidly into place. 'He's the one who intercepted the letters.' It was the only thing that made sense. Anything the boys wanted to send out was placed in a box on Mr Pritchard's desk, and he was the one who dished out the incoming mail every evening after they'd finished their homework and were given free time in the common room before bed.

'Yes, but I want to be clear that it was my idea. I thought that without the constant distraction of Isabel's letters reminding you of what you were missing at home you'd find it easier to adjust to the situation and settle in. I wanted you to succeed, Liam, to enjoy the advantages you'd been afforded.'

'Advantages I'd never asked for.'

Ray glanced down at the floor and then back up. 'You reminded me so much of myself and I simply wanted to help make things easier for you than they were for me.' He gave Liam an almost imperceptible smile. 'I know what it's like to be held back by lack of resources, at home as well as school. Trying to find a bit of peace and quiet in a house full of younger siblings. Being expected to look after them because your parents both worked full time to try and make ends meet.'

'My parents never *expected* me to look after the others, I was happy to do it. They were my little brothers and I loved them.' Liam shook his head. 'You think you know what my life was like, but you didn't have a clue. You projected your own experiences onto me. I was happy at home. Happy with my life and the plans I'd made for the future.'

'What plans? To work for your mother in the chandler's? Or follow in your father's footsteps at the harbour master's office?' For the first time there was a hint of belligerence in Ray's voice.

Liam pushed himself away from the wall and stood straight. 'You need to be very careful about what you say next, Ray...'

Ray's shoulders slumped again. 'I didn't mean to imply disrespect, only that with your natural intelligence and sense of hard work you were capable of achieving much more.'

'But what if I didn't want more? Did you ever stop to consider that?' From the startled look the old man shot him, it was clear he truly hadn't. Liam laughed, but there was no joy in the sound. 'All I ever wanted was to pass my exams, leave school and get a job. You're right that I thought about going to train under my father, or work for Pa at the boatyard like Uncle Ryan had done. I would've been proud to follow in their footsteps in other ways too. Get married, have a family of my own, raise them in a house full of laughter and love.' Liam choked over the last word. He'd lost so much because of one man's misguided ambitions. Almost lost it all.

Ray's eyes were haunted as he stared up at Liam. 'I'm so sorry. I wanted to tell you both earlier, but it was never the right time. You had your exams to focus on, then Issy lost her parents and it felt like too much to put on her. I thought if you came home after you'd finished at school, I'd say something then but you went off to university and then you met that nice girl and I assumed you'd moved on. I told myself it couldn't have been that serious between you and Isabel after all.'

'And eased your conscience in the process.'

'Yes. There was always an excuse not to tell you what I'd done if I looked hard enough for one…' Ray trailed off with a shake of his head as he dropped his gaze to the floor.

He looked broken, a shell of the man who'd opened the door to him earlier. Liam wanted to find it in himself to pity him, but he was too damn angry. 'You almost cost me everything, but Issy's right: I'm not going to waste any more time fretting about the past, not when I've got the brightest of futures possible.'

Liam crossed to the door and yanked it open then paused and glanced back over his shoulder to where Ray was still slumped on the bed like a puppet whose strings had been cut. 'I'm going to be around the hotel a lot for the foreseeable future and I think it would be in both our interests if you found yourself somewhere else to live, Ray.'

The other man nodded but didn't look up. Liam cast one final grim look around the room then left, closing the door softly behind him.

Issy took one look at him when he walked into the café and drew him into the privacy of the kitchen. The moment the door swung shut behind them Liam pulled her into his arms and held onto her like a drowning man clinging to a lifeline. 'I've been worried about you all morning,' she said, her hands stroking his hair, his shoulders, his back.

Letting out a shuddering sigh, Liam pressed his face into her neck and breathed in. She smelled delicious, like sugar and sweet things and everything good in the world. 'You've been baking,' he murmured.

Laughing, she drew back far enough to cup his face. 'I thought you might need something special.' Her expression grew serious. 'Was it awful?'

Liam nodded. 'Yeah. He didn't try and make excuses, just said he was sorry for what he'd done.' A strand of Issy's hair had escaped one of the clips she was wearing and he tucked it behind her ear, his fingers lingering to stroke the soft skin of her neck. 'The worst thing is he genuinely thought he was doing it for the right reasons. He was worried about how hard I was finding it at school and he didn't want me to throw away what he believed was an amazing opportunity.'

'Poor Ray.'

'Poor Ray?' Liam echoed, incredulously. 'How can you feel sorry for him after what he did to us?'

'Because he's obviously been feeling guilty about it. If he thought he'd done nothing wrong he would've tossed those letters out years ago. But he held onto them. Returned them to us so we'd finally know the truth.'

'Too late.'

'No!' Issy cupped his face and forced him to look at her. 'No, Liam, it's not too late. We didn't need the letters to bring us together, we did it ourselves. We found our way back to each other because those feelings we shared never went away.'

Leaning forward, he pressed his forehead against Issy's. 'I can't get the image of him sitting there out of my head. You should've seen his room, Issy. There's nothing in there.' He wanted to hold onto his anger, but it was already slipping away. 'I hope to God I never end up like that with nothing to show for my life but one photograph.'

Issy stretched up on tiptoes and pressed a kiss to his lips. 'That's never going to happen.' She stroked his cheek and smiled up at him. 'Why don't we change the subject for now and talk about something nicer?'

Now that was an idea he could definitely get on board with. Clasping her waist, he pulled her close. 'What exactly did you have in mind?'

She linked her arms around his neck. 'Let's go out tonight. We could go to the cinema, maybe grab a bite to eat. A little pre-birthday treat.'

He'd almost forgotten about that. 'Sounds good. Is there a film you especially wanted to see?'

Issy's mouth curved into a very cheeky, very tempting smile. 'A couple of hours in the dark together? I wasn't planning to concentrate much on the screen.'

Liam half-laughed, half-groaned as he ducked his head and claimed her lips in a long kiss. He really needed to find that nice hotel he'd promised to book for them. And soon.

25

By the time Issy arrived at Liam's house on Thursday evening, it sounded like his birthday party was in full swing. The front door was closed but even without the A4 directional sign pointing to the side of the house, the noise coming from the back garden would have drawn anyone arriving in that direction.

She rounded the side of the house and stopped in surprise. Liam had said it was just a small family thing, although given their numbers nothing to do with the Penrose family was ever that small. As she surveyed the crush of people on the back lawn it was clear to Issy that Rachel had got a bit carried away with her party plans because it looked like half the village was there. Clutching the present she'd bought, Issy went up on tiptoes and scanned the crowd, trying to spot Liam.

She eventually noticed him in a group with his brothers over by the barbeque and began to weave her way in his direction. Her progress was somewhat impeded by the number of people who paused to greet her, but eventually she made it close enough for Liam to spot her. The way his smile ratcheted up the moment he laid eyes on her sent her tummy dancing and she was immediately cast back to Tuesday night when they'd sat in the corner of the back row and snogged like a couple of teenagers. No, she thought with a silent laugh, it had been much better than anything their younger selves had ever got up to.

Striding away from his brothers, Liam closed the short distance between them and swept her up into his arms. She tried to ignore the oohs and murmurs of interest from around them and focus on the kiss, but she knew they'd be the number one topic of conversation in the morning. Let them talk. Issy had nothing to hide. 'You don't have to look quite so pleased with yourself,' she teased when Liam set her back on her feet.

'But I am pleased with myself,' he told her with a grin. 'Besides, it's my birthday and I should be allowed all the kisses I want.'

'Deal. As long as you're not thinking of claiming them from anybody else.' She gave him one more kiss then handed him his present. 'Happy birthday!'

'You didn't need to get me anything,' he said, even as he began ripping at the paper like he was an excited boy and not a grown man of thirty.

'I wasn't sure what to get you, but I thought you'd like this.' Discarding the paper at his feet, Liam lifted the lid on the rectangular box. 'It's a planner cover,' she explained as he lifted out the brown leather folder. 'There's a notebook already inside, but you can replace it with whatever you want. I thought you could use it for keeping your project notes for the hotel, and it matches your messenger bag, so, anyway...' She realised she was babbling and trailed off while Liam watched her with an amused smile.

'It's fantastic,' he told her, giving her a one-armed hug and stealing another quick kiss.

'You're sure it's okay? I wasn't sure if you already had something like it, but you just seemed to have all your notes in a loose bundle when you've been working in the café.'

'It's perfect, I love it.' He leaned down and claimed another kiss. 'Come and get a drink. Chloe and the others are here some-where. Can you believe this crush? I told Mum not to make a fuss.'

'She's just glad to have you home.' Issy took his hand and squeezed it. 'We all are.'

It was much later in the evening when Liam clambered onto a garden chair and raised his hands. 'Ladies and gentlemen, if I can have your attention please?' The noise and chatter died down and whoever was in charge of the music cut it off, casting the garden into a sudden silence. 'I don't want to interrupt your fun, but I just wanted to take a couple of minutes to thank you all for coming.'

A chorus of cheers and well wishes interrupted him. Liam smiled and raised his hands again. 'Most of all, I want to thank my mum for putting on such a great party.' More cheers. 'And my dad for not complaining about you all churning up his lovely neat lawn.'

'Don't remind me,' Jago grumbled to a chorus of laughter.

'Anyway, I know there's been a lot of speculation about my future, so I am happy to put you all out of your misery and confirm that I'll be staying in Halfmoon Quay to take over the hotel as per my Uncle Davy's wishes.' Liam paused and raised his glass towards where Davy and Maud were standing arm in arm. Nan was dressed in her party best; her neat bobbed hair had been dyed since the last time Issy saw her and the shocking pink strands matched the sparkles glittering on the front of her denim jacket.

'I've got a few things planned for the hotel, but it's my inten-tion to be open and honest with the community about it. My bril-liant design team from Penrose Duncan Design' – he pointed at

Chloe and Anya, earning him another cheer – 'have come up with a concept that I believe will improve and enhance the hotel and show it off to its best advantage. It's going to take a lot of work, but with the support of my family and friends' – Liam turned his gaze to Issy and raised his glass – 'and my girlfriend, I know I'll succeed.' The cheers this time were deafening and Issy was glad it was dark enough to hide her blushes as she raised her glass to toast him in return. 'Well, that's more than enough from me, so thanks very much for coming and please enjoy the rest of the evening!'

Liam climbed down from the chair and was swallowed up in a round of hugs and congratulations from his family. She saw him look around and raised her hand to give him a quick wave to let him know she was okay and happy to wait. This moment of reconnection with his family was important to him.

Liam eventually broke away and came and joined her, putting his arm around her. 'Are you having a good time?' she asked as she turned her face up for a kiss.

'Yeah.' He pressed his cheek to hers and whispered in her ear, 'But I'd rather it was just the two of us.'

Her heart started beating faster. 'Me too.'

He stared down at her, the heat in his eyes bringing a matching flush to her cheeks. 'I'll look into booking that hotel, yeah?'

She nodded.

Another cheer went up and they turned to see Jago climbing up on the chair. 'Oh, lord,' Liam groaned.

'Right now, folks, I won't keep you for long.'

'I hope not, cos my glass is empty,' a tall man with the ruddy cheeks of a life spent out on the water called from the back, earning a ripple of laughter.

'Sean Hamilton with an empty glass?' Jago clutched his hands to his heart. 'Whoever heard of such a thing?' The laughter was louder this time.

Jago raised his hands and the noise quietened down. 'Seriously, though, Rachel and I just want to take this opportunity to not only wish our beloved Liam a happy thirtieth birthday, but to also tell him how proud we are of him. He's worked bloody hard and achieved so much already. If he'd decided to return to London, well we would've supported that choice because that's all we've ever tried to do for all our boys.' Jago's voice cracked and he laughed and waved off a little chorus of 'Ah'. 'Behave yourselves! Anyway, Liam's made the decision that his future lies here in Halfmoon Quay.'

Jago looked down and took the bottle of beer his wife held up to him. Raising it high, he looked directly at Liam, a smile of pride wreathing his face. 'Welcome home, son!'

'Welcome home!' everyone chorused.

Swallowing a lump in her throat, Issy squeezed Liam's hand tight. 'Welcome home, darling.'

'Thank you.' Liam's voice was deep and husky and Issy wanted nothing more than to spirit him away from the party so they could be alone, but Jago hadn't quite finished, it seemed.

'Oh, and I've one last thing to announce! Now I've got my first mate back, Team Penrose will be competing in the Round the Rock race!' He pointed a finger towards the back of the crowd. 'So enjoy that trophy while you can, Sean, because it'll be me and Liam lifting it next month!'

The cheers that followed seemed to come from a long distance away as Issy felt her knees wobble. She was vaguely aware of the look of horror on Liam's face as he squeezed her hand. 'I had no idea he was going to say anything, I swear. After what you told me on the beach the other day I was going to speak to him and cancel, I just haven't had a chance.'

Before she could respond, Jago was there tugging Liam into a hug, his eyes shining with pride and excitement at their shared adventure to come. Not wanting to ruin the moment, Issy turned and slipped away as the guests converged on Liam and Jago to offer their congratulations.

She made it as far as the front driveway when a familiar voice called her name. 'Isabel, wait!'

After raising her hands to dash the angry tears from her eyes, Issy turned to face her nan. 'Not now, Nan.'

'Yes now, darling.' Maud extended her hands as she walked towards Issy. 'Where are you going in such a hurry? The party's still in full swing.'

Issy gulped. 'I, uh, I'm just a bit tired and I've got to get up early for work in the morning.'

'Without even saying goodbye to Liam first?' Maud took a step closer and Issy couldn't bear the tender understanding she could see in her nan's face.

'I can't, Nan...' Her next words were choked off as Maud enfolded her in a tight embrace and rocked her gently.

'Shh, shh, it's okay,' Maud murmured as she stroked Issy's hair. 'I know it's a shock, but it simply won't have occurred to them.'

'Issy?' She turned in her nan's arms to find Liam watching her with eyes brimming with regret. 'I swear I was going to speak to him. If I'd have had any idea what he was planning I would have stopped him.'

She nodded. A rational part of her brain knew she was overreacting, but it was being drowned out by the hypervigilant parts that were always braced for her enemy the sea to steal away her happiness.

It was Maud who spoke. 'She's just a bit upset about the race announcement, lovey. She wasn't expecting it and after what happened—'

'He knows, Nan,' Issy cut her off gently. 'Liam knows about my struggles with the water.'

Liam closed the gap between them and pulled her into a tight hug. 'I didn't want to embarrass Dad in front of everyone, but I'll talk to him in the morning and tell him I'm not doing it. He'll understand once I explain it to him.'

Issy leaned back enough so she could look up at him. 'No! You mustn't. I'm being silly, I know I am.' She sputtered a laugh through her tears. 'I just can't seem to stop bloody crying, though.'

He leaned down and kissed her. 'It's just a stupid race. It doesn't matter. I'll tell Dad I'm not doing it,' he repeated.

It would be so easy to accept, but she'd been so proud of herself the other evening just for being willing to dip her toes into the water and she'd be damned if she would let the fear ruin things for anyone else, most especially Liam. Reaching up, she cupped his face and forced herself to smile even as the fear began to gnaw at her belly. 'Listen to me, Liam. I want you to do the race. I remember how much it always used to mean to you and your dad.'

Liam shook his head. 'It doesn't mean enough to see you in a state like this, Issy. I swear to God I agreed to do it before I knew how hard it would be for you. I'll admit I was excited when Dad asked, but it's not that big a deal.'

'And what will you give up next time? And the time after that? This stupid fear has controlled me for far too long, I'll be damned if I'm going to let it control what you do. You can't spend the rest of your life never going near a boat because of me, because of this. I won't allow it.'

'I think I probably can.' He had a stubborn expression on his face, one she recognised of old. 'I'll speak to Dad—'

'No.' She pressed a finger to his lips. 'It'll spoil the evening and honestly I can't face everyone whispering behind my back when they find out why you've changed your mind.'

'I'll make up an excuse; they won't know it's anything to do with you,' he protested, and God she loved him for offering to do that.

'Let's not talk about it any more tonight, yeah? People will be wondering where you are.'

'I couldn't give two shits about anyone else, Issy!'

He sounded so outraged at the idea he'd care about something like that she couldn't help but laugh. 'How romantic!' It was enough to tease a reluctant smile from him and she soon coaxed it into a proper one with a few kisses. 'Come on, let's get back to the party.'

26

Though the party had ended later than anyone had intended, Liam found it difficult to sleep. He'd walked Issy home afterwards and it had been a struggle to leave her. She seemed a lot brighter and had insisted she was fine, but the sight and sound of her sobbing had haunted him all the way back home and for the rest of the night. He'd have to speak to his dad about the race. Issy had made him promise he would go ahead with it, but how could he, knowing she'd be petrified for his safety and imagining the very worst?

He hadn't been there for her when her parents died – another thing to blame Ray Evans and his bloody meddling for – and he simply couldn't imagine how awful it must've been for her. She always seemed so in control of everything, but the fear on her face as she'd taken those tentative steps into the surf had been painful to see. He'd been so proud of her courage, but it was a bloody long way from paddling ankle deep to expecting her to cope with him going out on the open water.

With a groan, Liam tossed the covers aside and rolled out of bed. There was no point in lying there counting off the minutes until it was a reasonable enough hour that he could go to Issy's and talk it over, so he grabbed his gym kit and his trainers and went out for a run.

The chill was noticeable the moment he opened the front door. The first hints of autumn were everywhere, from the coolness in the air to the dew covering the grass in a carpet of sparkling diamonds. A spider's web hung suspended between the fence and one of the neatly trimmed shrubs that lined the border next to the driveway, glittering like a priceless necklace. He hadn't been kidding about his dad being bothered by people churning up the back lawn last night. The garden was his father's pride and joy, though Liam wasn't sure how he found the time to keep it up. Liam and his brothers had spent hours when they were little pottering around behind Jago with miniature trowels and spades. He'd given them their own plot at the bottom of the garden where they'd planted easy-to-tend flowers. One year they'd even had a sunflower-growing competition and Liam could still picture the four golden and black-headed blooms bobbing high overhead. Still smiling over the memory, he began to jog.

To avoid the temptation of running straight along the seafront and banging on the door of the café at what was still an ungodly hour to many, when he reached the junction at the end of the street, Liam turned in the opposite direction away from the centre of the village and up towards the castle. He passed the entrance to his grandparents' road and made a mental note to fix that lunch date he'd promised Ma. They hadn't been at the party last night and he'd missed them, but though they were both still pretty fit and active, neither was a fan of crowds much these days. Maybe he could speak to Issy about it, get her to make up a nice lunch basket rather than expecting Ma to do all the hard work.

The irony of passing that labour onto Issy didn't escape him, but he would at least be able to pay her for it when he knew both

Ma and Pa would be horrified if he tried to give them any money towards their costs. It didn't matter that his income more than likely outstripped theirs, they still saw him and his brothers and cousins as their grandchildren to be treated and not the other way around. Well, it did at the moment. One of the other things Liam needed to sort out today was quitting his job in London. He had just over five weeks of his sabbatical to run, but Darren had always been a great boss and he deserved to know as soon as possible. He'd probably still have to go and serve some sort of notice period, which was another reason to have the conversation today so he knew exactly where things stood.

The thought of going back to London didn't exactly thrill him, but he also couldn't throw himself straight into refurbishing the hotel either. He needed quotes and advice, structural surveys, a solicitor, an architect to translate Chloe and Anya's concepts into technical designs to support the planning application. Adam would be able to help him with a lot of that, thank goodness. That was someone else he needed to have a proper conversation with, sound him out on how serious he was about their proposed partnership. His level of commitment would depend on how large a bank loan Liam would have to try and secure. He'd be able to use the hotel building itself as collateral once Davy officially transferred ownership to him, but a formal arrangement with someone of Adam's experience would go a long way to greasing the wheels.

Slowing to a walk, he took out his phone and opened his voice notes app and began dictating a list to himself. As soon as he thought he was done, something else occurred to him and he added that too. By the time he'd walked to the top of the promontory overlooking the Quay, Liam had enough items on his to-do list to scare even the most experienced project manager. There was a reason he'd never sought promotion and been happy to hide away at his desk in the corner and focus on the numbers.

Numbers made sense. They did what they were supposed to do – provided the person who'd inputted them had done it correctly, that is – and there was a logic to them, a predictability he knew and understood.

The hotel would be an entirely different prospect because he'd have to deal with people and that's where things had a tendency to get messy. He couldn't deny the thought of it made him nervous, but he was excited too because he would finally be accepting full responsibility for something. Staring out over the village below, his gaze alighted on one familiar building after another: the tall harbour master's office, where his father spent his days keeping everything safe and organised; the chandlery his mother ran; the café that Issy and Maud had built from scratch; the restaurant, where Russ Armstrong had battled for years to earn a coveted reputation and where Harry was beginning to earn his own plaudits.

Even the hotel looked impressive from this distance, gleaming white in the early sunshine, and Liam felt the first hint of satisfaction that he would be the one to bring it back to its former glory. Everywhere he looked he could see the impact of his family and friends upon the landscape, the evidence of their hard work helping to shape the village itself. Now it was his turn. A chance to leave his own mark on the place. To improve things and have something to pass on to the generations that followed. Was this what it felt like to be a grown up? Liam, who had avoided responsibility for much of his life, was surprised to discover how well it fitted him.

He turned away from the village and stared up at the impressive grey stone edifice of Boscowen Castle. Originally built as a coastal defence in the time of King Henry VIII, it had been in the same family ever since. Richard, the first Earl Boscowen, had been a loyal friend and follower of the king, so much so that he'd

earned the sobriquet 'The Hound'. The deadly, sharp rocks at the
base of the promontory that the castle sat upon had become
known locally as the Hound's Teeth. Rumour had it that the family's wealth had been improved over the years by the fortuitous
wrecking of a number of large trading ships, and a network of
tunnels was supposed to link the castle to caves at the base of the
rocks. No one in the village had a bad word to say about the
family because the Boscowens had turned a blind eye when those
caves had been used for the less-than-legal activities that had
given the Smuggler's Den its name.

It was one of the few castles in the area still in private hands,
many having been turned over to English Heritage or the
National Trust as the running costs and death duties became too
much for their owners to meet. Liam couldn't begin to fathom
how much money it would take to keep the lights on, never mind
everything else, and it put the responsibility of the hotel into
perspective.

He vaguely knew the current generation of the family, as
Rosamund and Felix had both attended the village school, but
those early friendships hadn't bridged the class gap for very long.
Their parents took their duties to the village and the surrounding
area seriously and would always be there with a smile to cut the
ribbon on a new business venture or judge the many competition
categories at a local fête. God, was there anything worse than
politely deciding who'd grown the best marrow?

Beyond the castle, the sea was a blanket of blue as far as the
eye could see. The Round the Rock race was three weeks away. He
was deeply concerned about Issy's reaction and wondered again
how hard it must've been for her to tell him she still wanted him
to go ahead with the race. Part of him still believed the easiest
thing to do would be to speak to his dad and call the whole thing
off. It would be disappointing, and not just for Jago, because Liam

had been really looking forward to spending a few hours alone with his dad. And if he was being completely honest with himself, he'd been looking forward to getting out on the water again because it had been too long.

If he pulled out of the race, it wouldn't solve anything, not in the long run, because there was no way he'd be able to promise Issy he'd never go out sailing again for the rest of his life. No, what he needed to try and do was help make her as comfortable as possible with the idea, and surely the best way to do that was to continue to help her tackle her fear of the water. Liam turned his back on the sea and began to jog back down to the village, his mind turning the idea over and over. There had to be something he could do between now and the race...

27

The Monday after Liam's party Issy was still trying to come to terms with her overreaction to him competing in the Round the Rock race. Her heart still beat too fast every time she thought about it. Liam had done his best to reassure her over the weekend, but somehow she'd only ended up feeling worse. It had been on the tip of her tongue more than once to ask him to drop out, but that would mean giving in to the fear she'd lived with for too long. She glanced out of the window at the blue sky and gentle waves. It was easy enough to think she'd get over it when the view looked so calm and peaceful, but she knew better than anyone how quickly the weather conditions could change.

A few people were busy at the far end of the beach and it looked like they were going to take advantage of the nice conditions to do some water sports from the equipment they were setting out. *Good luck to them*. Issy turned her attention back to the café. She didn't have time to gawk out of the window, it had been another busy weekend and she had baking plans.

Issy had just popped a batch of scones into the oven and set the timer when the kitchen door swung open and she looked up to see Maud walking in. She was dressed a little more conservatively than usual, her sparkles and denim replaced by a plain black T-shirt and matching soft trousers.

'Hello, Nan, what a nice surprise!' Keeping her floury hands clear of Maud's dark clothes, Issy leaned in to kiss her cheek. 'To what do I owe the honour?'

Setting a bag on the counter by the door, Maud reached for one of the spare aprons and hooked it over her head, tying the straps behind her with practised ease. 'I've come to take over.'

'Take over?' Issy frowned as she glanced towards the calendar on the wall. 'Have I got an appointment I've forgotten about?'

'You have now.' Maud pointed at the bag. 'I'm to tell you to take that upstairs and get changed and Liam will meet you by the front door in ten minutes.'

What on earth was he up to? 'I can't just skive off work and go out on a date.'

'Why not? It's not like you're answerable to anyone and I'll be here to look after the place.' Maud sniffed the air. 'What's in the oven?

'Umm, scones. And then I was going to do a couple of batches of flapjack and some chocolate chip cookies.' She shook her head. 'I wish Liam had talked to me about this first rather than assuming I can just drop everything.'

Maud planted her hands on her hips. 'Perhaps the boy is trying to give you a surprise. And you're not dropping everything, I'm here, unless you think I'm past it and won't be able to cope for a couple of hours?'

Wow. There was no guilt trip worse than a Nan-sized one. 'Of course I don't think you're past it, Nan.'

'Correct answer. Now grab that bag and get yourself upstairs.

You've got...' Maud checked the watch on her wrist. 'Eight minutes.'

Still not convinced it was a good idea, Issy grabbed the bag, surprised to find it was heavier than she expected. She peeked inside but whatever was in there was wrapped up in shiny pink paper. 'What on earth is he up to?' she muttered.

'Seven minutes,' Maud called as the timer went off and she grabbed the oven gloves. With a frustrated laugh, Issy left the kitchen and ran upstairs to the flat.

Entering her bedroom, she pulled the present out of the bag, knocking a folded piece of paper onto the floor in the process. She bent and picked it up, and her apprehension didn't lessen in the slightest when she unfolded and read the brief message.

Trust me. L xx

Setting the piece of paper aside, Issy tore the corner of the parcel open and her stomach dropped. She ripped the rest of the paper off and held up a brand-new wetsuit. A quick check of the label told her it was the correct size. She looked at the note, then back at the suit. The old fear began to tug at her. Whatever he had planned it involved the water somehow. Trust him? Bloody hell, he was asking a lot.

Twenty minutes later, she was too irritated to be anxious as she stomped out the front door of the café to find Liam pacing back and forth on the small patio outside. 'There you are!' he said, his relief obvious. 'I was beginning to think you wouldn't come.'

'I nearly didn't,' she said, tugging the bottom of the T-shirt she'd thrown on over the suit before stuffing her feet into a pair of old trainers. 'And ten minutes to get into a wetsuit? Are you mad?

It took me that long to find the talcum powder in the back of my bathroom cabinet!'

Laughing, Liam bent and gave her a kiss. 'I'd have been happy to come up and give you a hand if I'd realised you were struggling.'

Issy imagined him trying to help her squirm into the tight neoprene and blushed. 'Somehow I think you'd have been more interested in helping me get undressed.'

'Good point.' He took her hand and squeezed it. 'Come on, before I change what I had planned and help you straight back out of it.'

The anxiety roared back to life full force. She'd given him the benefit of the doubt this far, but there was a limit to how far she was willing to trust him. 'What *have* you got planned?'

Liam pointed down the beach to where two figures were standing next to the water sports equipment she'd seen being laid out earlier. One of the figures raised a hand and waved and Liam waved back.

'Who's that?'

'It's Rick, and Ed's with him. I thought we could try a bit of paddleboarding.'

'Are you serious?'

Liam turned towards her and took her other hand. 'We'll stick to the pond,' he said, referring to the shallow area marked out for children and families. 'And you don't have to do anything, you can just sit on the back of my board and I'll do all the hard work. Rick will be in the water with us and Ed's going to take a jet ski out just beyond the perimeter of the pond so there's no chance of us getting too far out without someone to help us.'

He looked so sweet and earnest and she knew he'd put a lot of effort into planning it, even down to arranging for Maud to cover in the café. She glanced back down the beach. The bright orange buoys clearly marked the perimeter of the pond and the surf washing up on the shore was barely more than a thin line of bubbles. The sun was bright overhead, but she felt nothing but cold as the fear teased down her spine. 'I'm not sure if I can.'

'It's okay if you can't, but will you at least come down and have a look? If the board is too much, we can have another little paddle instead.'

Now that she was sure she could handle again. She shot him a pleading look. 'You won't try and make me change my mind once we're down there?'

He shook his head. 'I'll never, ever try and make you do something you're not ready for. You seem so determined for me to go ahead with the race, I just thought it might help if we could build up your confidence around the water again.'

She glanced back to where Rick and Ed were waiting. 'You explained it to them already?'

'Yes.' Liam's voice was full of gentle understanding. 'And you can trust them.'

'I know.' Still it took a few more seconds before she could actually get her feet moving. Liam let her set the pace and didn't say anything when, rather than crossing the sand directly towards his brothers, she turned left and led them down to the shoreline. This time it was easier to get her feet wet even if the cold shocked a little noise from her throat. By the time they reached Rick and Ed she didn't even notice the cold any more and the anxiety had ratcheted down a few notches.

'Hey, Issy.' Rick's smile was warm and reassuring. 'Ready to have some fun?'

'I'm not sure that's what I'd call it, but I am very grateful to you for giving up your time to try and help me.' She glanced past him to Ed. 'You too.'

Ed bounced over like an over-enthusiastic Labrador, his limp barely noticeable these days. 'Anything for you Issy-Wissy!' She rolled her eyes at the annoying nickname he and Harry had come up with many years ago, but she turned her cheek up to accept a kiss. 'I'll head out now, shall I?' he asked Rick. 'That way any wake I generate with the ski will have time to settle by the time you're ready to go.'

Issy swallowed hard. 'I'm not sure I'm going on the board yet,' she confessed, feeling a tad embarrassed that they were going to all this effort on her behalf.

'Then I'll just have fun dicking around. Either way, this is better than being stuck with my nose in my books on such a beautiful day.' Grabbing one of the life jackets stacked at Rick's feet, he strapped it on in a couple of swift, practised moves.

She watched as the three of them waded out with the jet ski until they were knee-deep, Rick and Liam holding the ski steady while Ed hopped on the back and settled onto the seat. He watched over his shoulder until his brothers had returned to the safety of the beach before raising one hand in a quick wave. A flip of a switch and the ski growled into life and then Ed was off, skimming over the water. As he'd predicted, the ski churned the water up, sending large ripples washing up on the shore. The coloured buoys outlining the pond bounced and bobbled and Issy found her insides doing the same.

As though sensing her nervousness, Liam's warm hand closed around hers and he gave her a reassuring squeeze. 'Give it a minute or two.'

Even as they watched, the sea was already beginning to calm. She only wished her nerves would do the same. She pressed a hand to her stomach. 'I'm not sure about this.'

'It's okay.'

She knew he meant it and if she turned and walked back to

the café now, none of them would think any the worse of her. But what would she think of herself?

'We could take the board out and you could watch Liam have a go on it,' Rick suggested. 'The water in the pond isn't deeper than mid-thigh on me so at worst it'll be up to your waist, so your feet won't leave the ground.'

Her throat felt too dry to speak, so she nodded her agreement. Liam helped her with her life jacket when her fingers turned suddenly clumsy and she couldn't get the end of the zip into the stopper at the base. When he'd finished, he set his hands on her shoulders and held her gaze. 'You *really* don't have to do this.'

'I... I'll be fine.'

His hands shifted to her arms and he rubbed them up and down. 'You're shivering like a dog in a thunderstorm, Issy.'

Issy tightened her muscles, the action forcing her to straighten her spine. 'I'll. Be. Fine.' The message was for herself as much as him, but Liam accepted her assurance with a single nod.

In the end she didn't get up on the board, but that didn't matter. It was enough to be in the water and watch Liam and Rick. They started out sedately enough, paddling in slow circuits around the perimeter of the pond. It was too cold to just stand there, so Issy waded around, trailing her fingers through the water and letting memories of days long past drift through her mind. It was hard at first because they arrived with the usual stab of grief, but instead of resisting it, Issy let it come. When the tears came, she welcomed them too. When Liam looked over, she waved at his blurry outline then dipped both hands into the sea and splashed her face with the cold, salty water. The shock of it was enough to stop her crying and after that she began to really enjoy herself.

Unable to resist the natural-born instinct of brotherly competition, Rick and Liam ended up facing off on their boards, using the ends of their paddles to try and push each other off balance. They both ended up in the water more than once, but it didn't stop them scrambling back up and going again. Deciding to leave them to it, Issy waded back to the beach and settled on the sand to watch them messing around, wrapping herself in a large towel to ward off the chill. By the time they flopped down next to her a few minutes later, they were both soaked to the skin. 'Who won?' she asked with a grin as Liam snatched up a towel and rubbed at his wet hair.

'Who do you think?' The pride in his voice was unmistakable.

Rick snorted from beneath the towel he'd draped over his own head. 'I let you win, old man.'

'You keep telling yourself that if that's what your pride needs to hear!' They continued to bicker back and forth and they soon reached new levels of nonsense once Ed parked his jet ski up on the sand and joined them.

Issy had heard them tease and jest with each other a hundred times, a thousand more likely, but she knew she'd never grow tired of it. This was what love sounded like, and she'd missed being a part of it.

Her heart was full when Liam walked her back to the café a short time later. When they reached the patio she stopped and curled her arms around his waist. 'Thank you for today.'

He beamed down at her; his slightly too long hair was a tangled mess and there was a streak of white on his cheek from where the salt water had dried on it. He'd never looked more handsome, never felt more dear to her than he did in this moment. 'You're welcome.' Leaning down, he pressed a kiss to her neck and murmured, 'Do you want me to help you out of that wetsuit?'

She was tempted, oh so tempted, but then the reality of their situation came crashing back in. It would be lunchtime soon and she couldn't leave Maud on her own to deal with that. 'I wish I could.'

Liam sighed against her skin. 'I know, I would just really like some alone time with you.'

'Me too.' She hugged him close, a mixture of desire and frustration urging her to grab his hand and drag him upstairs. 'Sort that hotel out for us soon, okay?'

28

Though Liam had been disappointed by his failure to persuade Issy to let him help her with the wetsuit, he'd been buoyed by the urgency in her tone about arranging a hotel room. He hadn't really expected her to invite him upstairs, not when she'd already played hooky from the café for half the morning and the lunchtime rush was approaching. Still, it was getting harder to walk away each time, and their lack of a private space where they could be alone together was becoming a pressing frustration. Booking that night away would be at the top of his priority list as soon as he'd sorted a few things out at the hotel. While he and Issy had been down on the beach, Adam had messaged him with a list of requests for information.

Liam knocked on the frame of his great-uncle's open office door. 'Hey, Uncle D, have you got a few minutes to spare?'

His uncle set aside one of the red ledgers Liam had formed a love–hate relationship with and pointed at the spare chair. 'I've always got time for you, son, what do you need?'

'Adam's asked for the latest copies of a few things and I was hoping you'd be able to track them down.'

'Then we'd better get cracking.'

They worked side by side for the next hour, digging out as many of the things Adam had requested as they could find. They didn't have everything he'd asked for, and a couple of things, including the fire inspection report, were close to running out. Thankfully, it didn't take more than a couple of calls to get them booked in, but Davy was still annoyed with himself. 'I don't know how I've let that slip,' he muttered for the third time in as many minutes.

'It's fine, Uncle D,' Liam reassured him. 'No harm done.'

His great-uncle shook his head, clearly unwilling to let himself off the hook. 'I should've kept on top of things better.'

Liam knew he wasn't referring to a couple of nearly missed inspections. The signs of neglect were everywhere around the hotel. 'You've had a lot on your plate,' Liam countered. 'And nothing is that bad that it can't be sorted. Before you know it, we'll have this place looking good as new.'

'Better than new,' Davy said. 'Thanks to you.'

Reaching out, Liam patted his hand. 'Thanks to you, you mean. After all, you're the one taking a leap of faith and letting me take over.'

'Letting you? More like railroading you into it,' Davy said with a chuckle. 'You looked like a stunned mullet when I tossed the deeds in your lap.'

Liam laughed. 'I'll admit it was a shock at first, but it didn't take me long to realise it was too good an opportunity to pass up. Plus, you've given me the push I needed to do what I really want and that's to move back home.'

'And get yourself out of the clutches of that snooty little madam you got yourself mixed up with. Never liked the bloody woman from the first moment I laid eyes on her, looking down her nose at everyone.'

'Come on, Uncle D, Caro wasn't that bad.'

'You could've fooled me, boy!' Davy cackled, clearly enjoying watching Liam squirm. 'She was never going to fit in here, and we both know it.'

'It's not always easy feeling at home in a tight-knit community like ours,' Liam protested, still feeling the need to defend Caro a bit, though he wasn't sure why.

Davy made a rude noise. 'She never even tried. You know as well as I do that people fit in just fine if they're willing to make the effort. We're not one of those places that treat anyone not born here as permanent outsiders.'

Liam conceded the point with a wry laugh. 'Yeah, you're right.'

'And thank God you've come to your senses now and sorted things out with Issy,' his great-uncle added. 'I was worried you were going to make the same mistake I did when I was your age and let the best thing that ever happened to you slip through your fingers forever.'

'Well, not all of what happened in the past was in my control.' Liam hadn't set eyes on Ray since their confrontation, and he couldn't say he minded. He might not be angry with him, but Liam was a long way off from being prepared to think about forgiving him. It would be best all round if he stayed out of the way for the foreseeable future. 'But I am doing my very best to make up for lost time.'

'That's what I like to hear! So what are you going to do while the work on the hotel is being done? Are you staying at your mum and dad's or do you want to move in here?'

'I hadn't really thought about it.' Well, he'd considered the cramp his and Issy's current living conditions were putting on their chances to be alone together, but that was definitely not a topic of conversation he was keen to pursue with Davy. 'If I move in here then that's another room we can't rent out.'

Davy shook his head. 'You don't need to worry about that, because there'll be a couple of spare ones once Maud and I move out.'

'Where to?' It would certainly make things a bit easier if they had fewer people to work around, but he didn't want Davy to feel pushed out. 'You know you can stay as long as you want.'

Davy shook his head. 'Maud's had her name down on the waiting list at Blue Horizons for a while now. Someone's had to transfer into a full-time care home, so there's a flat available for us. It's being redecorated and we're getting new carpets fitted but we should be able to move in in a couple of weeks' time.'

'You kept that quiet!' Liam laughed. 'But if it's what you both want, I'm happy for you.'

'It is,' Davy replied. 'I'm not sure about all the activities she's planning on signing us up for, but if it makes her happy, that's good enough for me.' His smile was full of such affection, Liam felt it deep in his heart. 'Anyway,' his uncle continued, 'my suite will be there if you want it. It's nothing fancy but it'll be your own space, at least.'

Liam nodded. 'It would be good to be on hand while the redevelopment work is ongoing.'

'And nice not to have to try and sneak your girlfriend up the stairs past your parents, no doubt!'

'Give me a break, Uncle D,' Liam groaned, hiding his face in his hands. 'I am not discussing the logistics of my private life with you!'

Davy's response was a delighted roar of laughter.

* * *

He'd hoped to make it to the café before closing, but he'd got caught up chatting with Davy and Anya and they'd ended up getting a tape measure out and discussing the most cost-efficient way to reorganise the reception area so they could fit in some tables and chairs for guests. It was putting the cart before the horse a bit, but Liam hadn't minded at all because Davy had clearly been enjoying himself, for all his early protests that the changes to the hotel weren't anything to do with him.

The closed sign was up and the door was locked when Liam tried it. He cupped his hands to his eyes to get a good look inside, but there was no sign of Issy. He could faintly hear music playing and the lights were still on, so he knew she must be about somewhere. He knocked on the glass and waited. She appeared through the swing doors, her face lighting up when she spotted him. 'Hello, I wasn't expecting you!'

'You don't mind me calling in?' he asked as she ushered him inside.

'Not at all, it's a lovely surprise.' She went up on her toes and kissed him. The touch of her lips to his was an electric jolt and his arms went around her to hold her close so could he capture more of her lightning-in-a-bottle kisses. 'Is that why you came to see me?' she asked, eyes dancing with delight when he eventually let her go.

'It was certainly an incentive, but I wanted to see if you have plans for Friday night?'

'Not at the moment, but I'm hoping my boyfriend has some ideas.'

Liam laughed. 'Give me his number and I can call and ask him.'

'Silly fool.' Issy swiped his arm. 'What did you have in mind?'

'Well,' Liam said, gathering her close against him once more. 'Rick was telling me about a nice Italian restaurant over in Port Petroc. And then I was thinking about booking that hotel room we were talking about...'

'Oh, were you now?' Issy snuggled up against him in a way that made him groan.

'Don't tease me, woman, or I'll carry you over there and put that sofa in the Hub to good use!'

'Don't mind me!' They jumped apart at the sound of Kat's voice. 'Sorry to interrupt,' she said with a grin that said she wasn't sorry in the least for catching them up to no good. 'I just got home and wondered if you wanted me to sort something out for dinner, but I can see you're busy...'

'It's fine,' Issy said, tucking a stray strand of hair behind her ear. 'Liam and I were, uh, just making plans for Friday night.'

'So I heard,' Kat said with a laugh. 'But don't worry about wasting money on a hotel. I've arranged a girly night with Chloe. She's invited me over so we can drown our sorrows over our permanent spinsterhood and I'm going to stay the night.'

'Oh, you don't need to do that!' Issy protested. 'This is your home too.'

'But it's really very generous of you to offer,' Liam added quickly, giving Issy a come-on-this-is-too-good-an-opportunity-to-pass-up look.

'It's not a problem,' Kat assured them. 'I'll need to pop home and change before I go to work in the morning, but I'll text when I'm on the way to give you time to put some pants on, Liam.'

If it was possible to burst into flames from embarrassment, he might have discovered the truth behind the mystery of spontaneous human combustion. 'Why is everyone in this village obsessed with our sex life?' he grumbled to Issy.

'In my case, it's pure jealousy,' Kat said, clearly enjoying his discomfort. 'Of the sex, I mean, not who Issy's having it with!' she added, quickly.

'Well that's my ego crushed to pieces. Anything else?'

Kat laughed. 'No, that's everything for now, I shall leave you both to it. I'll see you upstairs in a bit, Issy.' She was gone again before either of them could reply.

Liam's laugh stuck in his throat as he glanced down at Issy to find her looking pensive. 'Hey, if you'd rather we went to a hotel, I'm happy to book one.'

She snuggled against him. 'We might need to think about it if you staying over becomes a regular thing. I know Kat says she doesn't mind giving us space, but I still feel guilty about it.'

Liam certainly intended for it to become a regular thing, so he needed to get his arse in gear. 'I'll do some research and find us somewhere nice, I promise.'

'Thank you. And I'll try and talk to Kat again, but for now, let's concentrate on our plans for Friday night.'

The soft warmth of her against him was irresistible and Liam slipped his hand under the back of her shirt to trace gentle circles against her skin. 'You still want to go out for dinner?'

Issy looped her arms around his neck. 'I was thinking staying in with a takeaway might be more fun.'

'Now, that sounds like a great idea.'

29

'You really don't have to stay at Chloe's,' Issy said as she watched Kat packing an overnight bag. 'I asked you to move in here with me and I want you to feel like it's your home too. You shouldn't feel pushed out. And it'll only be this once because Liam's going to sort out a hotel for next time.'

Kat paused in folding a pair of pyjamas and smiled at her. 'I don't feel pushed out, but you made that offer before things changed between you and Liam.' She crossed the room to Issy and gave her a hug. 'And tell Liam not to waste his money on a hotel. I promise that I feel at home here, but I'm also happy to give you both some space whenever you need it.'

Issy couldn't deny it would be nice to have some alone time with Liam, but still she hated the idea that Kat might feel she was somehow in the way. 'Well I appreciate you being so thoughtful.' She paused to study Kat's face. The dark circles beneath her eyes were livid purplish-black, almost bruise-like. 'Is everything okay at work?'

Kat's mouth twitched before she shook her head. 'I don't want to talk about it, okay?'

'Kat...'

She turned her back and returned to packing her bag. 'Seriously, Issy, just leave it.'

Though it went against her instinct not to press for more information when it was clear something wasn't right, Issy forced herself to leave the room. Hopefully Kat would unwind a bit with Chloe and be able to talk to her about whatever it was that was bothering her. If not, Issy was going to have to find a way to get Kat to confide in her.

She was still brooding about it when Liam pressed the buzzer about an hour later. 'Come on up,' she said through the intercom and pressed the button to unlock the lower door. Leaving the upper door open for him, she went into the kitchen and opened the fridge. She'd nipped out and bought a nice bottle of wine from the deli to go with the food Liam had picked up on the way.

'There you are!' Liam placed a white takeaway bag on the counter next to her and leaned down to give her a kiss. 'How was your day?'

'It was good, thanks – busy, but there's not anything I'm going to complain about. How about you?'

'Same. I had another meeting with Adam, just sorting out a few details about how things will work going forward.'

The mundane domesticity of the situation amused her. 'Listen to us chatting about our day like an old married couple.'

Liam grinned at her. 'Nice, isn't it?' He placed a cardboard tube on the counter in front of her, then dug in his coat pocket and pulled out a small square box. 'I got you something.'

'What's this?'

'Have a look and find out. Here, give me that bottle and I'll open it while you open your presents.'

Intrigued, Issy pulled the plastic cap out of the top of the tube and looked inside. There was something rolled up in there and she pulled it out with careful fingers and unrolled it. Her heart skipped a beat when she saw what she was holding. 'You got me a new map for my wall.'

Liam set the wine down and picked up the box, giving it a shake. 'And lots of pins so you can mark off all the places you want to visit.'

She shook her head. 'And when are we going to find the time to do that?'

He put an arm around her waist and pulled her closer. 'We'll make time.'

'Careful! You'll wrinkle my map.' Issy pushed him away with one hand so she could place her new treasure safely on the kitchen table before she turned back to him. 'And how will we afford it? I don't exactly have a holiday savings fund and you're going to need every penny to sort out the hotel.'

'Not every penny.' Liam gathered her close once more. 'I'm serious about making a fresh start, Issy, and that includes recognising what's really important. We need to work to live, not just live to work. I talked to my boss this morning and formally handed in my notice. He's not keen to let me go completely, so we've agreed that I'll switch to a zero-hours contract.'

'How will that help?'

'There's going to be a lot of waiting around, especially over the next couple of months while we wait for plans, surveys, planning permission. I can use that time to do some ad hoc project work for my old company. It's extra money I wasn't expecting and I intend to put it to good use. My boss has already ear-marked a project for me, and he's happy for me to work from home.' He raised a hand to her cheek. 'What do you say to celebrating our first Christmas together in New York?'

It was a crazy idea, reckless even to think about spending

money they should be saving. 'Don't you think we should put it away in a rainy-day fund?'

Liam leaned down and pressed his forehead to hers. 'We'll do that too, on the next contract, but what about the sunny days? Don't you think we deserve a few of those too?'

Her head said no, be sensible, but her heart? Oh her heart was yelling a big fat YES! 'Work to live, not just live to work,' she murmured, trying Liam's new motto out for size.

'Work to live,' he echoed as he tilted his head and claimed her mouth with a slow, tender kiss.

Issy melted into him with a sigh. 'I'm so glad you won't be rushing off anywhere tonight.'

Liam kissed his way along her jaw and down her neck to that spot beneath her ear that always made her shiver with delight. 'I feel like I've waited for this forever,' he murmured as he shifted his mouth lower until it grazed along her collarbone, sending her pulse racing.

Heat pooled low in her belly, desire flooding her entire body until she was all but vibrating with it. 'I don't want to wait another second, Liam.'

He raised his head, his eyes full of heat as they blazed into hers. 'Can I take you to bed?'

'Yes.'

They stumbled out of the kitchen, clumsy in their haste to reach her room and yet they couldn't make it that far before Liam's mouth was on hers again as he pushed her against the back of the sofa. By the time they fell back onto her bed they were both naked apart from Issy's bra, which dangled around her neck where Liam had shoved it out of the way, both of them too impatient to fiddle with the hooks. 'I'm sorry, I'm rushing you,' he said, as he braced himself over her. 'Give me a second to catch my breath and I'll take the time you need.'

The only thing she needed was him. Right now, right this second. She reached up and hooked a hand around the back of his neck, dragging him down on top of her. 'You can go slow next time.'

After the promised next time and a quick shower that would've developed into round three until Issy's stomach had given an embarrassing loud rumble, they ended up back in bed with their reheated takeaway and the bottle of wine. Issy was wearing Liam's T-shirt, having rescued it from where he'd left it dangling over the back of the sofa. The shirt smelled so deliciously of him that she'd already decided he wasn't getting it back.

'I can't eat another bite,' she declared, pushing aside her tray with a groan. Her plate looked like she'd hardly eaten anything. 'It's been ages since I had a Chinese. I forgot how filling it is.'

Liam pushed his own tray aside and climbed out of bed. Unlike her, he seemed entirely comfortable in his own skin, and as she let her eyes trace over the taut lines of his muscles, she found she rather liked this unexpected exhibitionist streak. 'Put your eyes back in your head and give me your tray,' he said, gesturing towards it with a grin.

She handed it to him then pushed the covers back with her foot to display the fact his T-shirt didn't quite cover her own modesty. 'Don't be long because I think I might have room for dessert after all.'

* * *

Issy woke early the following morning and was content to lie there for a while and simply listen to Liam breathe. His six-foot frame took up more than its fair share of her double bed, and she'd discovered he was a hot sleeper when she'd woken just after two feeling like she was boiling to death. She'd wriggled out from the heavy weight of his arm and thrown back the cover to cool down. Her respite had lasted all of two minutes before he'd raised his head from his pillow to grumble she was too far away and gather her in close. Well at least she wouldn't have to worry about her heating bill that winter, she supposed.

She lay there as long as she could until her body urged her to move, so she slipped out of bed and used the bathroom and washed her face and cleaned her teeth. It was early enough to still be dark outside and for a moment she was tempted to crawl back under the covers and snuggle with Liam and forget about anything else. But the siren call of the coffee machine was too strong to ignore.

When she entered the kitchen, the map he'd bought her was curled up on itself in the middle of the table. She filled the coffee machine and switched it on to brew then took out four mugs from the cupboard and carefully used them to hold the map open at each corner. She traced a finger over the wide expanse of the Atlantic, mapping a path from Cornwall to New York City. Had Liam really been serious about spending Christmas there? It was something she'd seen so many times in movies: couples bundled up in thick hats and coats as the snow drifted down over Times Square, holding hands as they ice-skated around the temporary rink at the Rockefeller Centre, using one of those bird's eye viewers to look over the city from the top of the Empire State Building. She knew some people would sneer at the touristy clichés, but she wanted to do them all.

'I woke up and you were gone.' Startled from her daydream, Issy glanced up to find Liam leaning against the door-frame. He'd put on his jeans but was naked from the waist up and the sight of his sculpted chest made her wish she'd gone back to bed after all. 'You've got my T-shirt,' he pointed out.

'I think you'll find it's mine now,' she said with a grin. 'Want some coffee?'

'Yes, please.' He shifted from the door-frame to next to the table while she poured them both a cup and accepted one with a smile of thanks when she handed it to him. 'Been making plans?'

'Not quite plans, but I've got a few ideas.' She leaned against him and he lifted his arm and placed it around her shoulders. 'You're really sure we can afford it?'

Liam leaned down and claimed a kiss. He tasted of minty toothpaste, coffee, and the future. 'I wouldn't have suggested it if I wasn't sure. You're not having second thoughts, are you?'

She smiled up at him. 'Not at all. It's lovely to have something to look forward to.'

'It is, isn't it?' He raised his coffee. 'I'm going to go take this and grab a quick shower if you don't mind?'

'Help yourself. Do you want me to fix you something for breakfast?'

'Coffee will be fine. I've promised to help Matt and Ed again at the cottage.' He put his arms around her and smiled. 'Although I could put them off for an hour or two.'

It was very tempting, but Kat would be home soon to get changed for work and Issy was already feeling a bit guilty about her staying away to give them privacy. 'I'm not sure we have time.'

'You could hop in the shower with me, help scrub my back,' he suggested with a filthy grin that promised much more than that.

It should probably have worried Issy how little willpower she possessed when he looked at her like that, but she was too busy grabbing his hand and dragging him towards the bathroom to worry about it.

30

'You're very quiet,' Jago observed as he and Liam moved around the small sailing boat, completing their final checks. The harbour was an absolute hive of activity, the other competitors busying themselves with their own preparations while spectators lined the dock, offering advice and jokes. The door to his mother's chandlery shop stood open, and a steady stream of people scuttled back and forth from the boats to pick up last-minute items they'd forgotten. 'Everything all right?'

Liam glanced up to find his dad watching him, his hands frozen in the middle of winding up a length of rope. 'Yes, fine. It's just been a while since I was on deck, so I want to make sure I don't forget anything, that's all.'

It wasn't strictly a lie, but he didn't want to confess his mind had been fixed on the worry he'd seen in Issy's eyes as she'd kissed him and sent him on his way earlier. Spending Friday night with her had become a regular thing because Kat had made a standing arrangement to stay over at Chloe's in spite of Issy's protests. Liam understood why she felt awkward about it, but he was grateful for the chance to be alone with her whatever the circumstances. Thankfully, Davy and Maud were due to move to Blue Horizons any day now, so Liam could take over his great-uncle's suite until the alteration works started. Issy could stay with him then, which would make life easier for everyone.

Jago eyed him for a moment, then his attention was drawn away by a call from a man in dark trousers and a short-sleeved white shirt with gold rank slides affixed to each shoulder. 'Final safety briefing in ten minutes, Jago!' Tony Reeves, the deputy harbour master, called out in his broad Scouse accent. A veteran of the merchant navy, he'd moved to the village after retiring and taken up his current post. Though his accent marked him out, Tony and his wife, Alison, had both slipped seamlessly into village life. It was like his Uncle Davy had said the other day: no one stayed an outsider in Halfmoon Quay unless they chose to.

'We'll be there.' Jago raised his hand in acknowledgement. Liam knew his father and Tony had written the plan together and Jago would know it inside and out. Still, he made sure they were front and centre when the competitors gathered in front of the harbour master's office. Sean Hamilton came over and clapped Jago on the shoulder. 'Lovely morning for it!' he boomed in his usual cheerful voice.

Jago turned and shook his hand. 'Enjoy the sunshine while you can, Sean, because you won't be smiling like that when Liam and I lift the trophy later.'

'In your dreams, mate!'

They joshed back and forth for a few more minutes, the banter spreading around the other competitors, and Liam noticed one or two private wagers being placed on who would finish where. Liam couldn't give two hoots about winning, as long as they got back safely and in a decent time so Issy wouldn't have to worry about him for too long. He pulled out his phone and wondered if he had time to give her a quick call and see how she was, but then Tony called them to order and he had to pay attention.

Towards the end of the briefing Tony handed out some printouts. 'This is the latest weather update. Now, I know it looks okay at the moment, but that storm that's been building over Ireland took a bit of an unexpected turn in the past few hours. We're still hopeful that it might miss us or we just catch the edge of it at worst, but please keep an eye on the situation and obey any instructions from the race marshals.'

Liam took the printout and studied it with a frown. Like many others, he turned his gaze to the north west. The sky was blue for a fair distance but there was no mistaking the smudge of grey on the far horizon. God he hoped it stayed fair until at least the race was over, because a change in the conditions would be bound to freak Issy out, and with good reason. Still, perhaps he'd better forewarn her.

Telling his dad he'd be back in a minute, Liam wandered to the other end of the dock where it was quieter and took out his phone again. Issy answered after a couple of rings. 'Hello! How's it going?'

'Okay, we've just finished the safety briefing and then it's final checks before everyone heads out to the start line. How's things with you?'

'Not bad. I've been keeping myself busy with some batch baking and there's been a fair few people in and out already, so it's kept my eyes off the clock if that's what you're worried about.'

'No, I'm not worried about that.'

She was quiet for a long moment then said, 'But you are worried about something.'

Liam sighed, wondering if he should've left her in peace but it was too late now. 'Tony gave us a weather update at the end of the briefing. The storm that's been developing out in the Atlantic might come a bit closer than expected.'

Her voice dropped to a whisper. 'How close?'

He raised his eyes to the horizon. The dark smudge was still there but it didn't look to have moved any closer. 'We might catch the edge of it, a shower or two before the race ends if we're unlucky.'

'Oh. Well, you'd better make sure you've got your waterproofs on!' Her voice was unnaturally bright and he wasn't fooled by it for a second.

'You don't have to pretend that everything's okay, Issy, not with me. There's still time to drop out.'

'I'm sorry, I just didn't want you worrying about me worrying about you. A couple of showers, you reckon?'

'With any luck.'

'Then I'd better keep my fingers crossed, hadn't I?'

'*Issy*.'

'No, Liam. If you drop out of the race, then what? I need to find a way to conquer this and you going out with your father and coming back safe to me later is going to go a long way towards helping me.'

Liam stared back up at the sky then out across the sea, which was as calm and placid as anyone could hope for in October. 'Are you sure?'

'Yes. I'm sure. Thank you for warning me about the storm, now go and have fun and next time I see you, you'd better have a nice shiny trophy in your hands. I don't want people thinking I'm dating a loser now!'

'Aye, aye, Captain!' Liam laughed. 'I'll be back before you know it.'

It was a chaotic fifteen or twenty minutes to get all the boats clear of the mouth of the harbour and on their way out towards the starting line marked by two motorboats. His dad had the helm and it was Liam's job to raise and lower the sails and basically do whatever else Jago told him to do without getting in the way. There were still a few boats making their way towards the start, so they tacked and sailed in a slow loop to avoid crossing too early and causing a false start. It put them towards the back of the jostling vessels but gave them a clear view of the field ahead.

Three sharp blasts from a horn and the starter had them underway. Jago steered them towards the top end of the course and the boat all but skipped forward as the sails caught the wind at just the right angle and they raced over the top of the waves. The salt sting was exhilarating and Liam let out a laugh of delight as they skimmed past several other boats. 'You've got it now, Dad!' he called out to his father, glancing back over his shoulder.

Jago beamed at him from the helm seat. 'I knew it'd come back to you.'

Though it was called Round the Rock, the rock was actually the second point of a triangular route, so they initially sailed away from the brooding crag, racing parallel with the village and following the coast in the direction of Port Petroc. The race ebbed and flowed, first one boat and then another finding an advantage.

By the time they approached the first marker buoy, Liam reckoned they were in about fourth or fifth position. He eyed the horizon nervously. It wasn't only the other boats they were racing, the tiny smudge of grey had spread to cover a large part of the blue sky and the wind had picked up, sending white horses dancing over the surface of the water.

They'd almost reached the buoy when one of the other yachts pulled a very dirty manoeuvre, cutting right across their racing line and forcing them to steer sharply away to avoid a collision. All they could do was watch in frustration as their sails lost the wind and they slowed dramatically, losing places as their fellow competitors zipped past on either side.

To add insult to injury, the radio crackled and Sean's familiar voice boomed out of the speaker, 'You snooze you lose!'

Jago snatched the handset up. 'Now we know how you've managed to win so many times, you dirty cheat!'

The radio crackled again, followed by a burst of laughter. 'All's fair in love and sailing, Jago!'

They had no choice other than to wait for room to turn the boat before they could clear the buoy. By the time they rejoined the race they were well towards the back. 'Well, that's that then,' Liam sighed.

'We're not giving up that easily,' his father yelled. 'Come on, where's your competitive spirit?'

They were racing into the wind now, forcing them to tack constantly to make any headway. The boats ahead of them followed similar zig-zag patterns across the waves and slowly they began to make up a few places. A sharp gust of wind sent a blast of salt water over the edge of the boat, catching Liam full in the face. He sputtered and shook his head, blinking rapidly against the stinging in his eyes.

He cast another look to the sky then gestured towards the ominous dark cloud bearing down on them. 'Looks like that storm is going to catch us after all,' he called to his dad.

Jago nodded, but kept his eyes fixed on the water ahead. 'I've seen it. We might get a soaking, but we've had worse.'

Liam eyed the skyline. The storm looked closer still and the wind was definitely picking up. 'Yeah, I suppose so.'

'What's the matter? You're not scared of a bit of rain are you?'

Liam shook his head. 'No, it's not me I'm worried about.' Jago tacked the boat, losing the wind once more so they slowed down.

Liam frowned back at him over his shoulder. 'What are you doing? You'll lose all the progress we've been making.'

Jago shook his head. 'I'm not fussed about some stupid race. Something's been bothering you all morning. What is it?'

'It's Issy, she was upset after my birthday when she found out we were entering the race. She... uh, she still has a lot of unresolved stuff around the way her parents died.'

Jago's face fell. 'Bloody hell, I didn't even think about that; why didn't you say something? You know I'd have understood if you wanted to pull out of the race.'

Liam sighed. 'I know, Dad, and I told her as much when I realised how stressful the idea of me going out on the water was for her, but she insisted. I called her again before the race after we got the weather update, but she still didn't want us to drop out.'

Now they'd slowed almost to a standstill it was noticeable how much colder the wind was. The sky was darkening by the minute and Liam feared they were going to catch a lot more than just the edge of the storm. 'I should've gone with my gut instinct and called it off, but I was worried it would be more harmful to her, reinforce her fears of the ocean.' The rock loomed ahead, the last couple of boats in front of them making busy preparations to sail around it.

'Watch your head!' Jago called out and Liam ducked instinctively as the boom began to swing as his father began to turn the boat.

'What are you doing?'

'We're going back,' his father announced in a voice that brooked no argument. 'Now.'

Liam couldn't deny the relief that washed through him as they caught the wind and the sails swelled, carrying them back towards the direction of the quay. 'Thanks, Dad. I'm sorry about the race. I should've said something earlier but you were so excited when you asked me to take part.'

Jago chuckled. 'Silly boy, I never gave two hoots about the race. I only suggested it because I thought it'd be a nice way to spend some together.'

Liam leaned over, stretching out a hand so he could touch his father's leg. 'It means a lot to me to get to hang out with you, Dad. We'll find some other way to do it.'

A squally gust of wind showered them in icy raindrops. Liam shuddered and turned up the collar of his waterproof jacket, zipping it up under his chin as far as he could. His father did the same. 'Come on, son, let's get the hell out of here.'

Liam cast one final glance towards the rock. All but one of the other boats were well clear and were racing towards the final buoy. Like them, the back marker wasn't making much progress, but not by choice. They'd lost control of their mainsail somehow and it was flapping wildly in the wind. 'Hold on, Dad, I think they might be in trouble.'

A second later the radio burst into life. There was no laughter in Sean's voice this time as he shouted, 'Mayday! Mayday!'

Liam didn't even have to ask what they were going to do. Ducking low, he waited for their own sail to pass overhead once more as his father turned the boat and they headed back towards the rock.

31

Issy tried her best to stay busy and not think about Liam. Or, to be more accurate, she tried not to think about him getting caught in the storm he'd forewarned her about. It was easy at first because the café was buzzing from the moment she opened the doors as both locals and visitors from the surrounding towns and villages flooded the seafront to enjoy the spectacle and she was rushed off her feet.

Things calmed down on that front when Kat arrived with both Chloe and Anya in tow. 'We thought you could use the company,' Chloe had said with a sympathetic hug. 'And it looks like we've arrived just in time as well. It's a madhouse in here.'

'What can we do?' Anya asked.

'There's spare aprons in the kitchen. Can you and Chloe grab any dirty plates and cups you can find and give the tables a wipe over, please?' Issy answered with a grateful smile.

'I'll hop on the coffee machine, shall I?' Kat offered. 'It's pretty much the same as the one we have at Java Brava, and then you can look after the till.'

'Thanks, Kat, you're a lifesaver.' She turned to look at them all in turn, feeling a little teary. 'Thanks for coming.'

'As if we would leave you on your own.'

As soon as they'd regained control and cleared the queue, Issy left the other three to keep an eye on things while she nipped into the kitchen to whip up a couple of batches of quick-to-bake items like scones and some cookies to make sure the display counter stayed topped up. She popped her phone on the counter and turned on one of her favourite podcasts, hoping the cheery banter of the two comedians bemoaning their everyday domestic disasters would help keep her brain occupied. Issy glanced at the window several times. The dark line on the horizon didn't seem to be spreading, so she allowed herself to hope that Liam was right and the storm front would miss them.

After the fifth time she'd looked outside in as many minutes, she grabbed the string on the side of the blind and let it down to block out the view. It meant putting the light on, but she didn't care. Anything was better than gawping out the window and wondering what Liam was doing right then and there.

Maud arrived about forty minutes later and joined Issy in the kitchen, ignoring her protests that she could manage. 'As if I'm going to sit on my backside and watch you all running around,' she said, giving Issy's arm a fond pat. 'Besides, it gives me an excuse to get away from Davy for a bit.'

'Trouble in paradise?' Issy teased with a laugh.

'Something like that. Oh, he's fine for the most part but his hip always gives him gyp when there's rain on the way. I couldn't stand him grumbling and griping so I've left him behind the counter at the hotel.' Her eyes were soft with understanding as she smiled at Issy. 'I didn't just want to get away from his moaning; when I realised the forecast was wrong and that storm was heading for us, I didn't want you to be on your own, though I see your friends had already had the same idea.'

Issy ran to the window and yanked up the blind, her stomach dropping away as if she was plunging down the steep rails of a roller coaster as she saw how much of the sky had been swallowed by a deep layer of grey-black clouds. 'How long until the race finishes?' she asked, eyes already turning towards the clock.

'They're not normally back before two.' Maud tucked an arm around Issy's waist and gave her a squeeze. 'I'm sure it looks worse than it is, darling.' She obviously read the panic in Issy's face because she raised a hand to cup her cheek. 'I shouldn't have said anything. I know what you're thinking and you need to get that out of your head right now. Liam and Jago are going to be fine.'

Issy nodded, trying not to let the panic overwhelm her. 'I'm sure you're right. I might just nip out the front and have a proper look though.' Before her nan could say anything, Issy dashed out into the café. The first thing she noticed was the yellowy glow from the overhead lights. The second was the almost solid wall of black filling the sky beyond the quay. 'That's going to be more than a shower.' She walked towards the windows facing out across the beach and the ocean beyond. White horses thundered atop the waves to crash onto the sand and send a wash of bubbling foam up towards the high-water line. The flags flying above the lifeguard station whipped back and forth as if fighting to rip free of their moorings. People outside were no longer strolling and smiling, their postures hunched against the wind as they quickened their steps.

She opened the door and stepped outside, a shiver rippling through her as the cold wind bit at her skin. Unheeding of the people around her, she pushed her way through to the sea wall until she had a clear view out over the water. She strained her eyes. She should be able to see the boats on their way back by now but the white-capped waves looked too much like sails to be sure.

Remembering an old pair of her father's binoculars in an upstairs drawer, Issy hurried back towards the café, where Maud was waiting in the doorway. 'There's nothing we can do other than wait for them to get back,' her nan said as she reached for Issy's hand.

Issy stared back out across the water. She didn't want to think about Liam and Jago getting tossed about on the waves, didn't want to think about the wind driving them off course. The biggest danger would be in the vicinity of the rock itself. Would they be clear of it by now? God, she needed something to do other than think about all the things that could go wrong.

Maud squeezed her hand. 'Come on in, darling, before it starts to rain. No point in you getting cold and wet as well.'

'They'll be cold and wet,' Issy repeated, an idea beginning to form.

'I know, but Jago and Liam are smart enough to have dressed for the weather.'

Issy turned to her nan. 'No, Nan, not just them. Everyone will be cold and wet, not just those out on the boats.' The race organisers and volunteers down on the quay would be in for a soaking too. She couldn't do anything to prevent the storm, but she could take care of everyone when they got back safely.

If they got back safely.

No. She would not think about that. Everyone was coming back in one piece, and when they did she was going to damn well make sure they had some hot food and dry clothes waiting for them. 'Come on, Nan. We've got work to do.'

The first thing she did when she walked back inside was to make a beeline to where her friends were standing behind the counter. 'The weather's going to turn bad any minute and everyone involved in the race is going to be freezing by the time it's over.' She turned to Anya. 'We're going to need towels and blankets. Is there any chance you can get some from the hotel?'

'Do you really think that's necessary?' As if in answer to her question, the first rattle of rain struck the windows. Anya immediately reached behind her and unfastened her apron. 'I'll head over to the hotel now. I need to ring Ma and Pa, too. They were going to take Freya down to the quay to watch the boats set off. I want to make sure they got back to their house okay.'

Issy grabbed her hand. 'Do that before you do anything else. Go in the back where it's quieter.'

Anya nodded and hurried off through the door into the kitchen.

'She'll need help transporting everything down to the quay,' Chloe said. 'I'll give Dad a call and see if he can bring the van.'

'Good idea. I've got a load of premade soup in the freezer. If we can find somewhere down on the quay to plug in the large kettle and the hot water urn we can at least make sure everyone gets something hot to eat and drink as soon as they get off the boats. I'm going to call Rick and see if there's room in the chandlery.' She turned to Maud. 'Can you look in the cupboard under the counter and see how many takeaway cups we've got in stock?' They'd be much more practical than lugging a load of china down there.

'Leave it with me, and don't worry about this place. Kat and I will hold the fort, won't we, dear?'

'Of course we will. You go and sort out whatever you need and we'll keep an eye on things here.'

Knowing they had things under control, Issy led Chloe into the kitchen. Anya was off the phone, looking a lot happier than a few moments ago. 'They're safely back at Ma and Pa's. They're happy to keep Freya there as long as I need, so at least I don't have to worry about them.' She glanced towards the window where the rain was coming down in earnest. 'Well, I'd better make a run for it and sort things out at the hotel.'

Chloe shook her head. 'I'm going to call Dad and get him to come and pick us up.'

While they arranged that, Issy headed for one of the large upright freezers and began removing the three-litre containers she used for batch-freezing soup. She decided tomato was the simplest option because they wouldn't need spoons to eat it. They wouldn't need a huge portion either, just something to warm them up, and with the hot water urn to provide tea and coffee, it would be better than nothing.

'Dad's on his way. What can we do in the meantime?'

'There's a couple of large insulated bags in that bottom drawer on the right. Put the soup containers in there and I'm also going to need one of those tubs of instant coffee and a large bag of tea bags from the pantry shelf. A bag of sugar as well and there's some long-life milk in there somewhere.'

While Chloe and Anya dug out the things she'd requested, Issy put a call into Rick and quickly explained her plan. 'There's a small staffroom in the harbour master's building. I'll go and speak to Tony now. Do you need a hand with transport?'

'No, everything will go in the back of my car, I reckon. And your uncle's going to give Chloe and Anya a lift down with towels and blankets from the hotel.'

'Seems like you've thought of everything. I'll run and speak to Tony then meet you at the car park by the quay.'

Kat poked her head around the kitchen door. 'Ryan's here.'

'We'll see you down there shortly,' Anya said, giving Issy a quick hug.

'Thank you. You're the best.'

'Friends forever, remember?' Chloe said with a wink before following Anya out.

Kat was still holding the door open. 'Maud checked the cupboard and there's only one tube of paper cups.'

'Damn, are you sure?' What the hell was Issy going to do, because that was never going to be enough.

'It's fine though, because I called my dad and he's arranging for a load to be brought down to the dock along with a couple of boxes of napkins.'

'How on earth did you persuade him to do that?' And what had it cost her friend to ask him for his help when they were so at odds with each other?

Kat's smile held more than an edge of cynicism as she shrugged. 'I pointed out what good advertising it would be for Java Brava and he was all over it.' Her smile softened. 'Don't worry about him. Are you okay?'

Issy shook her head. 'No, not really but sitting around fretting isn't going to make me feel any better. At least this way I'm doing something.' She just hoped to God it was enough and that no one would be in need of anything more than a hot drink and a blanket.

32

By the time Liam and his father had made it to Sean's boat, he and his sailing partner had managed to get the loose sail under control and lowered it, leaving the mast bare. The wind was blowing even harder, whipping up the waves and rocking both vessels from side to side and making it impossible for them to get too close without risking damaging one or both of the boats. Liam tried not to think about the looming menace of the rock behind them as he huddled against the side of the boat to get what little shelter he could from the pelting rain and waited for his father to issue instructions. 'Everyone all right?' Jago asked over the radio.

'I'm okay,' Sean replied. 'But Bob took a nasty thump to the head from the boom when the sail ripped loose. He needs looking at sooner rather than later.'

Liam exchanged a worried look with his father, but Jago's voice was calm as he spoke into the handset. 'I've already spoken to Tony and the lifeboat's on its way from Port Petroc, so they'll be here soon. How bad's the damage to the sail?'

'It's knackered. We'll need a tow to get back. If the lifeboat's on the way then there's no need for you to risk yourselves out here.

We'll be fine.' Sean did his best to sound his usual hearty self, but Liam wasn't buying it and he didn't need to see the look on his father's face to know he thought the same.

'Don't talk rubbish. We're going to get a line across to you. We can't tow you back to the harbour under sail power alone, but we can keep you clear of the rock, which will make the lifeboat's job that much easier.'

It took several attempts and a lot of swearing, but they got a line secured eventually. Thankfully the wind was blowing away from the rock and they managed to get the stricken yacht a safe distance away by the time they spotted the bright orange and dark blue lifeboat through the rain.

The coxswain and Jago were old friends, but there wasn't time to do much more than exchange the briefest of pleasantries before the crew shifted into action. 'We can take it from here,' the cox assured Jago. 'Are you going to be all right getting back under your own steam, or do you want one of my lads to give you a hand?'

His father looked at Liam. 'What do you reckon?'

It was raining hard now, but the wind seemed to have steadied out a bit. Now they knew Sean and Bob were in safe hands, all Liam could think about was getting back to Issy. 'We'll be fine. Let's go home, Dad.'

Jago beamed at him. 'What a bloody good idea.'

As soon as they were underway, Jago radioed Tony in the harbour master's office and gave him an update.

'Ask him to call Issy and let her know we're okay,' Liam said.

When his father relayed the request, Tony laughed. 'I don't need to call her, she's downstairs with most of your family, turning our staffroom into a bloody soup kitchen. It's like the Salvation Army down there with everyone wrapped in blankets and towels. You'd better get your arses in gear and get back if you want something, because that tomato soup of hers is disappearing at a rate of knots!'

'Tell her to save us some!' Jago replied before signing off. He shot Liam a grin that wasn't diminished in the slightest by the wind doing its best to throw him off balance. 'Sounds like she's got everything in hand.'

They were the last boat back by some stretch and Liam had expected the quay to be mostly deserted. He couldn't have been more wrong as half a dozen people rushed to help them secure alongside, including Rick. The rain was still hammering down, but everyone was smiling as they grabbed the ropes and tied off the boat. 'What's going on?' Liam asked as Rick held out a hand to help him ashore.

'Go and ask your girlfriend, it's all her doing,' Rick replied with a grin as he nodded towards the harbour master's building. He turned back to their father, who was still on board, fussing around. 'Leave it, Dad. We'll sort it. Go and get warmed up.'

They didn't need any more urging, and the two of them hurried along the quayside to the tall building that dominated the harbour entrance. They barely made it through the door before half a dozen blanket-wrapped people descended on them and started asking about Sean and Bob. Leaving his dad to field the barrage of questions, Liam headed straight down the corridor towards the staffroom. He'd visited his father often enough over the years to know the exact layout.

It was packed inside, every chair occupied with people wrapped up, clutching paper cups with the distinct brown and red Java Brava logo on them. Several turned and greeted him, but Liam didn't respond. He only had eyes for one person. Issy gave a cry the moment she spotted him, abandoning her spot behind a large table at the back of the room to run over to him. 'I'm soaking wet!' he warned her as she flung herself at him.

'I don't care! Oh God, Liam, I was so worried about you.' Tears shone in her pretty green eyes as she clutched his face in her hands and dragged him down for a kiss. 'You're freezing!' She released his face and reached for the zipper on his jacket, yanking it down so she could shove the heavy, wet coat off his shoulders. 'Someone get me a blanket,' she called, not taking her eyes off him.

'Here you go.' They both turned to find Ray standing there holding a neatly folded blanket and a large towel. Issy took them off him and he retreated at once.

'What's he doing here?' Liam asked as Issy bundled the blanket around his shoulders.

'He was at the hotel when Anya and Chloe went to fetch the blankets and towels and asked what he could do to help. I wasn't exactly going to send him on his way.' Issy barely gave the older man a glance as she shook out the towel and stretched up to try and dry Liam's hair.

Laughing, Liam took it out of her hands. 'Leave it, I'll do it.'

'Come and sit down and let me look at you.' She all but towed him over to the table where a chair had miraculously come free and she pushed him none too gently into it. 'Are you sure you're okay?'

'I'm fine. Everyone's fine apart from Bob, who got a whack on the head. He was up and talking when the lifeboat arrived so I don't think he's too badly hurt, but he's probably on his way to the hospital as we speak.'

'Where's your dad?' Issy's eyes went wide as she glanced around the room.

'He's in the hall. He's fine,' Liam reassured her.

'He'll need a blanket. And some soup. I'll get you both some soup. I brought tomato because I thought it'd be easiest and there's tea and coffee. Do you want a cup of coffee?'

Liam laid the towel over his lap, reached up to grab Issy around the waist and pulled her down onto his knee. 'Issy, stop a minute, okay?' Her eyes met his and he could see the slight glassiness of the fear that must've been tormenting her all day. The fact she'd been able to put it aside and bring so many people together at short notice was a miracle. He reached up to brush a strand of dark hair off her cheek. 'I'm here, Issy. I'm okay. Everyone's okay, you can relax now.'

Her shoulders dropped and he could see the tension drain away as his words finally sank in. 'You're okay. Everyone's okay.'

'Everyone's okay,' he repeated, placing a gentle hand on the back of her neck as he drew her against his chest. Her arms came around him and her body shuddered as the tears she must've been holding back for hours finally broke free. Liam held her tight, rubbing his hands over her back in slow circles as he tried to soothe her.

Movement on his left caught his eye and he watched as Ray leaned down to the people at the next table and spoke softly. They glanced their way for a second before standing and heading towards the door. Ray moved to the next table, and beyond him Anya and Chloe took his cue and began to guide people towards the door. The room emptied quickly; the last person out was Ray, who paused to give Liam a sad smile before closing the door behind himself, leaving Liam and Issy alone. It would take a hell of a lot more than that before Liam was willing to forgive the man, but nonetheless he was grateful for his thoughtful actions.

It didn't take long for Issy to cry herself out, and Liam coaxed her to look up with a gentle hand on her cheek. 'I must look a mess,' she said, wiping her face with the cuff of her sleeve.

'You look beautiful,' he assured her. 'Absolutely perfect.'

'You're a terrible liar,' she said with a laugh that ended on a sniffle. 'But thank you.' She glanced around with a puzzled frown. 'Where is everyone?'

Liam touched her cheek, drawing her attention back to him. 'No one else matters, only you, only me.' Leaning forward, he pressed a kiss to her mouth. 'Only us.'

She curled her arms around his neck. 'You scared me today.'

'I know, I'm sorry. I promise I won't ever go—'

She silenced his words with a firm finger against his lips. 'Don't promise something you'll regret later.'

He was silent for a long moment before he conceded the point with a nod. 'No more storms.'

'No more storms,' she agreed. 'And maybe stick to the pond for a bit, just in case.'

Liam laughed. 'You've got yourself a deal. Hey, I've got something for you in my pocket.'

Issy's eyebrows rose. 'If you think I'm going to stick my hand in your pocket, you can forget it!'

'Behave yourself. Stand up a minute.' He kept one hand on her waist as she stood between his spread thighs, while he reached into his pocket and fished out the present. 'Hold out your hands,' he instructed.

She cupped them together, laughing when he placed one of the plastic containers from the gumball machine in her hands. 'Where did this come from?'

'I stopped at the newsagents this morning on my way to the harbour. Open it.'

Issy prised open the container and tipped out the contents into her palm. Next to the bright bubblegum ball sat a miniature racing car.

He stared at it in disappointment for a moment, before giving a resigned shrug. 'Oh well, better luck next time.'

Issy shook her head. 'How much money are you going to waste in that silly machine?'

'As much as it takes until I hit the jackpot and find you a replacement ring.'

Issy straddled his thighs and curled her arms around his neck. 'I don't need a ring, because I've already hit the jackpot.'

When they emerged from the staffroom sometime later, the hall was empty. They stepped out the front door to find it had stopped raining and everyone was enjoying the small sliver of sunshine that had broken through the bank of grey-black clouds. A rainbow hung over the quay, its colours shimmering. Smiling, Issy turned and put her arms around him. 'Maybe Nan was right about that wish after all.'

Liam didn't have a chance to ask her what she meant because she'd leaned up to kiss him and he couldn't think about anything other than the touch and feel of her in his arms. It was still hard to believe sometimes that she was truly his. He'd only been home a couple of months but everything had changed. As Issy drew back to smile up at him, Liam corrected the thought. Not everything had changed. Issy was the same girl he'd loved since he'd first held her hand in the playground twenty-five years ago.

And if he had his way, they'd be holding hands for the next twenty-five years, and every year after for the rest of their lives.

EPILOGUE

Monday morning rolled around again far too quickly for Issy's liking. The break in the storm hadn't lasted long, but it had given her the perfect excuse to drag Liam back to the café for a hot shower. She'd got in with him so she could check him over and reassure herself he really was okay, of course. They'd woken on Sunday to find the rain still hammering down, which had given Issy the perfect excuse to keep the café closed, and keep Liam in bed where she could keep an eye on him. In her head she knew he was okay, but her heart had taken a lot more convincing. She'd only reluctantly let him go that morning because he and Adam had a meeting at the hotel with a surveyor friend of Adam's.

Moving to the window she looked down the street towards the large white building, picturing in her mind's eye the pretty sketch Chloe had drawn of a patio full of people enjoying drinks in the sunshine. Hopefully she'd get to see the real thing by next summer, maybe even relax out there with Liam and their friends and family. As she watched, someone stepped out of the front door of the hotel and began walking towards the café. It didn't take her long to recognise Ray, his normally purposeful gait still hampered by whatever he'd done to his leg. She'd noticed him limping on Saturday when he'd arrived to help, but she'd been too busy, and honestly still too upset with him, to ask if he was okay.

As he drew closer she spotted the bouquet of pink roses in his hand and she couldn't help the wave of sympathy that washed through her. He was on his way to the cemetery for his weekly visit to see Denise. She glanced at the empty table by the window. He still hadn't been back in since their falling-out.

Issy kept one eye on the clock and when she spotted Ray on his return trip about forty minutes later she hurried outside and called out to him, 'I've got a carrot cake baked fresh this morning. I reckon it'd go down very nicely with a pot of tea.'

She thought he would carry on walking, but instead he limped across the road to join her, his slow progress making her want to wince. 'I wasn't sure my custom was welcome any longer, Isabel.'

'Well, I won't deny that you pissed me off, Ray.' She used the bad language deliberately and was quietly amused at the way he closed his eyes, no doubt disapproving of her appalling manners. 'But you still owe me an apology and things like that always go down better with a cup of tea.'

'I truly am sorry, Isabel.'

'That's a start, but I think I'm going to need to hear it a few times more before I accept it.' Without waiting for a reply, she walked to the door and pulled it open. Ray studied her for a moment or two longer before giving a single nod and hobbling slowly inside.

As she'd hoped, Ray headed straight for his usual table while she went behind the counter to brew his tea and cut him a generous slice of cake, which she set before him with a smile. 'Thank you,' he said. 'Though I'm not sure I'll manage all that.'

'Take your time with it, because I'm not letting you leave until I'm satisfied with that apology. I'll give you a few minutes to compose something suitable and then I'll be back.' Issy took a couple of steps then stopped as something occurred to her. 'Has someone had a look at your leg?' When Ray raised his eyebrows at her, she folded her arms. 'That look might have worked when I was still in school, but not any more.'

He set his fork on his plate with a sigh. 'You get more like your grandmother every day.'

'Thank you.'

The laugh that earned her was more than a touch exasperated. 'In answer to your enquiry, yes I have seen the doctor because I developed a small infection where I hurt my leg. I've got some antibiotics and I'm seeing the nurse twice a week to get it dressed, but it's progressing slower than I'd hoped.'

'I'm glad you've seen someone, and hopefully it'll mend soon.' It was on the tip of her tongue to ask if he needed any help but then she remembered she was still supposed to be upset with him. Damn it, she was terrible at holding a grudge against anyone for long. Except for Liam, she thought to herself with a smile.

Having served a few more customers – and given Ray long enough to stew in his own regret – Issy returned to his table and sat down. 'How's that apology coming along?'

Ray pushed aside his cup and empty plate. Issy noted with quiet satisfaction that he'd managed to finish off the cake after all. He folded his arms on the table in front of him. 'What I did to you and Liam was unforgivable.'

'Agreed.'

Ray swallowed and nodded. 'And if I could go back in time I'd change what I did, find a better way to help Liam settle in—'

'Or maybe actually take the time to listen to what he'd wanted instead of believing you knew what was best for him?' she suggested, softly.

He closed his eyes. 'I'm not sure I was capable of listening back then. I was so sure I was doing the right thing.' When he opened his eyes, there was nothing but pained realisation in them. 'But I did the wrong thing. For him. For you.'

Issy wished she could ease his guilt, but it was too soon for her to say she forgave him because she wasn't a liar. 'I do believe you did what you did for the right reasons.'

'That's kind of you to say so, but it doesn't change what I did.' He sighed. 'I just wish there was some way that I could make amends, but I know that's not possible.'

He dropped his head and she was reminded once again how much he'd diminished since Denise's passing. She hated to see him like this, so sad and fragile. He was almost twenty years younger than her nan, but in that moment he looked so much older. As hurt and upset as she was with him, she hated to see him like this. It was as if he'd given up and was just waiting for the day until he could join his wife. If only there was something she could do...

The wrong thing for the right reasons. Apart from Denise, teaching had been Ray's entire life and he'd given it all up to take care of her. She thought about the way he timed his daily visits to when the café was full of children, the patience he'd always shown as he'd explained a maths problem she simply hadn't been able to get her head around. If only there was a way for him to help others the way he had her. He was probably too old now to go back to full-time teaching, but maybe he could speak to Morwenna, the head of the village school, about a support role. But he'd always specialised in teaching older children and as much as he seemed to take comfort from the chaotic joy of the little ones playing and laughing in the Hub, dealing with that all the time might not suit someone as naturally reserved as Ray. The seed of an idea began to form in her mind. Excited at the possibility, she leaned forward. 'Are you serious about wanting to make amends?'

Ray's head shot up, his red-rimmed eyes shining with hope. 'Of course.'

'We have kids' club in the Hub twice a week for the younger children, but we don't have anything for the older ones.'

Ray frowned. 'That's true...'

'What if we could provide a service that would help them? A homework club, maybe. Somewhere they could come and hang out after school, get a snack and a drink.' She captured his gaze. 'Maybe have someone on hand to help them if they're stuck or struggling.'

It took a moment for the suggestion to hit. 'You can't possibly mean me?'

Issy sat back in her chair and folded her arms. 'Why not? It's not like you've got anything better to do, is it?'

Ray shook his head, his expression incredulous. 'But why would you want me to do this after what I've done?'

'Because this time I know you'd do the right thing for the right reasons. The Hub was created to serve the entire community, but we've been neglecting a core part of that.' Issy's heart began to beat faster. This wasn't about helping Ray any longer, this was something that could truly make a difference. 'What do you say? Do you want to help?'

Ray swallowed hard, then nodded. 'I'd be honoured, Isabel. Truly.'

'That's settled then.' She stood. 'I'd better get us another pot of tea because we've got plans to make.'

* * *

MORE FROM SARAH BENNETT

The first book in another heartwarming series from Sarah
Bennett, *Where We Belong*, is available to order now here:
    https://mybook.to/WhereWeBelongBackAd

ACKNOWLEDGEMENTS

I'm having so much fun building this community and bringing the Penrose family and all their friends to life. My aim is always to create somewhere special that my readers can escape to for a few hours. I hope you enjoy exploring this pretty little haven on the Cornish coast over this book and the rest of the series to come.

My grateful thanks to my lovely editor Emma Beswetherick for all her hard work and support. x

Shout out to my brilliant, innovative publisher Boldwood Books, and everyone on the team who has helped to put this book in your hands. Huge congratulations to them on being awarded Independent Publisher of the Year!

Many thanks to Candida Bradford (copyeditor) and Helen Woodhouse (proofreader) for their eagle-eyed expertise.

Huge thanks as always to Alice Moore for bringing Halfmoon Quay to life with her beautiful cover designs. x

Special thanks to all the other #TeamBoldwood authors. It's a joy to be part of the same publishing family. x

I have the best friends and cheerleaders any author could wish for in the shape of Phillipa Ashley, Jules Wake, Bella Osborne, Rachel Griffiths, Donna Ashcroft, Pernille Hughes, Rachel Burton, Jessica Redland and Portia MacIntosh. Love you all. x

Saving the best for last, my thanks and love go to my wonderful husband. xxx

ABOUT THE AUTHOR

Sarah Bennett is the bestselling author of several romantic fiction trilogies. Born and raised in a military family she is happily married to her own Officer and when not reading or writing enjoys sailing the high seas.

Sign up to Sarah's mailing list for news, competitions and updates on future books.

Follow Sarah on social media:

facebook.com/SarahBennettAuthor

x.com/Sarahlou_writes

instagram.com/sarah_bennettauthor

bookbub.com/authors/sarah-bennett-b4a48ebb-a5c3-4c39-b59a-
09aa91dc7cfa

ALSO BY SARAH BENNETT

Mermaids Point

Summer Kisses at Mermaids Point

Second Chances at Mermaids Point

Christmas Surprises at Mermaids Point

Love Blooms at Mermaids Point

Happy Endings at Mermaids Point

Juniper Meadows

Where We Belong

In From the Cold

Come Rain or Shine

Snow is Falling

Halfmoon Quay

Just the Beginning

Everything Changes But You

Boldw⊙⊙d

Boldwood Books is an award-winning fiction publishing company seeking out the best stories from around the world.

Find out more at www.boldwoodbooks.com

Join our reader community for brilliant books, competitions and offers!

Follow us
@BoldwoodBooks
@TheBoldBookClub

Sign up to our weekly
deals newsletter

https://bit.ly/BoldwoodBNewsletter

Printed in Dunstable, United Kingdom